Texas Land

Julian Green

Disclaimers

This is a work of fiction. Unless otherwise indicated, all of the names, characters, businesses, places, events and incidents in this book are either the product of the author's imagination or used in a fictitious manner. Any resemblance to actual persons, living or dead, or actual events is purely coincidental.

This work contains highly controversial views, ideas and concepts. These are not necessarily those of the author or publisher.

Texas Land

Julian Green

8 Ask me,
      and I will make the nations your inheritance,
      the ends of the earth your possession.
9 You will break them with a rod of iron
      you will dash them to pieces like pottery."

Psalm 2, New International Version

Chapter 1

Encampment

Another hot, bright July day in Southern California. Cliff rode his electric bicycle up the stony path into the hills between Spadra and Pomona. Camping in the hills was more effort than camping in the city, but it was worth it. He preferred to live outside the city, with other vets. Homeless vets looked after themselves, kept their tents and the area around them tidy and kept active. Life in the military had been tough, but being homeless was tough also. Long rides into town to look for work and get supplies kept Cliff fit. That day had still not yielded any work. Still, he had collected his pension and some food and water. It always felt good to have some cash and supplies.

He reached the top of the hill and the bicycle started to coast down the other side, towards the trees, where he camped. The remote settlement of tents had grown to 11, all vets. They took turns going into town, so that there was always someone to keep an eye on the camp. Grayson, or Gray as he was known, was Cliff's next door neighbor. It was easy to tell when he was home, as the sound of a HAM radio could usually be heard, coming from his tent. No one asked whether he had a license for the radio, because no one wanted to know. Anyway, Gray never transmitted, just listened in to other people's conversations. Truckers, road work crews, even air traffic control came over the radio from time to time. Cliff's mode of communication was his trusty Fujitsu Life-book, with his Android phone, as a hot-spot. He parked the bicycle beside his tent and unloaded the bags of tins, pasta and water from his back rack. A few minutes later and a meal of spaghetti and a ground beef and vegetable stir fry was on the gas double-burner. The strong sun light of Southern California did a good job of charging his laptop and LED light via the small solar panel outside his tent. That was another advantage of living in the hills, as such things would go missing, in the city.

Cliff had grown up in Pomona and had come home, after traveling all over the world on classified missions, in the Special Forces. He was an only child and his Mom was a single parent, but he had never gone without. But, he had never imagined himself living homeless, a few miles from his childhood home. The secrecy of his military career

2

had driven a wedge between him and his mother. For much of his twenties, no one even knew which country he was in. Anyway, she no longer lived in Pomona. Nancy had married Chuck and moved with him to Tallahassee, Florida. Two decades of working night shifts as a nurse and raising a hyperactive son made marriage to an ex-army helicopter pilot a good proposition, despite the re-location to his home town on the other side of the country. Cliff and Chuck had a lot in common. Both had been in the army, Chuck was quietly envious that Cliff had made it into the Special Forces, Cliff was envious of Chucks Victory Vegas Jackpot motorcycle.

After dinner, he stretched his 6'3", 210 pound frame out on his sleeping mat for a while and listened to the internet on his laptop. He had gradually become used to the homeless lifestyle, after his military career was cut short by an IED. He was now the proud owner of a steel, transtibial leg. That had made learning to ride a bicycle again a challenge. Learning to ride a motorcycle was now out of the question, according to Chuck. But, Cliff had a habit of doing things that were out of the question. His long term plan was a home stead and some kind of business. He had been a demolition specialist in the Special Forces and just needed to work out how to translate those skills to the corporate sector. Demolition companies around the Greater Los Angeles area had so far given him the cold shoulder. Some casual work pulling parts in a scrap yard had provided some extra cash, but was not a long term solution. He had been fifteen years in the military, from basic training to discharge. He had saved hard for all of that time, but was reluctant to

3

dig into his savings until he had figured out what he was doing. On days when he was at the camp all day, he would trawl the internet for job vacancies. Building a resume from a career of black ops was tricky, but somehow he had managed and was working hard at getting it in front of agencies and employers.

*

The next day was Friday. Cliff's alarm went at 7:00 am. He had an interview for a job as an assistant at a scrap metal dealer's. He put on a pair of black denims and a navy-blue polo, that he had been keeping clean for such an occasion. It was in San Bernardino, which was too far to cycle, so he walked down the hill to West Mission Boulevard and caught a bus to the railway station in Montclair. There, he boarded an Interlink Train to San Bernardino and took another bus the last few blocks. The business was on a large industrial estate, in a 'big box building'. There, they sorted industrial scrap, stripped paint and cleaned the material. Cliff did not have exactly the right experience, but had some transferable skills. The interview went well and they said they would let him know, in a few days, whether he had secured the role. That was good, except he had heard the same thing several times before, but was still looking. Job hunting was tricky when homeless.

Luckily, Cliff had some friends in Pomona and they let him use their address for mail. He had hoped that someone might have a spare room for him, that he could rent, but all of his school friends had married and had kids. The military had been Cliff's family.

Rents in the greater LA area were high, at least a thousand bucks a month for a tiny studio apartment. Cliffs loss of his leg qualified him for a pension, which was a percentage of his salary, but was not much more than an entry-level rent. On top of that were taxes and bills. And food. For him, a pension did not mean retirement.

*

Weeks went by. It was now August, five months after Cliff had arrived in the camp, six months after he had left the military hospital in LA and nearly a year after his injury. He had not made any real progress in that time. He had become used to the homeless lifestyle, he had put his field craft skills to use in looking after himself. But, he had no job on the horizon and could not afford housing where he was.

Cliff booted his laptop and connected to his phone. He opened the mail client and worked through the day's emails. Job-related stuff, one or two from friends, spam. Later in the day, once he had dealt with them, he opened a browser, navigated to an alternative media site and started a news program streaming. He lay back on his sleeping mat and closed his eyes. Space Force. Markets. GM crops. He listened to the interviews, the discussion. He drifted off to sleep. He awoke suddenly. He sat up and looked around. It was dark. He could hear Gray's HAM radio going, a few tents away. He got out of bed, grabbed his flash-light and unzipped his tent door. He shone the light around the camp and into the trees, around about. Nothing. Oh well. He went back inside and put the flash light down. The pod cast was still playing. They were talking about the crypto currency market. He had missed the beginning of the discussion, but it sounded like the market was booming. He clicked on the dot and dragged it back up the progress bar a little. He listened.

*

Friday morning. Cliff arose at 7:00 am, after only a few hours sleep. He had been up late, selling off most of his crypto portfolio. He sat in his deck chair, heating his kettle on the gas stove, for a cup of tea. His head was foggy and he was slowly starting to realize – he was no longer poor. Overnight, literally, he had gone from four figures savings, to six figures in the bank. Now, he had options. He poured water into his mug, added some milk and drank. He could start a business, buy a house. Still, his money would go further, if he moved inland. California was expensive. First priority was to get transport. He would not get far on his bicycle.

Later that morning, he arrived at a car dealers, on Mission Boulevard, in Pomona. He stopped his bicycle near the gate and put the stand down, then walked around the lot, looking at cars and trucks, wondering what to buy. He fancied a sporty sedan, but had a feeling that he should get something more practical. He started to look at SUVs and trucks. A salesman came out to meet him. "Alberto." "Cliff." Fist pump. "What sort of car are you looking for, Sir?" Alberto asked. "I'm looking for a truck." Cliff said, without thinking. "Do you have a monthly budget in mind, Sir?" Pause. "I'm buying for cash."

Cliff said. Alberto showed him several trucks. He looked inside, under the hood and underneath.

A few hours later, after a bunch of paperwork and a bank transfer, he hit the road. His bicycle lay in the flat bed, under the tonneau cover. He headed back, towards the camp. The leather seat was the most comfortable thing that he had sat on, for months. He chuckled as he cruised down the boulevard, in his 2017, GMC Sierra 3500 Dually truck. It was in Raven Black, with a 6.2 liter V8 diesel engine. A previous owner had blacked out the windows and fitted Fuel FF19D chrome alloys. He arrived at the trail head, of the stony trail, up the hill. It was for walkers and cyclists only and had a barrier, to prevent access by motor vehicles. He parked the GMC in the small parking lot and got out.

Back in the camp, he talked to Gray and explained his financial wind fall. A few of the other guys joined the group and they chatted a while. They helped him get his things down the hill. He had dragged things up the hill, one at a time, months ago. Tent, sleeping mat, sleeping bag, solar panel, stove, chair, laptop etc., went into the back of the truck. He transferred a few hundred bucks to each of the guys and said farewell.

A little later, he checked into a reasonably priced motel, in Chino, a suburb South-East of Pomona. He showered and ordered dinner. He sat in his room, eating take out and watching a pod cast on his laptop. After he had eaten he crashed on the bed. It was the most comfortable bed that he had been in, for months. Suddenly, his life had changed. He felt a little sorry for the guys, back at the camp, still homeless, still sleeping in tents. Maybe he should have given them a bit more than a few hundred bucks each. Still, maybe he could employ them, if he started a business. Teach a man to fish. His mind turned to business. What was he going to do? Where was he going to go? A thought struck him. He remembered one of his buddies, from the Army. Kirk had left a little before Cliff had, for reasons that he kept to himself. He was from Portland, Oregon and had gone back there. Cliff sat up and grabbed his laptop. He wrote a quick email to Kirk and sent it. Then, he went to sleep in the ridiculously comfortable bed.

*

The next morning, he awoke at 7:00 am. He showered, dressed and had breakfast at a cafe next door to the motel. After, he returned to his room and booted his laptop. He opened the mail client. Kirk had replied to his email and had invited Cliff to go to his house, in Portland. Cliff hurriedly packed up his things and checked out of the motel. He was going to Oregon.

Chapter 2

Urban Blight

Cliff walked out of the main entrance and approached his truck. He suppressed a grin as he walked towards it. It looked the biz. A mean looking, all black GMC Sierra. And it was his. He opened the driver's side rear door, to put his hold all inside. The first thing that he noticed, was that there was too much daylight inside the cab. The rear seat was covered in smashed glass. He looked at the window on the opposite side. Someone had smashed it in. His truck had been broken into. Damn. He opened the drivers door and slung his holdall into the front passenger seat. He closed the door and walked around the outside of the vehicle. There was a gap between the tonneau cover and the bodywork of the truck. He looked at the rear of the truck. There were scratched and gouges in the steel of the tail gate. Someone had used a pry bar to pop the tonneau cover open. He lifted it up and looked into the flat bed. His bicycle was gone. His solar panel was gone. His tent was gone. His folding chair was gone. His sleeping mat remained. The bag of tinned food remained. Luckily, he had taken his laptop into the motel with him, in his holdall. How had they done all that, when the truck was parked right outside of his window? He must have been in a ridiculously deep sleep, in the ridiculously comfortable bed.

11:11 am, Interstate 210, Northbound. Cliff cruised at 75mph in one of the middle lanes. He had found a hardware store and bought various items to patch up his truck. The rear nearside passenger window was now made from MDF board, glued in place. A cheap, plastic dustpan and brush had enabled him to remove the glass from the rear seat. The tonneau cover was secured with a padlock. A cordless drill had enabled him to make holes in the cover and tailgate, then he wrestled the large padlock into place. What remained of his belongings were now secure-ish. All done in a suburban street, in Chino. No one had paid any attention to the guy patching up his truck, outside a hardware store. Such things were common place in SoCal.

Navigating the suburban streets and finding his way to the freeway had kept his mind busy. Now that he was on the freeway, he fancied some radio and went to turn it on … but found only a gaping hole in the dash. The thieves had also taken the truck's radio.

Less than 24 hours after purchase it had been broken into. SoCal. He realized that he had forgotten to log a ticket with the police. He would have to turn back, if they wanted to interview him. Screw it, he would not bother. The insurance would not pay out without a ticket number, but a window and a tail gate would not break the bank. He drove on.

He hit the I5 and headed North, past Santa Clarita, into the hills. Scrubby, arid hills. Blue sky. Mile after mile of sunny freeway. Tire noise. Cars. Trucks. Hypnosis by wind-shield. Cliff took his Android phone from his khaki cargo pants pocket and swiped the screen with his thumb. He thumbed in the device password, being careful to stay in lane, then tapped on the Ready icon. He tapped on a podcast and it started to play. He turned the volume up and stashed the phone in the centre console. The GMC was an auto, which was lucky, because he could not operate a clutch with his prosthetic leg. He had set the cruise control and all that was required from the driver was a hand on the steering wheel, to keep it between the yellow and white lines.

Cliff stopped for diesel and food in Bakersfield, at around 1:00pm. He brimmed the truck, chose a sandwich, pack of olives and a bottle of water from the chill cabinet and paid in cash. He parked the truck in a space, at the side of the gas station and ate. He was in a good mood, despite the break in. For the first time in months, he was making some progress. Kind of. A little later, he hit the road again, heading North on Highway 99.

Late afternoon, he arrived in Modesto. He found a hotel and checked in. He had been driving most of the day and was tired, so booted his laptop and ordered pizza online. He showered and put pants and shirt on. The reception rang to say his food was there. He went down to the hotel lobby, gave the driver a $20 note and took his food up to his room. He ate pizza and watched a pod cast, on his laptop. After dinner, he wrote an email to Kirk.

Hi Kirk,

Thanks for your invite. I am en-route and should arrive later tonight. How much do you charge per night, for a single room? I would like to stay a few nights.

Regards,

Cliff.

*

9:00 am, Sunday. Cliff drove through Sacramento on Highway 99. He joined the I5 and continued North. It was an overcast day and was starting to rain. The road was dead quiet, with few cars around, early on a Sunday. A few semi-trucks traversed the freeway. He left the cities behind and headed out across the plains of Northern California. The rain became heavier and heavier as he drove. It lashed down. The GMC's wipers swished to and fro. Cliff peered though the screen and continued up the road, at a steady 60mph. Spray from semi's washed over his truck. People said it never rains in California. Apparently, they were wrong.

Late morning, he approached the town of Red Bluff. It was still raining as he turned onto the off lane. Something caught his eye. The was something lying on the lane, a few yards ahead. He slowed and swerved, to avoid it. Then he realized that there were multiple things, lying on the road surface. He tried to avoid them, but the truck's rear wheels ran over some of the things. A rumbling sound came from the rear of his truck. Damn, something was wrong. He pulled onto the hard shoulder, to the right of the lane. He stopped and turned off the engine, then got out of the truck. He looked back up the road. The things on the road were planks of wood. He walked back and looked at them. It was a load of scrap wood, some of it with nails. He picked them up and threw them to the side of the road, before another vehicle went over them. He went back to his truck and looked at the rear tires. He could not see anything wrong. He, but knew from his time in the military, that a rumbling sound from a tire was usually caused by a puncture. He stooped under the rear of the truck and tried to hear a hissing sound. He could not hear anything over the sound of the rain. He pressed the walls of each of the tires, with his thumb. The inside tire on the near side of the truck was soft. Shit. He would need to change the tire, in the lashing rain. His khaki pants and grey-marl t-shirt were already wet. He got back into the cab and took his camouflage rain suit from his hold all. He manoeuvred his prosthetic leg and struggled into the suit. A few minutes later, he was at the rear of the truck. He broke the lug nuts loose, with the truck's breaker bar. Then, he put the bottle jack under the axle. He pumped the leaver, until the tires lifted off the tarmac. He spun the nuts undone, then lifted off the outer wheel. He laid it, flat, on the road surface and slipped it under the diff, next to the jack, in case the old jack gave way and let the truck down. Then he pulled off the inner wheel. Luckily, the previous owner had put the wheels on with copper grease, so they came straight off. He lowered the spare from the chassis, at the rear of the truck. It was a steel spare, unlike the after-market alloys that the previous owner had fitted. He wrestled it onto the hub, then took the outer wheel from under the diff and put that on the hub. He spun the nuts back on, let the bottle jack down and torqued the nuts. He opened the tail gate and put the punctured tire and wheel into the flat bed, then put the jack and tools away.

A few minutes later, he pulled into a gas station, nearby. He struggled out of his rain suit and hung it from one of the roof handles in the rear, to dry out. He was damp, sweaty and dishevelled. He brimmed the tank with diesel and went inside to pay. He scrubbed his hands in the restrooms and bought lunch. He parked at the side of the gas station, ate and rested. Two incidents in 48 hours. Only Cliff Miles had luck like that. But, he was still on the road and could reach Portland that evening, if he made good time for the rest of the day.

He hit the road and headed North again, on the I5. The rain cleared and he made good time, cruising at 75mph on the damp freeway. The road past through the hills, forest and deserts of Northern California. About 3:00pm, he crossed the border into Oregon. For the first time in nearly a year, he had left his home state of California. The road became twisty as it went through the densely wooded hills of Southern Oregon. The radio played; music, jabber, music, jabber.

About 5:00pm, he arrived in Eugene. He found a diner and stopped. He ordered steak, fries and salad and booted his laptop. He opened Thunderbird and found a reply from Kirk in his inbox.

Hi Cliff, if you want to stay a few nights I will not charge you. It'll be good to see you again, buddy. Kirk.

His dinner arrived. He thanked the waitress, plugged ear plugs into his laptop and listened to some news while he ate. After dinner, he paid, tipped the waitress a few dollars and hit the road. The I5 crossed the Willamette River and continued North. It was dead straight, through a large, agricultural, river basin. The Sun went down and it started to get dark. He turned on the headlights. The previous owner had fitted projector beams, which did a good job of lighting his way. He reflected on what a good deal he had gotten. Low miles, tip-top condition, full dealer service history and loads of after-market goodies. The only down side was that the stainless steel sports exhaust made a drone, at freeway speeds. Still, overall, he was pleased with his purchase.

He arrived in Portland in the evening. The GPS took him off the freeway, onto Highway 26, then into the suburban streets of Centennial. The road took him deep into the suburb. He arrived at his destination and parked the truck at the side of the road.

He got out and took his hold-all from the back seat. He pressed the lock button on the fob, the doors locked and the turn signals flashed. He turned and looked at the house. It was a large, old house, of white clap-board. Silhouettes of large pines towered over it, just visible against the night sky. The Oregon evening air was fresh and humid. He walked up the path. A few men sat on deck chairs, on the lawn in front of the house, smoking and talking in low tones. They glanced at Cliff. "Howdy." Cliff said. They echoed his greeting. "This Kirk's place?" He asked. "Sure." An old man with a large beard said. "Just go in and ring the bell." Cliff went in and rung the bell. He put his hold-all on the tiled floor and looked around the hallway. The wallpaper and wood work were a little tired looking. A sign hung on one wall 'Welcome to Columbia Guest House'.

Someone got up and walked towards him. The door opened and Kirk appeared. "Hey Dude!" he greeted Cliff. "Long time!" Cliff grinned. Man hug. "Follow me." Kirk said and lead Cliff deeper into the large house. "I've given you a room on the ground floor, wasn't sure how you get on with stairs, with one leg." He said. Cliff laughed. "I've been living in a tent, on a hill, for the past few months. But thanks anyway!" Kirk gave him a key to the room. "I'll let you settle in, come and catch up whenever you are ready." Cliff showered and changed, then went to the living room. "This is Dorothy." Kirk introduced his wife to Cliff. "This is my best buddy, from the Army." He introduced Cliff to Dorothy. "Just call me Dot." Dorothy smiled. She was a good looking lady in her late twenties. She wore a t-shirt and jeggings. "Have you eaten?" She asked. "Thanks. I had a steak dinner on the road." He replied. "Like a beer?" Kirk asked. "Sure thing." Cliff replied.

He sat in an easy chair. Kirk and Dot sat on the sofa. They drank beers and talked. "What's been happening the last few years?" Kirk asked Cliff. "Well, when I came back from Afghanistan, I got into the Special Forces, did their training, then started going on missions, overseas. I did that for a few years, then I had an altercation with an IED, lost my leg." "Shit, man, that's harsh. What happened then?" "I was in a field hospital, then I was flown back to the US. I was transferred to a hospital in LA, where I had surgery. I was in there for a few months, all told. I was discharged earlier this year." Pause. "What then?" Dot asked. "I didn't have anywhere to go. My Mom has moved to Florida, some years back, to live with her new husband." Pause. "You did not go to stay with them?" Dot asked. Pause. "Nah. Didn't fancy that. I ended up homeless. I started out in the city. Bought a tent and camped under freeway overpasses and suchlike, for a few weeks. It wasn't good. There were a lot of other people in the camps and many of them were users. Then I was talking to a guy who knew the city and the homeless scene. He said that vets tended to camp outside of the city, in the hills. I thought that sounded more like my kinda thing, so I took a chunk of my savings and bought an electric bike. I rode out to Pomona and explored the hills around about. I found a camp, with a few other vets and set myself up there. It was home, for the last eight months or something like that." Kirk and Dot watched him intently, listening to his story. "What about you? I did not hear much from you, after we split in Afghanistan, what, like, five years ago?" Cliff asked. "Well, I basically quit the Army. I'd had enough. I remember you told me you were going into the Special Forces and I thought that sounded interesting, but we had bought this place already, by then and settled down." Cliff looked at Dot. "What's your back ground?" He asked. "I was in the Women's Army Corps. I did a tour of Afghanistan. Then I met Kirk and we decided to quit and do something different." "How did you come to start a guest house?" Cliff asked. Kirk and Dot glanced at each other. "We needed a place to live and a way to make a living and sort of merged the two." Dot said. "We lived with my folks for a while and looked around for an affordable place." Kirk added. "Portland does not have a lot of affordable property, but we found this place. It was a foreclosure and needed a load of work." He added. "Lucky someone likes to get his hands dirty." Dot shot a grin at her husband. "The place was pretty run down. As soon as we got the keys, we cracked on with repairs and decorating. We did the whole place in … about a month?" Kirk glanced at Dot. "The hallway still needs decorating." Dot pointed out. "Yeah? I thought decorating was your department." Kirk replied. Dot laughed. "You get plenty of business here?" Cliff asked, changing the subject. Pause. "We have to turn people away. We are always fully booked." Kirk said. "How many rooms do you have?" Cliff asked. "We divided the basement into two, have another two in the extension and two upstairs." Kirk replied. "We mostly cater to vets, but take other tourists as well. Our rooms are much cheaper than the hotels in the down town, which charge one-fifty plus, per night." Dot added. "It's a nice place. Seems quiet, suburban." Cliff replied. Pause. "The area is actually kinda rough." Kirk said. "The whole of Portland has gone down hill, over the past few years." Dot said. "There are so many homeless people around now. And most of them are users. We have to be real careful to keep everything locked up." "Perhaps not as bad as

Southern California." Kirk added. "Ha! You bet. My truck was broken into, less than twenty four hours after I bought it." Cliff replied. "What did they take?" Kirk asked. "Most of my stuff. My gas stove, my solar panel, my tent. They left my tinned food and other odds and ends. Luckily, my laptop was in my hotel room." "How did you get a truck, after eight months of being homeless?" Dot asked. Pause. "When I was in hospital, I had loads of time to spare. The guy in the bed next to me was some kind of trader, investor, whatever. He said he was going to make his fortune trading crypto currencies. I asked him, what was a crypto currency? After that, he never stopped talking about them. So, I bought myself a cheap laptop, off eBay and started buying all sorts of cryptos. Whatever he bought, I bought. Not financial advise. Just what I did." "I heard that the crypto market is real bullish at the moment." Kirk replied. Pause. "I made a good chunk." Cliff said. "What are you planning to do next?" Dot asked. Pause. "I want to go self employed. I have not figured out what. Maybe a work shop, or something. I have been doing some work for a wrecking yard, over the summer, pulling parts. I'm not a time served mechanic, but I know my way around a car or a truck." "There is always work in the motor trade." Kirk replied. "I also want to move inland. The West Coast cities are way too expensive, for someone starting out. In Southern California, you need, like, quarter of a million bucks for a single wide." "Where are you thinking of going?" Dot

asked. "I dunno, maybe, Idaho, Utah, Montana."
Cliff mooted.

Chapter 2A

Computer Says No

Monday, early doors. Cliff had breakfast with Kirk
and Dot. He asked them where to find a salvage
yard, to get some replacement parts, for his damaged
truck. They told him that there was a yard in Cottrell,
a suburb East of Portland, a few miles out of town,
not far from Highway 26. He hit the road. He
stopped at a hardware store on the way and bought a
small half inch drive socket set and a set of
screwdrivers. A little later, he found the yard. He
parked on the wide gravel lot at the side of the road
and went into the office. He joined the queue of
locals. The queue moved forward and his turn came.
The man behind the counter put his license number
into the PC and found that they had an GMC Sierra
3500 in stock. He priced the parts for Cliff. Cliff
agreed and the man gave him directions to the truck.
Cliff thanked the man and went back outside to his
truck. He took his tools and walked into the yard.
They did not allow customer vehicles in, for security
reasons. He took a cart and found the truck, near the
rear of the yard. It was maroon color, so the parts
would not match his truck. Never mind, he could
paint them some time in the future. He unbolted the
hinges and took the tail gate off. He put it on the cart

and started work on the tonneau cover. Ten minutes later, that was on the trolley as well. He unlocked the truck and opened the rear, near side passenger door. He pried the door card off, leaving the window switch connected. He put the key in the ignition and turned it to the on position. He hit the window switch. Nothing. The trucks battery was flat. Damn. He thought about it. How to get the window out, when it was firmly in the frame. Then he went to work. He unscrewed all the screws and removed the mechanism from the door, complete with the window. He carefully pried the glass from the mechanism and left the mechanism in the rear floor of the truck. He locked it and headed back to the office. "Get what you want?" A member of staff asked, as they past on the dirt road. "Sure thing. Thanks. Here's the key to the truck." "Thanks. Have a good one." "You too."

Cliff paid for the parts, then drove back towards Portland on Highway 26. He had the parts he needed and Kirk had offered the use of his drive way, to carry out the repairs. All good. The road went through the suburb of Holly Brook. Various businesses lined the sides of the road; fast food, gas station, motels, convenience store, thrift store, gun store.

Gun store. Mirrors, signal, manoeuvre. He parked the truck in the gun store's lot and got out. He locked the truck and went inside. He had some money now, so he may as well spend some on something that he could use, to protect what he had. He found the pistols and browsed. CZ, Glock, Springfield,

Kimber, Ruger, Smith & Wesson, Taurus … He was spoiled for choice. Then he remembered, he would need to go through the background check. And he had been of no fixed abode, for the last eight months. This might be tricky. Still, worth a try. He went to the counter. The store was busy with customers and he waited his turn. A woman behind the counter finished with a customer. "How can I help you?" "Hi, I'm looking for a pistol, for concealed carry." Cliff said. "We'll need to do a background check." She said, logging into a PC, behind the counter. She opened the background checks application and logged into the State Police database. "Can I see your drivers license?" He handed her his license. She keyed in his driver number and watched the wheel whirl. "What's your home address?" She asked. Pause. What was his home address? Oh yes. He gave her the address and ZIP code for his friends in Pomona, where his mail had gone, for the past eight months. "That does not match the address on your drivers license …." She replied. Damn. His drivers license still had his address at the base. He had not updated it since he had been discharged from the military. He thanked the lady and left, empty handed. He bought a sandwich and a bottle of juice, at the convenience store, next door, then sat and ate, in the truck.

He arrived back at Kirk and Dot's place, in the early afternoon. Kirk's Chrysler 300 wagon was not on the drive. He parked his truck on the drive, by Dot's Focus. Kirk and Dot ran a handyman business, alongside the guest house and Kirk was no doubt out on a job. Cliff took his tools from the rear seat of the truck and started swapping the tailgate and tonneau cover. Then he replaced the rear window. By late afternoon, he was done and the truck was repaired. It was now a black truck, with a maroon tail gate. He put the old, damaged parts in the truck's flat bed and his tools into his tool box, leaving Kirk and Dot's driveway tidy. Kirk returned and parked the Chrysler, next to Cliff's truck. "Hey, Dude, how's your day been?" Kirk asked. "Well, I fixed my truck." Cliff nodded to the tail gate. "Looks better. Wrong color, though." "Yeah, I'll spray it, once I have sorted a place to live." Cliff replied.

They went inside, showered and changed, then went to dinner. Dot had cooked Salmon and fry bread. They tucked in and talked. After dinner, they all crashed on the sofa. "Awesome dinner, thanks." Cliff said to Dot. "An old Oregon favourite that my Mom taught me, years ago." Dot replied. "Well, it sure hit the spot." Cliff replied. "You had a job on, today?" Cliff asked Kirk. "Sure. Just a yard tidy. Regular customer, I cut his grass. Today, he wanted all his trees and bushes tidied, so that was a full day. He has a massive yard, must be an acre, or something." "There are some wealthy people around." Cliff said. "Oh, sure. But, they have to be careful, about security. There are countless thieves out there. And homeless users are not put off by CCTV notices, or stuff like that." Kirk said. "I went into a gun shop, on the way home. I thought I should have a concealed carry, after what happened. Next time, I might come face to face with the thief."

"Yeah. That's not a bad idea. What did you get?"
"Nothing. I still have my military drivers license, which is different to my other ID, so they wouldn't sell me anything." Cliff replied. "Ha! Of course. Don't worry, I can hook you up. Come with me." Kirk got up from the sofa. Cliff followed him out of the room. Dot put the TV on.

Kirk lead Cliff outside, to the cinder-block garage, which was at the rear of the house. He keyed a PIN into a pad, by the door and they went inside. He flipped on the light. Cliff looked around at the ladder-rack shelving, with tools and equipment of every kind. Kirk went to the rear of the building and unlocked a large safe, which was bolted to the wall. Cliff looked into the safe. Hey, man! Quite a collection!

Chapter 3

The Heartland

Monday, 3:00pm, late August. Vicki drove up the I5, through Southern Oregon. Her yellow, 2005 Chevrolet Monte Carlo cruised comfortably on the freeway. The 3800 supercharged V6 purred, under the hood. Her luggage was in the trunk. She had left her home in Southern California, the day before, to travel to Portland, for a few days work. Her double-wide was locked up and the CCTV turned on.

Pretty, average height, curvy build, Victoria Wisconsin, aka 'Vicki', was used to travel, having been all over the country and to Europe. She worked as a model, made good money and saved much of it. She had a vague idea that she wanted to settle somewhere, quiet and rural. She was born and raised in Wasilla, a city in Alaska, North of Anchorage. Her parents were not impressed with her career choice, but she went her own way, anyway, relocating to Southern California in her late teens, where she had lived ever since. She kept her outgoings as low as possible, within reason, to maximise her savings. She had booked a room in a reasonably priced guest house, in Centennial. She did not know what it would be like, but had stayed at all sorts of establishments, through her career.

Later afternoon, she stopped in Eugene, brimmed the car with gas and went into a diner. She ordered steak, fries and salad and dealt with emails, on her laptop, as she waited. After dinner, she hit the road again and arrived in Portland, shortly after dark. Her GPS guided her off the I5, onto Highway 26, then into Centennial. She arrived at the guest house and parked her car at the side of the road. The house was a large, old clap-board house, surrounded with pines. On the drive were several cars, including a GMC Sierra and a Chrysler 300C. She got out, took her hold all from the trunk and locked the car. She walked up the garden path, to the front door, which was open, went inside and rang the bell. A woman of a similar age came and greeted her. "Hi, I'm Dot." "Vicki." Fist pump. Dot showed her to her room, which was on the first floor. She showered and changed into fresh leggings and a t-shirt, then grabbed her vape pen and headed outside.

Outside, it was dark, but still a balmy late August night. She found a bench in the front yard, sat and vaped. The Sierra had gone from the drive, but the other cars were still there. She looked through a few messages and emails on her Android phone. A little later, the GMC truck returned and parked in the street. A man got out of the truck. He was tall and athletically built. He had a shaved head and a large beard. He wore a red and black check shirt, khaki cargo pants and desert boots. He was carrying a large pizza box. "Howdy." He greeted her. "Howdy." She echoed.

*

Saturday, early September. A black Sierra and a yellow Monte Carlo headed East on Highway 84. The GMC lead the way. It was a clear, sunny day. The traffic on the road was light, a semi here, a car there. Blue sky, pines and the Columbia River slid by the windows of their vehicles. Cliff and Vicki both lived in California. They both wanted to move inland. They both had savings; her from her modelling work, him from his crypto windfall. They were both single. In under a week, they had decided to have a new start in life. Neither of them had skills that transferred very well, into flyover country, but, they had enough capital to buy a house, so that was a start. They would find some work, or start a business. The week had gone by, working on his truck and her car, moving money around, looking at houses for sale, online.

Kirk had sold Cliff his Rock Island Armoury 1911, with a California spec 10 round magazine, from his collection of pistols and revolvers. It was in as-new condition, with only a few mags fired. He sold it to Cliff for $200, with a spare mag and some Hornady, .45ACP ammo included. Kirk declined any payment for Cliff's stay, at the guest house, as they went back a long way. But Cliff felt good that he had bought something from his old colleague and friend. Cliff and Vicki promised to have Kirk and Dot for a few days, once they had a place to live.

They stopped in Baker City for fuel a sandwiches. They parked in spaces at the side of the gas station. She sat in the passenger seat of the GMC. They ate, chatted, the radio played beats, the Sun shone on the mountains in the distance. "What kind of music do you like?" Cliff asked. "All sorts. Mostly club stuff, house, garage, baseline, techno, drum 'n' base, that sort of thing. You?" "Same. And country." "My folks listen to country." Vicki replied. "I listen to it occasionally." Early afternoon, they set out again, on the 84. A little later, they crossed the border into Idaho and continued. The road took them through Treasure Valley and they arrived in Boise at around 4:00pm. They found a motel in West End and checked in for a few nights, then went to find dinner.

They found a diner in the down town and went inside. One of the waitresses seated them and brought them beers. She ordered chicken cordon bleu, a favourite from her time in Europe. He ordered lamb shank. They waited and worked on plans. He booted his laptop and they looked at

houses online. "Twin falls looks like nice, small town." Vicki said. "Yeah." Cliff agreed. "But it's about eighty miles from Boise. That's a long commute. I wonder how many jobs there are in the small towns?" Pause. "We can make our own work. Start a business, maybe?" She suggested. Cliff was unsure. "I think we would be better somewhere near a city, so that we can get work, or enough customers for our business. How about Mountain Home?" Vicki typed 'Mountain Home' into the real estate website. They looked at a few houses and manufactured homes. "A double wide's good value for money." Cliff pointed out. "But, I'm not sure if that's your cup of tea." Vicki looked at him. "I live in a double wide, in San Bernardino. Have done for the past decade, minus a year in Germany." "Ah, OK. I imagined you'd have a condo or something." "Well, it beats a tent, either way." She quipped.
*

Sunday, mid afternoon. Vicki's Chevy pulled up, at the side of the road, in a tree-lined residential street, in Twin Falls, Idaho. Cliff was in the passenger seat, his truck parked in the parking lot, back at their motel. "Seems like a nice neighbourhood." Vicki commented. "I wonder what the locals will make of a Special Forces vet and model, moving into their neighbourhood?" Cliff mooted. A late model, silver Ford Fusion stopped behind them. A middle aged lady in a grey skirt-suit got out. "The realtor's here." Vicki said, looking in her rear view mirror. They got out and met the realtor. "Hi, I'm Lucy." She introduced herself. "Vicki." "Cliff." Fist pumps.

They turned to the house, which was a white, clapboard bungalow, surrounded by overgrown lawn, with chain link fences and mature trees. At the right hand side, was a long driveway, with a garage at the rear. Lucy lead them up the garden path and unlocked the front door. They went inside. It smelled of old house. Damp, well used. They looked around. It was empty of furniture, the previous occupants had taken everything, when it was foreclosed. The floors were bare wood. The kitchen was shabby, the bathrooms grotty. It had been scrubbed up, by professional cleaners, hired by the sellers, but it still looked well used. It had a large living room, kitchen diner, 3 bedrooms and 2 bathrooms. They went down to the basement. "That combi boiler looks nearly new." Cliff said. He checked the sticker on it. "October twenty seventeen. About two years old." He confirmed. They thanked Lucy, left and drove back to their motel in Boise.

*

Early October, Friday, mid day. Cliff's truck pulled up outside their new, old house in Twin Falls. Behind it, a U-Haul box trailer. Cliff carefully reversed the trailer down their driveway and parked. They got out and looked at the house. "Ha! What have we done!" He quipped. "We'd better get busy." Vicki replied and unlocked the door. They went inside and looked around. It was theirs now, after $99,000 dollars, plus fees. "Let's put the furniture in the middle of the rooms, so that we can get around it, to decorate." Vicki suggested. They were both tired, after a day and a half driving, from her place in San Bernardino, but there was work to do. They emptied the trailer, as quickly as they could, taking an end each of sofas and chairs, the dining table, washing machine, cooker and fridge. Her king-size bed frame was in pieces. "I'll build that first, so that we have a bed, for the end of the day." Cliff volunteered. "Cool. I'll go get some cleaning things." Vicki went out to her car. It started first time, after having sat in the street for nearly a week. She found a hardware store and bought gloves, cloths and bottles of harsh chemicals. When she returned, Cliff's truck and the trailer were gone. She checked her phone and found a text. 'Gone to take the trailer back.' She looked in the master bedroom and found the bed was built and the mattress in place. She made the bed, then went to scrub the bathroom. Shortly, she heard the rumble of a V8, as Cliff's truck pulled onto the drive, behind her car. Cliff appeared at the bathroom door. "Can you fit the appliances?" She asked, without looking up. "Sure thing." Cliff went out to his truck, got his toolbox, then went into the kitchen. An hour later, the cooker was wired in, the fridge was plugged in, waiting for the refrigerant to settle and the washing machine was plumbed in. The weekend was a blur of paint rollers, carpet tiles and flat pack furniture. By Sunday night, they had a home.

Cliff had been working as a courier, delivering parcels in and around Boise, using his truck, for the month and a bit that the house purchase had taken to go through. Vicki tried and failed to get modelling work in the area, then took a temporary job as a waitress. Their earnings covered their motel room and other outgoings, helping to preserve their savings. They had gone halves on the purchase and still had a good bit behind them, with no mortgage. Her double wide was on the market. They were in good shape.

Sunday evening, Vicki sat on her bench, in the back yard. It was cool and was starting to get dark. She had on leggings, a fleece and sat cross-legged, vaping. Cliff appeared with two bottles of beer, one each. He sat down next to her. He looked around. It was a low-density neighbourhood. The houses were all on large lots. Lawns sprawled everywhere, bounded by chain link or wooden fences. Mature trees towered over the houses. Long driveways lead to multi car garages. Cars and trucks of every kind sat on the driveways. Two months ago, he had been sleeping in a tent, on a hot, dry, hill, outside of LA. He could hardly believe it. Now, he was somewhere. Vicki chatted to him about this and that. He half listened. He looked at the next door neighbours driveway. They had a black Chevy Impala and a blue Cavalier sedan. GM people. Good start.

Weeks went by. Boise was a two hour commute, of which they soon became tired, especially as their hours were different, his through the day, hers in the evening, so they either had to use both cars, or one had many hours hanging around, waiting for the other. They jacked the jobs in and found other temporary jobs, him in a recycling plant, her in a convenience store. Evenings and weekends were filled with DIY. Cliff bought a brush cutter and tidied up the yard. They bought ladders and rollers and painted the exterior of the house. They had a tipper truck deliver a load of chippings and gave the driveway a top-up. Their old house started to look much newer.

*

Friday evening, some time in October. There was a knock at the door. Cliff got up from the sofa and went to answer it. He opened the door and found a couple standing on the doorstep. They were about the same age as Cliff and Vicki, early thirties. "Hi." The man said. "We're your neighbours. I'm Jesse. This is Sophia." "Cliff, come in." Fist pumps. "This is Vicki. Vicki, our neighbours." Vicki arose. Fist pumps. They all sat down on the sofa's. Vicki brought a tray, with beers, glasses and snacks from the kitchen. They ate, drank and chatted. "You guys just moved in, right?" Jesse said. "About two weeks ago." Cliff replied. "Where are you from?" Sophia asked. Pause. "I'm from Alaska, originally, but I've been living in San Bernardino for about a decade." Vicki said. "I'm from Pomona." Cliff said. "Ah, OK, so both from California, then." Sophia said. "What brings you to Idaho?" Jesse asked. Pause. "The cost of living in California ..." Cliff said, a little un-easily. "And all the social problems that California has now, crime, homelessness ..." Vicki added. Cliff had expected the neighbours to be locals, but as Jesse and Sophia spoke, he realized that they had West-Coast accents. "How long have you lived here?" He asked. They glanced at each other. "About seven years?" Sophia said. "We moved here in our mid-twenties." Jesse added. "Where did you move from?" Vicki asked. "We're from San Francisco, Mission Terrace, specifically." Sophia said. "What do you do for a living?" Cliff asked, knowing that the reciprocal question would put he and Vicki in a awkward place. But, he had to ask and hoped that the career gap was not too large. "I'm a web developer, self employed." "I'm a teacher." Sophia added. OK, their turn. "I was in the military, Special Forces. I was medically discharged, about a year ago. I've been doing various things since then, courier, van driver, etc." Cliff replied. Vicki's turn. They looked at her. "I have been a model, for most of my career. I have a retail job just now." Pause. "Ah. OK. Cool." Jesse replied. "You're very pretty." Sophia smiled at Vicki. "Thanks." Vicki replied, a little awkwardly. At least they had not asked what sort of modelling. "What brought you to Potato State?" Cliff asked. Pause. "Same kind of issues as you." Sophia said. "San Francisco is so expensive nowadays. Our generation can't afford to buy a house there. Plus the other issues that you spoke about. Crime and suchlike." She added. "And we wanted to live somewhere that'll be safer when, you know, things really go South." Pause. "How do you mean, 'go South'?" Cliff asked. Pause. "Well, our countries economy is built on a Keynesian fiat monetary system. And, if you know anything about economics, you know that it will not last forever." Jesse said. Pause. "You mean, like two thousand

and eight?" Cliff asked. "Like that, times a hundred." Jesse replied. "That sounds scary." Vicki replied. "You definitely don't want to in a big city when it happens." Sophia said. "And you want to be prepared." Jesse added. "Do you think there are many people, moving from California into the Rockies?" Vicki asked. Jesse and Sophia laughed. "Half of this street is from Cali." Jesse said. "Actually, that's an exaggeration. But there are quite a few people from the West Coast here. And there are more moving in all the time." He added. "And now, there's the Calexit Party, who don't like the Arcana Administration." Sophia said. "If they continue to gain support, more people will leave California and move inland."
*

Early morning, Monday, the following February. Cliff drove up the I15, through the Mojave Desert, towards Las Vegas. His trusty GMC had a fifth wheel installed in the rear flat-bed. The tailgate and tonneau cover were back home, in the garage. Behind him, his Big Tex, 30' goose-neck trailer. On the trailer, a customer's Datsun 280Z hot rod. The customer was retiring to Utah and needed a professional to help with the move. The neighbours talk about inter-state migration had seeded a business idea in Cliff's mind. Something had guided him to buy a truck, instead of a sedan, back in the summer. Now he knew why. He had become a hotshot truck driver. Cliff and Vicki started the business with the capital from the sale of her double wide. He drove, she dispatched, from home and sometimes came along. Being careful to find loads for both directions of most of his journeys, they made a reasonable living at it.

Cliff turned off the freeway in Las Vegas and stopped for diesel. He brimmed the Sierra's tank and went inside to pay. He paid for the fuel and bought a sandwich. When he went back outside, an old-timer, in a plaid shirt and blue jeans, was eye-balling the 280Z. "Nice car." He said. "Thanks!" Cliff laughed. "I used to have one, oh, forty years ago." "It's not mine. I'm moving it for a customer." Cliff replied. "He races it?" The man asked, looking at the cars slick tires. "I believe so." "Oh well, I better let you go. Have a good day, son." "You too." Cliff climbed back into his truck and parked at the side of the gas station to eat.

Later that afternoon, Cliff drove into a residential street, in Alta Vista, Salt Lake City, guided by the GPS. He spotted a U-Haul, up ahead and pulled up, behind it. He turned off the Sierra and sent Bob a text to say that he had arrived. The house was a recently built red-brick and part timber frame colonial style. A minute or so later, the front door of the house opened and Bob came out. Cliff got out of the truck. "How was the journey?" He asked. "It was fine, thanks." Cliff replied. "How is she?" Bob walked down the side of the trailer and looked at his race car. "She's fine. There were no issues on the road." Cliff replied, undoing the ratchet straps. He lowered the ramps at the rear. "You want to drive her off?" He asked. "Sure thing." Bob replied. Cliff handed him the key and he climbed onto the trailer. He opened the door, got in and started the engine. The V8 rumble gave away the car's engine-swapped status. Bob carefully reversed the car off the trailer onto the tarmac. Cliff put the ramps back and stashed the ratchet straps in the tool box. "Cash OK?" Bob asked. "Sure." Cliff replied. Bob handed him a thick brown envelope. "There you go." Cliff took it. "Thanks." "You're welcome. Wana come in for a tea?" "Thanks. I'd like to. But, I want to get back home to Twin Falls this evening." "No worries. Any time you're going past, come in for a cuppa." Bob said. Fist pump.

10:00 pm. Cliff turned into the street that he lived on. He stopped outside his house, then reversed the trailer into their drive. He turned off the engine and got out into the cool, February Idaho air. It was dark. The light was on in the living room. He put the trailer's feet down and unhitched the truck. He went inside. Vicki greeted him with a hug. "Dinner's ready." They went into the kitchen. Cliff sat and Vicki served onion-apple pork chops and rice. They sat and ate. "How was your journey?" She asked. "It was fine. Went smoothly. Customer was happy." Cliff replied. "That's the main thing." Vicki said. "When's my next job?" He asked. "Nothing booked for a few days." Vicki said. "That's good. Been manic recently, huh?" "You need a few days off." "The truck is due an oil change as well." Cliff said. "You're an awesome cook, by the way. That really hit the spot."
*

36

Tuesday, early. Cliff put the truck on ramps and drained the oil into a drain can. He replaced the sump plug and tightened it with his torque wrench. He broke the oil filter loose with his oil filter wrench and spun it undone, then fitted the new one. He got back on his feet and got into the truck. He let the parking brake off and rolled it off the ramps, then put the parking brake back on. He took a tub of new Pennzoil Platinum semi synthetic 5w-30 from the garage and filled the engine, through a funnel. He checked the dip stick and added a little more, then put the cap back on the engine. He tidied up and took the old oil to the recycling centre. He arrived back home mid-morning. Jesse was standing on his drive. "All OK?" Cliff asked. "You got some spare time?" Jesse asked. "Sure." Cliff closed the trucks door and locked it. He followed Jesse into his house. Jesse opened a door and lead Cliff down a flight of stairs, into the basement. It was dark. Jesse turned on the light. Cliff blinked and looked around. "You're opening a supermarket?" He asked. "No. Sophia and I are preppers. This is our stock of food." Cliff looked at the goods on the shelves. Rows and rows of tins. Beans, ham, sausages, tuna, sweet corn, peas, tomatoes, pineapple, bags of rice, pasta, ready meals, protein drinks, water, batteries, candles, cleaning products and toiletries. Cliff knew all about prepping. Colleagues in the military had talked about buying a cabin in the woods a living off grid. But, he had not pictured a prepper living in a suburban setting. "Good effort. That's a pretty good stock." He said softly. They went back upstairs. Jesse took

Cliff into the house's built in garage. He unlocked a safe, which was bolted to one wall. He took out a rifle and handed it to Cliff. "You must be familiar with these, being a military man." Cliff looked at the AR15. "Palmetto State Armoury. Nice. What calibre?" "Thiry-oh-six." "You hunt with it?" Cliff asked. "Dropped a dozen deer, over the past two years. We have plenty of venison in the freezer." "Awesome." Cliff handed the rifle back. Jesse put it back in the safe and turned to Cliff. He put his hands on Cliff's shoulders. Cliff looked at Jesse with raised eyebrows, as if to say, 'what?' "Listen. We are well prepared, but we can't feed the whole neighbourhood. You and Vicki should stock up." Pause. "OK. But what about the rest of the street?" "We have been here years and I have spoken to most of the street. Most people are on board." "A little prepper enclave?" Cliff asked. "Pretty much, dude. You won't regret moving here. But, you need to turn some of that haulage money into food. And get armed. Do you and Vicki have any guns?" Pause. "I have a nineteen eleven. Vicki has a Glock seventeen." "You should get a rifle. I can give you contact details for a guy that I buy from. And for storable food."

*

The following took place in a few nano seconds. Think of this as a slow motion paragraph.

"All yours." Jesse said softly. Cliff had been there before, but different. He lay on the large outcrop, feeling the cold stone, through his camouflage jacket. Jesse crouched behind him. In his hands, a recent purchase. A Palmetto State Armory AR15, chambered in .308 Winchester. The wind was moderate. The range was just right. A hundred and something yards, across a hill side. He slowed his breathing. He lined up the cross hairs. His finger stroked the trigger. The sear ... let go. The firing spring pushed the pin forward. The pin struck the primer. The primer ignited. The propellent ignited. The pressure built inside the chamber. The 170 grain bullet started to move. Slowly at first, then faster. It ploughed into the rifling. The ridges gripped the soft lead as it accelerated down the barrel. It left the barrel, travelling at 3,000 feet per second. It blazed across the hillside, then smashed into the brachial plexus of the stag. The bullets ballistic tip expanded it to several times it's original size. The stag's legs went out from under it and it crashed to the ground.

Cliff breathed again. "Nice work." Jesse said. Cliff stood up and they walked through the snow, towards their quarry.

Chapter 4

Machinations

Late October, 3:00am, Atlanta, Georgia. A blue Hyundai Sonata turns into a shopping mall parking lot and stops. The driver gets out. She is wearing a grey hoodie, grey track suit bottoms, white sneakers and a phlu-mask. She glances around. There is no one else around. She goes to the rear of the car and opens the trunk. She reaches into the trunk and lifts out a carrier bag. She closes the trunk and walks towards the stores. None of the stores are open. She steps up the curb, onto the side walk and walks under the covered walk-way. Next to one of the pillars is a ballot drop box. She stops next to it. She takes her Android phone from her pocket and opens the app. She takes a wad of envelopes from the bag and glances around again. No one is around. She scans the QR code on the top envelope, then slips it into the slot in the drop box. Then the next one, then the next … Oops, two went in at once. They got one for free. After a few minutes, the bag was empty. She walked back to her car and drove out of the parking lot. The next drop was a mile or so down the road. She turned off the road into the parking lot. She stopped, got out and looked around. There were a few cars in the lot, but no sign of any people. Probably just cleaners, or security staff. No matter. She opened the trunk and took the next bag out. She closed the trunk and walked towards the stores. She found the drop box and started to scan envelopes in. After a few minutes, she was finished and walked back to her car. Eleven down, two more to go. Then she would be finished for the night. The next day was Friday. Her pay would go into her account, from the strange company, that she had never heard of, based in Beijing. She did not care about the anonymity, it was best for all concerned. Plus, she needed the money, to buy Christmas presents for her kids.

*

Mid November, late morning, Wednesday. Cliff drove down Highway 50, between Austin and Eureka, in Northern Nevada. Behind him, his trusty goose neck trailer, with a new addition to the business. It was fitted with a 12-bike frame. The frame held the bikes securely, mounted cross-ways on the trailer. In it, were 8 bikes, the entire collection of his customer. A Harley-Davidson Fat Boy, a Victory Octane, a BMW GS1200, a Moto Guzzi Breva 1100, a Kawasaki H2, a Yamaha FZ09, a Kawasaki GPZ750 Turbo and the piece de resistance, a stretched and lowered, nitrous equipped Suzuki Hayabusa GSX1300R drag bike. The customer was a wealthy software developer and was re-locating to Denver, Colorado. People in the software business could live and work anywhere that there was internet. Many of them had figured that out and were moving to safer, cleaner cities, inland. The customer was nervous about entrusting his cherished collection to a transporter. The collection that he had been building for over three decades. Cliff had assured him that he had been in business for over a year and had moved dozens of vehicles without a scratch on any of them. The customer had agreed, on condition that Cliff did not stop for the night, between San Francisco and Denver. 19 hours drive, with nothing but a stop for diesel and food here and there. Vicki had insisted that she come along and share the drive with him. She had driven the truck a few times, including once with the trailer. Cliff did the

California and Nevada section, Vicki would take over somewhere in Utah.

The radio played, music, jabber, music, jabber. Vicki was in the passenger seat, reading news on her Android phone. Suddenly, she reached for the volume knob on the truck's dash and turned the volume up. The news reader was reading the news. The election count had taken several days longer than usual, but now the result was in. Incumbent, President Derek Arcana had lost the race to Sebastian Frank, of the Plebiscite Party. Vicki looked at Cliff. "Did you hear that?" She asked. "Yeah, I heard. How can that be?" "Unbelievable. Arcana was ahead in the polls." Vicki said. "And he had countless rallies, with tens of thousands of people." Cliff added. "There must have been shenanigans." Vicki replied. "So, we're gonna have President Seb Frank." Cliff said. "I wonder what that will mean for our business? No more Calexit." He pondered. Pause. "There will still be people who want to move. The West Coast had been in decline for years." Vicki suggested. They drove on.

They stopped for dinner and diesel in Delta, then hit the road again, with Vicki behind the wheel. They joined the I15 and headed North for a few miles, then exited at Scipio and headed East-South-East on Highway 50 again. At Salina, they joined the I70 and headed West. It was dark and the silhouettes of mountains loomed, either side of the road, against the starry night sky. They drove in silence, the radio playing quietly. Both wondered what the change of administration would mean for them.

They arrived in Denver at around mid night. The GPS guided them to the street, in Lakewood and they pulled up outside their customers new house. There was no removal truck outside, in this case, as they had unloaded some hours ago. The lights were on in the house. Cliff called the customer and told him that they were outside. Todd came out. Cliff and Vicki got out of the truck. The street was quiet and the air cool. Vicki took the ramp and latched it onto the side of the trailer. Cliff walked Todd around the trailer, Todd looking at his bikes. "Shall I take them off for you?" He asked. "No, thanks. I'll do it." Todd climbed on the trailer and started the HOG. It's V-twin rumbled into life. Todd carefully backed it down the ramp, using the front brake to control the speed. It rolled off the ramp, onto the tarmac. Todd rode it up his driveway and parked it in front of his garage. He did the same with each of the bikes. Cliff and Vicki stood by and watched, moving the ramp one place, after Todd had removed each bike. By 1:00am, all of the bikes were off the trailer. Todd pinged a piece of Bitcoin to Cliff, as agreed. "Thanks. Great service. I'll give you a good rating on Turkey Shoot." Fist pumps. They parted company. Crypto jobs were always good. The customer would pay a premium, to get a service for a chip of something that they had bought years ago, for pocket change. Cliff could cash the coin in and get paid twice his normal rate, or more. If the market crashed around the same time, he would hold it for a while, then cash it in later when the exchange rate was in in his favour. Cliff and Vicki drove through the streets of Denver, found a motel and checked in for the night.

*

Next day, 9:00am. They hit the road and headed North, on the I25. Vicki had fixed up another load for them, a caravan, from Fort Collins to Ogden, which would minimize their unpaid mileage. They picked up the load, from a caravan dealers and headed up Highway 287, across the plains and through the hills, towards Laramie. At Laramie, they joined the I80 and headed West. The radio played, music, jabber, music, jabber. The news came on. Vicki turned up the volume. President Arcana was making preparations to hand over to the new administration, in January. Seb Franks crowd was celebrating. The internet was talking about fraud. "Damn, do you think the Plebs might have stolen it?" Vicki asked. Pause. "Dunno. Maybe. Anything is possible, in the world of politics, I guess." Cliff replied. Vicki logged onto her Android phone and read news articles, online. "Some of the Constitutionalist Party candidates have hired researchers to investigate the election count." She said. Pause. "They must be pretty sure that it was stolen." Cliff replied. "They are going to have hearings. They have witnesses that have come forward, claiming that they saw malpractice in the polling stations." "Like what?" Cliff asked. Pause. "Like the same ballots being run through the machines, over and over." Vicki replied. "That would definitely skew the result." Cliff said. "Where did it happen?" He asked. "Michigan, Pennsylvania, Georgia, and Arizona." "All the purple states." Cliff said. "The ones that are easy to flip." Vicki said. "And that make the difference between a win and a loss." Cliff added. "No need for widespread fraud, just targeted fraud." Vicki added. "Each of those states are worth a dozen or so college votes. Change the outcome in them and you change the outcome of the whole election." Cliff mused.

They delivered the caravan to the customers lot, then continued up the I84, to Twin Falls. They arrived home in the evening, both tired from several days on the road. Cliff parked the trailer, whilst Vicki went inside and heated two ready meals, in the microwave. They sat at the dining table eating macaroni cheese and drinking cold beers. Theirs was not the easiest life, or the most glamorous, but it was their house, their truck, their business. At the back of their minds, was a question; what did the future hold?

*

The following March, early Saturday morning. Cliff drove East bound on the I40. He was moving a 1957 Chevy Bel Air project car from Albuquerque, New Mexico to Amarillo, Texas. The job was some distance from Twin Falls, but he would take work wherever it came up. He had stayed in a motel over night, after delivering another load in the area, the day before. It was a cold, clear day, with a mostly blue sky. Traffic on the interstate was light. The Sierra cruised comfortably at 50mph. Arid plains and distant mountains slid by. Cliff was alone, as Vicki had elected to stay home and work on various spring cleaning and DIY projects. The radio kept him company.

He stopped for diesel and food at Tucumcari, then hit the road again. Around 1:00pm, he crossed the border, into Texas. The news came on. The Texas independence referendum was going ahead and polling was that day. The Texit party had lobbied the Texas State government and the government had agreed to hold a referendum. The Texit Party had also lobbied for paper ballots and a hand count to be used. The news said that few people had turned out to vote.

About an hour later, Cliff arrived in Amarillo. The GPS guided him into the residential streets. He drove past a school. A long queue of people were lined up, outside the school. Near the entrance, a sign read 'Polling Place.' Cliff arrived at the customer's address. He sent a text, to say that he had arrived. The door of the house opened and John came out. Cliff got out of the truck. "Hi, how was the journey?" John asked. "Fine thanks." Fist pump. John walked around the trailer, looking at the car that he had bought online. Cliff put the ramps down and unhitched the ratchet straps. He walked up the ramps and got into the car. The old V8 motor span over and reluctantly fired. It rattled and chugged. The exhaust blew. Cliff carefully reversed it, down the ramps, onto the tarmac. He put the parking brake on and got out. "I'll leave it running for you. It can be hard to start." "Thanks." John got in and drove the old car onto his driveway. He stopped the engine, got out and paid Cliff. "You've got your work cut out." Cliff said. "Yeah. It'll keep me busy."

Cliff put his ramps back onto the trailer, the straps in the toolbox and hit the road. He past another school, on the way out of town. It also had a long queue outside. The news was wrong. Texans were taking the referendum very seriously. It had been scheduled for a weekend, as fewer people would be working on the weekend, in order to maximise turn out. The plan seemed to be working.

Amarillo to Twin Falls would take around 17 hours. It was mid afternoon and he did not want to drive all night. He went back up the I40, West bound, driving a little faster, with the trailer empty. His phone rang. It was Vicki. He answered and put it to the car phone. "Hi Babe, hows things?" "Fine and you?" "Yeah, fine. Dropped the car in Amarillo and got paid." "Cool. I've got another load for you. Can you take a load of lumber, from a sawmill near Albuquerque, to a ranch near Moab?" "When do they want it collected?" Cliff asked. "Tomorrow morning. The sawmill is open seven days, I checked with them." "OK. I'll stop the night in Albuquerque. I should get there about six anyway." "OK. See you tomorrow night."

Cliff drove on and arrived in Albuquerque, just after dark. He stopped at a motel. He parked the trailer in one space, the rear end overhanging the grass verge, then unhitched the Sierra and parked it in the next space. He put his security chain through one of the wheels of the trailer and set the alarm. A disadvantage of being a hotshot trucker was that his truck had no sleeper cab, so he had to stay in motels. He went inside, paid and went to his room. It was a ground floor room and he could see his truck and trailer from the window. Perfect. He ordered a takeaway online and showered. Dinner arrived and he sat in the tub chair, eating burger and fries and listening to the news, on his laptop. The news was still saying that turnout was low, for the Texas Independence Referendum. They also said that exit polling showed that it would be a 'no', albeit by a slim margin. He finished his dinner and closed the news. He opened a new tab in the browser and went to an independent news website. He started the live stream on the page, got into bed and closed his eyes. He lay in bed, listening to the discussion. The turnout to vote in the referendum had been enormous, the largest turnout for any vote in Texas's history. The count had started and it looked like it was going to be a 'yes'. Cliff drifted off to sleep.

*

Sunday, 10:00am. Cliff's Sierra and trailer pulled into the yard of a sawmills, on the North side of Albuquerque. He parked and went inside. He spoke to one of the staff, explaining that he was to pick up a load for a customer. The man used the forklift to load the lumber onto Cliff's trailer. Once he was done, Cliff tied the load down, with ratchet straps. He hit the road and headed North-West, on Highway 550. The road meandered through the arid hills of the Four-Corners region.

Cliff listened to the radio as he drove. The news came on. The Texas referendum was a yes. But, the news anchors were talking about a re-count, saying that it did not make sense, as the exit polling had showed that it would be a no. They interviewed a few politicians from DC. They all made similar remarks; a sad day for Texas, a sad day for the USA, there would need to be a re-count, etc.

Early afternoon, he stopped in Shiprock, for diesel and food, then headed North on the 491. He crossed the border into Colorado, then, mid-afternoon, into Utah. He crossed so many state lines, as part of his work. He wondered if other States would hold independence referenda? If they all gained independence, he would fill up his passport, with stamps, rather quickly.

Late afternoon, as it was getting dark, he arrived at the ranch in Spanish Valley. It was down a narrow road, off the main highway. Irrigation booms loomed in the dusk light. Craggy mountains were visible in the distance, against the late afternoon sky. He parked in the yard and the customer came to meet him. "Cliff." "Otis." Fist pump. Cliff unhitched the ratchet straps and Otis brought a tractor, with a fork on the front and lifted the lumber off. He paid Cliff and offered dinner. "Thanks, real nice of you to offer, but I want to get back to Twin Falls tonight." He replied.

Cliff hit the road and headed North, on Highway 191. The trucks projector beam headlights lit the road well. But, the desert roads were lonely at night. Occasionally, he would see headlights up ahead, coming towards him. A car or a semi would pass. The truck's heater kept him cosy. The radio kept him entertained. He wondered about Texas. Would it really become an independent country? It had been one, after it won independence from Mexico, before joining the USA, but that was a century and a half ago. If it did, how would that effect his business? Would people start to move to Texas in larger numbers, now? Would they need a visa and work permit, after it became independent? He did not know. No matter, his business had diversified in the year and a half that he had been running it. Now, much of his work was agricultural machinery, lumber and numerous other items. He drove on.

He passed through the populated region of Utah's Central Valley, through Provo and Salt Lake City and on through the hills of Southern Idaho. It was nearly mid-night when he arrived home. He was used to long days and went through his usual parking and unhitching routine on auto-pilot. Vicki came out to greet him. "Dinner is ready when you are." She said. He hugged her and they went inside. They sat at the dining room table, eating steak and potatoes and drinking beer. Vicki was always full of news. He was tired, but he liked to hear his woman talk. It was always good to be home, after several long days on the road. "I had a video call, with my folks, this afternoon." She said. "Oh yeah? What's new in Alaska?" He asked.

*

Mid afternoon, Tuesday, May the thirty first. Cliff and Vicki drove North-East on the I10, in Arizona, between Benson and Willcox. Arid plains and distant mountains went by. The radio played techno, with news once an hour. On the trailer, four monster truck wheels and tires. The load was going from San Bernardino to San Antonio, a long haul, but on the same Interstate, all the way.

Cliff was behind the wheel, Vicki in the passenger seat, reading some news on her Android phone. She was a news hound and did a good job of keeping Cliff up to date with all that went on in the country. "Oh em gee!" She exclaimed. "Seriously?" "What are you reading?" Cliff asked. Pause. "An article on nulla-sepe.com. The Army International have taken over the State Capitol, in Austin." Vicki said. "Seriously? Damn." Cliff replied. "They took it just after mid-night, last night. Government workers came to work this morning and could not get in to the building." Vicki said. Pause. The Frank administration was talking about securing the Texas Capitol. I did't think that they would actually do that." Cliff replied. "Yes. It was DC that sent them. They are there to keep Texas in the US." Vicki added. "Shit. This could lead to civil war." Cliff said. "The Texas Government have temporarily relocated to an office building, in Austin. They've tried to get access to the Capitol, to get IT equipment and documents, but the Army International are not allowing them in. They are arguing with the DC government, now." They drove on, Vicki relaying more details about the Texas situation, to Cliff.

They crossed the State line, into New Mexico and arrived at Lordsburg around 5:30pm. They stopped at a motel. Vicki went in and paid for a room while Cliff parked the trailer at the rear of the building, out of sight of the road. He unhitched the Sierra and put the trailers alarm on, to protect the customers property. Vicki came back. "Got us a room right there." She knew the routine. Get a room on the same side of the building that the trailer was parked, to see it from the window and hear the alarm, if anyone tried to steal the trailer, or the load. She unlocked the door of their ground floor room and they went inside. "What do you want for dinner?" Vicki asked. "Just whatever you're having." Cliff showered first, while Vicki ordered dinner online. Vicki showered and Cliff took delivery of their dinner.

They sat in tub chairs, eating Hawaiian pizza and watching news, online. A reporter stood in front of the Texas State Capitol, in Austin, talking about the situation. Behind her, were white, Army International tanks and armoured cars. The camera showed various scenes from the area around the Capitol. A steel fence had been erected around the Capitol building. Troops in camouflage uniforms and blue berets stood around concrete blocks, on roads leading to the building. They carried FN FS2000, bull-pup rifles, that Cliff recognized, from his time in the military. The anchor thanked the reporter, then went on to interview a civil servant in DC. He spoke about plans to put a DC controlled government into the Texas State Capitol. He said that he could not give details, at that stage. She asked him about the Texas Government and the referendum. He said that the referendum was illegal and was not recognized by the Government in DC. He said that the Texas Government were subversives and the DC Government would not negotiate with them.

They finished dinner and opened bottles of beer. "Shall we watch some independent news?" Cliff asked. "Yeah. I need a break from this." Vicki hit pause and opened a new tab on her browser. She started a video streaming, from an independent news site. The news reader, Abe, started a feed from a reporter, who interviewed members of the public, on the streets of Austin. People had various opinions on the situation. Many were disappointed that the DC Government had not recognized the result of the referendum. Some were angry. Only one supported the DC Government and the AI.

Back in the studio, Abe said that he had tried to contact someone in the Texas Government, but had been unable to. Instead, he interviewed a former employee, with some knowledge of the inner workings of State Government. Madison said that the government had relocated to an office building, which they were renting, in Austin. She did not give the exact location of the office building, but said that it was in the down town. Abe asked her how they were going to raise tax and govern the new country. She had heard, from contacts, that they were looking at various ways to finance the Texas Government.

*

Next day, they set out early. Vicki took a turn behind the wheel, as Cliff had done most of the driving, the previous day. About 9:00am, they reached Las Cruses and the I10 turned South. They drove down the Can-Am Highway and crossed the Texas State line. "We're now in a different country. I think." Vicki said, as they passed the 'Welcome to Texas' sign. "Sure. June the first is the day that the Texas Government set to formally leave the USA." Cliff replied. "No border control. We did not need to bring our passports, after all." Vicki said, then started to brake. Up ahead, a cars brake lights went on. They were approaching a queue. A sign at the side of the freeway read 'Border Control Ahead'. Below, it read 'Goods vehicles keep right'. They were in the right lane. Cliff looked at the GPS screen, on the dash. They were just North of Westway. They slowed to a stop, at the rear of the queue. Other vehicles pulled up, behind them. The queue moved forward, a vehicle length at a time. After ten minutes, they arrived at the border control. Red and white barriers had been placed across the road. A dozen or so men in military uniforms, carrying M4 rifles, stood near the barriers, checking drivers papers and looking under the vehicles, with mirrors on long handles. One of the men came towards Cliff and Vicki's truck. Cliff put the window down. "You're transporting goods into Texas?" The man asked. "Four tires and wheels." Cliff replied. "Do you have ID?" The man asked. Cliff handed him his and Vicki's US Passports. The man opened them and looked at their details, then handed them back. "I'm going to let you through, but we need to have a look at your load. Please pull into the lay-by, just past the barrier." The barrier went up and they drove through, then turned right into a recently built, roadstone lay-by. Another man in uniform stopped them. A few men climbed onto their trailer and looked at the tires. Cliff and Vicki watched them, in the trucks rear-view mirrors. The men scanned the tires, with portable X-ray scanners. After a few minutes, they were done and one of the men waved them on. They hit the road and continued into Texas.

The I10 weaved through El Paso, then out of town, into the arid plains. It followed the Rio Grande and the Mexico border, then turned East, deeper into Texas. They talked, as they drove. "So, there was border control, after all." Vicki said. "We are now in a foreign country." She added. "Did you notice their uniforms?" Cliff asked. Pause. "What about them?" Vicki asked. "They were US Army, OCP uniforms. I used to wear exactly the same thing, when I was in the Army, before I went into the Special Forces. They had taken off the US badges and sewn on 'Texas Guard' ones." Pause. "So, they're former US soldiers, now serving the Texas Government?" "Seems so." Cliff replied. "Or,

could they be working for Army International?"
Vicki suggested. "No. There would be no reason for
them to secure the border between Texas and other
US states." Cliff replied. They drove on.

Early afternoon, they stopped at Fort Stockton, for
diesel and lunch. After, they traded places, Cliff
taking the wheel and Vicki taking a break, in the
passenger seat. They drove down the freeway,
listening to music and news on the radio. Traffic was
light, semi-trucks and cars here and there. Late
afternoon, they left the arid region of Western Texas
and entered the forested region. Around 9:00pm,
they arrived in San Antonio. The GPS took them
into an industrial estate, in the Skyline Park area of
the city. They came to a rail road crossing and a train
was approaching, so they stopped and waited. Cliff
turned the engine off and they watched dozens of ISO
containers go by, at barely 20mph. After the train
past, they drove on and found the customer's
business unit. It was a large unit, built of grey box-
profile, with a high roof. They parked on the large
concrete area, in front of it. Vicki phoned him and
advised that they had arrived. He said that he was at
home and would be there in a few minutes. A few
minutes later, a red Ford 150 Lightening pulled up,
near them. The driver got out of his truck. They got
out of theirs. "Howdy. Carlos." "Cliff." "Vicki."
Fist pumps. "Here are your wheels and tires." Cliff
lead Carlos to the trailer. Carlos looked at his
internet purchase, then went to the door of his unit.
The door rolled up and he went inside. The lights
went on. All sorts of vehicles were visible inside:

cars, trucks, Jeeps and sand rails. Around the outside were benches with tools and equipment. Some of the vehicles were on lifts. Cliff and Vicki removed the ratchet straps from the load. Carlos got into his forklift and drove out to the trailer. Each of the tires was on a forklift pallet. He carefully lifted each tire from the trailer and took it into his unit, setting it on the concrete floor. After a while, all four tires were inside the unit. Carlos packed the forklift and waved Cliff and Vicki into the unit. They went into a small office, in one corner of the unit. Carlos put his thumb on the biometric scanner of his cash safe and the door popped open. He took a brown envelope out and reached into it. He asked Cliff to confirm the fee. Cliff confirmed and handed Carlos a receipt, from the border guards. "Plus that." Carlos looked at the receipt and started to count out notes. He handed a wad of notes to Cliff. Cliff looked at the notes. "Texas Dollars?" He asked. "Yes. Nineteen hundred and fifty dollars, plus the import duty that you paid in El Paso." "I quoted in US dollars." Cliff said. "Actually, you just said dollars." Carlos replied. Handed the notes to Vicki. She looked at them closely. They were polymer notes, with a design featuring Texas's historical characters and landmarks, all identical. "One sec." Cliff said. He took his phone from his pocket and looked at the pdf document that contained the quote, for Carlos. His figures had a dollar sign, but nowhere did it specifically read 'US dollars.'

*

Thursday, early doors. They pulled up outside a portable office, near Midland, Texas, just off the I20. A notice over the door read 'Exchange Bureau'. They got out of the truck and went inside. They were both a little nervous. Carlos had promised them that they could exchange Texas currency for US currency, at any of the new bureaus that had opened, around Texas. Vicki had searched the internet and found one, on their route home. But, how good was his promise. They joined the queue, inside. There were two desks, with perspex screens. Behind them were smartly dressed women, counting notes and entering data into PCs. Customers seemed to be getting one currency changed for another, which was encouraging. They reached the front of the queue and one of the women called them forward. "Can I change this for US dollars, please?" Cliff slipped his brown envelope under the level 3 acrylic screen. The woman took the notes out and ran them through a Cassida currency counting machine. She opened a drawer below the counter and put the notes under a clip. "Can I see some ID please?" Cliff handed her his passport. She scanned it into the PC, then slipped it back under the screen, to Cliff. She typed some details into the PC. She took another wad of notes and counted out $2,100 US dollars, then slipped them under the screen, to Cliff.

Ten minutes later, Highway 349, Northbound, towards Lubbock. Oil derricks went to and fro, in the distance. Irrigation booms watered crops, on the agricultural plains. Cliff drove, Vicki counted. "Two thousand, one hundred dollars." She said. "United States dollars?" Cliff clarified. "US dollars." Vicki confirmed. "Just like that, huh?" Cliff said. "We're actually in a foreign country." Vicki replied. "How did they print a currency, when they only got independence yesterday?" She mooted. Pause. "They must have printed it before independence." Cliff suggested. "They don't even have a formal government, yet. The Capitol is still occupied by the Army International." Vicki said. Occupied. She used the word, that they were both thinking, but neither had said out loud. "Occupied." Cliff replied. "I like that." They drove on.

Chapter 5

Fence Around a Fence

Late June. Cliff and Vicki had several months of almost solid work. Everyday, trips across the Rockies, between California, Arizona, New Mexico, Nevada, Utah, Colorado, Wyoming, Idaho, Oregon, Washington, Montana and the new country, IST, the Independent State of Texas. They had a week off, to recoup and do all the odds and ends that did not get done, when they were on the road. Vicki went with Cliff, on about half of his trips, to share the driving and make the days a bit less long, for him. On the shorter trips, he went alone, she stayed home and did admin, scheduling and odds and ends. She bid on whatever loads she could find, to minimize their unloaded mileage.

It was gradually sinking in, for most Americans, that Texas was now a separate country. The Government in DC and the media in New York were still insisting that it was not. They were playing down the fact that they had not been able to recruit any bureaucrats, to work in the AI guarded Texas Capitol. People were checking in and out, on the Texas border, daily. People were exchanging Texas Dollars for US Dollars, daily. The New York media did not talk about Texas Dollars. Not a mention. Neither Cliff nor Vicki could work out where the Texas Dollars actually came from. They each dug, on the internet, when they had some spare time. But, they could not find an answer. The new countries government was mysterious. It existed, on the internet and for ordinary people, but it did not exist, for the DC establishment. And it did not have a street address.

Saturday afternoon. It was a warm summer day. Cliff did another oil change and fitted a new alternator belt, on the Sierra. He checked the lights and fluids, looked at the tires, brakes and suspension. He could get another trip out of the tires. Everything else was good. He had replaced the front pads and disks, a few months back. Vehicle maintenance was a year-round thing, on a vehicle that could clock up a few thousand miles in one week. Cliff kept on top of it. "You done yet?" Vicki called, from the door way. "Just gotta tidy up." Cliff replied. "What's the hurry?" "Barbecue, next door, remember?" She called back. He tidied up his tools, closed the garage door and went inside. He showered and put on fresh denims and a polo shirt. They went next door. "Howdy!" Jesse greeted them. "How you doing?" Cliff asked. "Awesome, you?" "Yeah. Good." "How's business?" "Been really busy, recently. Got a bit of a gap, now. Just a week or so." "What're you up to?" "Bit of work on the truck, other odds and ends." Sophia served drinks. Jesse tended the barbecue. Vicki chatted to other neighbors. "Been anywhere interesting, recently?" Jesse asked. "Been to Lone Star State, er, country, a few times." Cliff replied. "What's that like?" Jesse asked. Pause. "Like going to a foreign country. Border checks. Currency exchanges." "Because it is a foreign country, now." "Sure. I guess. Not sure what the deal is with their government. Based in a rented office block?" Cliff mooted. "Ha! Really? You think so?" Jesse asked. Pause. Jesse filled rolls with hot dogs and burgers and continued to talk to Cliff. "No, man. They are not based in an office block. Don't you have internet in your house?" Jesse quipped. Pause. "I've looked all over the internet, but I can't find an answer." Cliff admitted. Jesse handed him a hot dog. Cliff helped himself to fried onions and mustard. Other guests talked, ate and drank. "Killeen." Jesse said. Pause. Cliff knew where that was and what it was. He had been there. He was not sure why he had not guessed, before Jesse had told him. "A military government?" Cliff mooted. "Apparently so." Jesse replied. Pause. "No office block." He added. "Try cog dot com."

*

Later, that evening. They thanked Jesse and Sophia
and invited them to dinner, the following weekend.
They sat together on the sofa. Vicki watched TV.
Cliff booted his laptop and opened a browser. He
found the website that Jesse had mentioned and
started to read the home page. The content was
written by an Army vet, who was from Texas. He
had contacts in the military, who kept him up to date
with current events. He could not give details, for
security reasons, but could write in general terms.
Cliff clicked on a link, to another page, on the site,
titled 'Texas Government'. Texas based regiments
had broken away from the US military and were
helping the Texas government to run the country.
The government was based on a military base, North
of Austin. They had not brought in an income tax,
but were raising money from import and export
duties, on the borders with New Mexico, Oklahoma,
Arkansas, Louisiana and Mexico, as well as at ports
on the Gulf of Mexico. The money was being used
to finance the usual business of government; they
were maintaining roads, border security, emergency
services and the military. The government staff were
taking basic salaries, not what they were used to, but
enough. Everyone pulled together, because they
believed in the new country. Major investments were
on hold, until a more permanent tax set-up could be
worked out. Cliff clicked on another link, to a page
titled 'Texas State Capitol Situation'. It was a long

article, with photos of the Army International vehicles and troops, that he had seen already, through various news sources. He skimmed through the text, reading the most interesting paragraphs. The Texas government were not fighting the Army International. They were ignoring them. If the DC government wanted to secure an empty building, so be it. The current situation was a stand off. The Texas Army had erected sections of steel fence, in the streets around the Capitol and parked tanks and armoured cars behind the fences. Some streets had gates, to let supplies in to the Army International. The AI had to pay import duties to the Texas Government, to get their supplies. The media had not reported that fact, anywhere, at any time. The government in DC still claimed that they controlled Texas, from the State Capitol. Cliff clicked on another link, to a page titled 'Other Independence Movements'. He started to read. "Oh em gee!" Vicki grabbed the remote and turned the volume on the TV down. "What?" She asked. "Alaska is holding an independence referendum, in the first week of July. That's about a week away." Cliff said. "I know. I told you that, months ago." Vicki said. "So you did. I forgot. Too much going on." Cliff replied. "Damn, if they get a 'yes', your folks will be in a different country, to us." "Yep. We'll need our passports to go see my folks." Cliff kept reading. Vicki turned the volume back up. "Oh em gee!" She turned it back down. "Idaho is having a referendum in August. About six weeks away." "I heard that as well, but I didn't know it was in

August." Vicki replied. Cliff opened another tab and searched for more info about the Idaho referendum. He found the official Idexit Party website. The Idaho State Government was organizing the referendum the same way as the Texas one; paper ballots and a hand count. He read on. "The Idexit Party want people to help with publicity."

*

July, early Sunday morning, Jerome, Idaho. Most people were at church, or still asleep. An immaculate, 2000, black, Chevy Impala turned into a quiet, residential street and pulled up, at the side of the road. Four adults got out. Jesse popped the trunk and they all gathered around. Jesse took a wad of leaflets from the cardboard box and handed them to Sophia, then another wad and handed them to Vicki, then another wad for Cliff, then one for himself. He closed the trunk. "Girls West, boys East?" Sophia said. "Okay." Jesse replied. The girls crossed the Street and started walking the Avenue. "You wana get the South side, the side-walk looks better?" Jesse asked Cliff. "Sure thing." Cliff replied. Jesse knew about Cliff's injury and his transtibial prosthesis, because he had spotted Cliff's very slight, barely perceptible limp and asked him about it. Cliff took the South side of the Avenue and Jesse the North. They each walked up the path to a house and put a single leaflet through the letter box. Then, onto the next house. And the next. And the next. The morning wore on. They worked their way around the streets. Some people were outside, cutting grass, working on cars, heading out for this or that. They handed a leaflet to some people, who they encountered, on paths and driveways. People said 'thanks', politely, took the leaflet and looked at it. Some took some time to read it. Others glanced at it, snorted and scrumpled it. Mid morning, the boys arrived back at Jesse's car. The girls were already there. Jesse put their remaining leaflets in the trunk. Cliff got into the front passenger seat. "How long have you been here?" He asked the girls, who were in the rear of the car. "Just a few minutes. How did you get on?" Sophia asked. "We got most of ours out." Cliff said. He drank some water from his bottle. "Did this Avenue, the ones North and South and several streets East of here." He added. "We did the same, West of here." Vicki replied. Jesse got into the drivers seat. "How'd you all get on?" He asked. "We did eight blocks in total." Sophia said. "Cool. Same as us." Jesse said. "My turn to get us lunch." Cliff said. They discussed what lunch would be that week and settled on Mexican. Jesse started the car and drove to a Mexican restaurant. He parked and they went inside. The waitress seated them at a table by the window and took their orders. "Any feedback?" Jesse asked. "Most of mine just went through letter boxes." Cliff said. "I handed a few to people, no one said anything." He added. "I had a few laughs, from people." Sophia said. Pause. "What sort of laughs?" Jesse asked. Pause. "Derisory, I guess. But only a few and I handed leaflets to quite a few people." She answered.

"Hmm. OK." Jesse replied. "One of the guys, that I handed one to, said we have his vote." Vicki volunteered. "Oh cool." Jesse said. "All we can do is put the leaflets out. People who are dead against will not change their mind." Sophia said. "I have a good feeling about it." Vicki replied. "To me, Idaho has the feel of an independent country."

*

Mid August. Early, Saturday morning. Jesse's Impala turned into the school parking-lot. "Damn, it's busy." Vicki observed, from the back seat. "No spaces." Cliff said. "Need to try the street, then." Jesse replied, turning the car around. He drove back out and down the street. A few blocks away, they found a space. Jesse parked. They got out and walked back, towards the school. "Everyone got their ID?" Sophia asked. Everyone confirmed. They arrived at the school. The queue came out of the building, down the path, out onto the street. Hundreds of people. People in the queue talked and laughed. The atmosphere was good. "Good turnout." Jesse said, softly, to the others. "Our leaflets worked." Sophia replied. The Queue edged forward, one person at a time. They talked to each other and looked at news and emails on their phones, to pass the time. The queue edged forward, one person at a time. Vicki found a music mix online and plugged her ear buds in. She had been a regular at clubs in LA in her younger years and some organ house made any task easier. The queue edged forward. Cliff talked to someone on the phone about a load that he was moving, through the week. The queue edged forward. Sophia texted a friend. The queue edged forward. Jesse read articles on nullasepe.com. The queue edged forward.

Eventually, they reached the building and went inside. Jesse went first. He handed the assistant his driver's license. She scanned it into the PC and handed it back, with a ballot. He took it and the ballot and went to a booth. This was it. What he had been working towards, for months. He read the writing on the ballot.

Please read the following question carefully and mark your choice clearly, with an X, in the box.

Should Idaho;

A. Remain a member of the United States of America, governed by the Federal Government, in Washington, District of Columbia.

B. Secede from the United States of America, become an independent country, governed by the State Government, in Boise, Idaho.

Jesse took his Biro and put a solid, black X in the box, next to B. He folded the ballot and put it into the ballot box. He walked out of the school and waited, on the side-walk, for the others. Vicki appeared, then Cliff, then Sophia. They walked back to the car. "Well, that's four votes for

independence." Sophia said. "Fingers crossed."
Jesse said. "About twenty four hours from now, we
will know." Vicki added. "I wonder if DC will send
the Army International, to Boise, if we win?" Cliff
mooted.

*

A few days later, Tuesday evening. Vicki sat alone
on the sofa, with her laptop. Cliff was on the road,
somewhere in Nevada. He would text or call her,
once he was at a motel. She opened the video app
and clicked on her Mom's account. Her Mom, Amy,
answered. "Hi Sweetie!" Amy said. "Hi Mom."
"Hi Vicki." Larry greeted his daughter. "Is Cliff
there?" Amy asked. "No. He's away, in Nevada."
Vicki said. "How are you two keeping?" Amy
asked. "We're fine and you?" "Yeah, we're good."
Amy replied. "We heard the news, about Idaho."
Larry said. "Yeah! We did it!". Vicki replied. "Did
you vote to leave?" Amy asked. "Are you kidding?
Yeah. Me and Cliff both. And we put out hundreds
of leaflets, for the Idexit Party, over the last four or
five weekends." Vicki replied. "Well, you know, I
have been for Alaskan independence for many years
and I always said Alaska would be the first State to
secede, but I was wrong. First Texas, now Idaho."
Larry said. "You had your referendum about a month
before we did." Vicki pointed out. "Sure, but our
leave date is in December, yours is in November."
Larry pointed out. "Oh right. I didn't know your
leave date." "The leave dates are not far off. The

governments don't have long to get everything organized." Amy said. Pause. "Well, actually, Cliff and I have been digging on the internet and found all sorts of interesting stuff. Apparently, many of the State governments have been preparing for secession for years; planning, researching the law, talking to the military and so on." Vicki said. "But DC still seem to have control of Texas." Larry said. "Yeah, they *seem* to have control. But, the Texas Government is actually running Texas, from a military base, outside of Austin." Vicki said. "Wow! Where did you find that?" Larry asked. "Our next door neighbour, Jesse, told Cliff about a website, with all sorts of info on the secessions. Cliff read some of the articles on it. I have read some. I'll email the link to you later." Vicki replied. "All right. Thanks." Larry replied. "So, in your view, Texas is an independent country, now?" He asked. "Oh, sure." Vicki replied. "Cliff and I have been there, towing loads. We had to show passports at the border. The customers paid us in Texas Dollars and we had to change them, to US Dollars, at an exchange." She explained. "What are Texas Dollars like?" Amy asked. "They're polymer notes, here." Vicki took her purse from beside the sofa and took out a note. "I kept one." She held it up to the camera. Larry and Amy looked at it. "Oh, very nice design." Amy said. "Stephen F. Austin, right?" Larry said. "Uh, yeah. Think so." Vicki said. She looked at the note closely. "Yeah. It says so, on the note." "Nice. Wow. Texas Dollars, huh?" Larry said. "And in a few months, Alaskan Dollars." He added. "Do you think that Idaho's secession will affect your business?" Amy asked. Pause. "I don't know." Vicki replied. "Cliff doesn't think so. Our trade is so varied, there is always enough work." She added. "What sort of things do you haul?" Larry asked. "Anything that can go on a goose neck. Cars, bikes, vans, caravans, farm machinery, lumber, small sheds, portable latrines, whatever job comes our way, really." Vicki replied. "He does most of the driving. I bid on the jobs, do the paperwork and share the driving on the really long journeys." She added. "He has been doing festival work, over the summer. Hauling tents and equipment, for gigs, in the desert." "Well, I started at the Port of Anchorage, when I left school, hmm....over forty years ago, so I have been in the freight business all of my career. We dealt with cargo, not just from the US mainland, but from Japan, China, South Korea and other places. International borders do not stop trade, they just involve some paperwork and in some cases, import duties." Larry said. "Sure. Like I said, we have taken goods into Texas, since it's independence." Vicki said. "Hey, you went self employed, though didn't you? So you are in the same position as us." She added. "Sure, I left the Port and started as a freight forwarder, after you left home." Pause. "A freight forwarder?" Vicki asked. "What is that?" Pause. "Well, I organize the shipping of goods, from producer to market." "By ship?" Vicki asked. "By whatever means. Might be truck and one end, then ship, then rail, then truck for the last bit." He said. "All from home, on my computer." He added. "Hey, so, I am kinda like a freight forwarder, when I organize loads for Cliff?" Vicki asked. "Well, yeah, kinda." Larry replied. "Thanks, Dad, you've given me an idea."

*

Mid November, Thursday morning. Cliff headed North on the I84, near Baker City, Oregon. It was a bright, snowy day. The road was clear, from gritters and traffic, but the ground had a few inches of snow.
Behind him, a load of animal feed, for a ranch near Pendleton. After that, a drive to Portland, to pick up another load, to go to Montana. And it was Idaho's independence day. Jesse and Sophia were having a party, at the weekend and had invited he and Vicki, as well as various other Idexit Party members. Cliff was looking forward to it. The Idexit Party were an interesting crowd and would be in good spirits, after their win.
Road and scenery slid by. There was little traffic, just a few cars and trucks here and there. Cliff noticed some trucks on the opposite carriageway, in the distance, up ahead. As the gap between he and them gradually closed, he saw that it was a large convoy of vehicles. They were all painted white.
There were semi-trucks, with flat-bed trailers. On the trailers, were tanks and armoured cars. Cliff had seen military convoys many times, when he was in the military. Military vehicles were usually painted in olive green, or camouflage. He remembered the photos, on news sites, of the Army International

vehicles, around the Texas State Capitol. That was an Army International convoy, heading South, on the I84. It did not take long, for him to work out where they were going. Damn. Boise was getting the DC treatment, now. He drove on, until he found a rest area, then left the Interstate and stopped. He grabbed his phone and called Vicki. "Hey, it's me." "Everything OK?" She asked. "I just saw the Army International, on the Interstate, heading for Boise." He said. "Oh! Really? Oh em gee!" "Yes. Dozens of vehicles. Tanks, armoured cars, the lot. Listen. Go and tell Jesse. He needs to know. He can tell someone in the IP. They can tell the Idaho Government they have company." "Uh? Oh, OK, right." "You got that? Go speak to Jesse, right now."

*

Vicki did a Ctrl+S on the document that she was in, got up from her desk in their spare-room office and went into the corridor. She grabbed her fleece from the peg and put on. She slipped her boots on and went outside, into the snow, pulling the door closed behind her. She walked down the drive, around the end of the chain link fence and up the drive to Jesse and Sophia's house. She knocked on the door and waited. Sophia would be out at work. Jesse mostly worked from home. He answered the door, in a red and black plaid shirt and black jogging pants. "Hi, I just got a call from Cliff, need to talk. Can I come in?" "Come in." He closed the door behind her.

"What's up? Is Cliff OK?" "Yeah. He's fine. He told me that he saw the Army International, on the Interstate, heading for Boise." Pause. "Really?" "Dozens of vehicles, tanks, armoured cars, the lot." "OK. Right. Thanks." Jesse went into the living room and Vicki followed him. His desk was in the corner of the room, with his PC and two monitors. There were numerous applications open on the screens, with lines of code visible, in a text editor. He grabbed his Android phone, from the desk and called someone, in his contacts. "Grab a seat." He said to Vicki, as the phone rang. She sat on the sofa and waited. "Hey... I'm OK... listen. Next door neighbor just got a call from her man, he's on the road, he saw the AI on the I84, Southbound... yeah, no shit.... Huh? You know?" Long pause. "Ah, right.... OK....awesome....right. I'll let you get on then. Have a good one." Jesse hung up the call and turned to Vicki. "That was, er, someone in the Idaho Government. Sorry. I mean the Idexit Party. He says they expected the AI to come to Boise. It's all fine. The Idaho Government is not in the Capitol, they are....elsewhere. So, it won't be a problem." Pause. "You mean like the situation in Texas?" Vicki asked. Pause. "Yeah. Something like that."

*

Cliff arrived at the ranch, near Pendleton, around 2:00pm. The farmer used a forklift, to take the palletized feed bags from Cliffs flat-bed and store them in his barn, then paid Cliff in cash. Cliff thanked him and went on his way. He headed East, on the I84. The trailer was empty and he averaged 60mph on the Interstate. It started to get dark, as he drove along the Vietnam Veterans Memorial Highway, though the Hood Mountains. He arrived in Portland in the early evening, took a ramp off the freeway and headed South, into the suburbs. He arrived at Kirk and Dot's house and found a space in the street, a little way away, big enough for the Sierra and the trailer. He checked that everything was locked, set the alarm and took his hold all. He walked up the sparsely lit street, then up the path. Several men sat on benches and chairs, on the front lawn. They glanced at Cliff. "Howdy." Cliff said. "Howdy." They echoed. He went inside and rang the bell. Footsteps came his way and the living room door opened. Kirk appeared, in a red and black plaid shirt and blue denims. "Hey man!" "How're you doin'?" Man hug. "Awesome! Hey, I left my truck and trailer on the road, about forty yards that way, at the side of the house with the tall fir hedge. I have not blocked anyone's drive." "Cool. That's fine, just one night anyway, huh?" Kirk showed Cliff to his room, on the ground floor. Cliff showered, then went to the living room. They had dinner, Dot's Guinness beef stew, at the dining table.

"So, your a foreigner now, Idaho-an." Kirk quipped. "Ha! Yeah. I guess so." Cliff replied. "You're welcome in our country, though." Dot said. "Thanks, I appreciate that." Cliff said. "I just saw something on the news, about the Army International arriving at the State Capitol, in Boise. Same kinda deal as in Texas, by the look of it." Cliff glanced at the TV, at the other end of the living room. On the screen, he could see a reporter, with the Capitol building behind her. Around it, were white tanks and armoured cars. He turned back to the table. "Yep. Looks like the same deal. I saw them on the Interstate, earlier today." "You know about Texas, though, right?" Kirk asked. "About the Texas Government? Sure. They're based at a military base." Pause. "Yeah, but now they have moved into the Texas State Capitol. The AI left Texas, a few days ago." Kirk said. Pause. "So, that's the same crew, from Texas, going to Boise?" Cliff mooted. "Dunno. More likely the Texas crew are going on leave for a bit. Probably the ones going to Boise are different." Kirk replied. "I heard that they docked in Seattle. Some people saw them disembarking from a ship, in the harbour. The troops appeared to be from the Far East." Dot said. "Wow. Foreign troops on US soil. Or Idaho soil." Cliff said. "Hopefully, your guys have a plan, like the Texas Government." Kirk said.

Cliff took his phone from his pocket. "Excuse me one sec, just want to check my messages." There was a text, from Vicki.

'Jesse says all OK. IG were expecting AI. They are elsewhere. Vicki.'

"It's fine. Vicki says the Idaho Government is at another location." Cliff said. "Probably at a military base." Kirk replied. They finished dinner. Kirk cleared the table and loaded the dishwasher. They sat on the sofas and watched some news. "All about the Idaho Capitol." Dot said. "Nothing about Texas." She added. "Where did you hear that the Texas Government had moved to the Capitol?" Cliff asked. "On cog dot com." Kirk replied. "You should follow that site. It keeps up to date with everything independence related." Kirk said. "I do. But, I have not been on it for a few days. Been busy." Cliff answered. "I wondered if you had heard from anyone still in the army." "Yeah. I hear all sorts from guys still serving. What about you?" "Well, I was in the Special Forces. Most of the guys that I worked with, in recent years, are involved in overseas stuff. So, they're not really up to speed on the Texas situation." "Fair enough. If you want any inside info, just ping me a text or an email and I will see what I can do." Kirk offered. "Thanks, that's awesome." Cliff thanked Kirk. "How is Vicki?" Dot asked. "She's fine. She keeps busy. We both do. She is always looking to ways to grow the business." Cliff replied. "What are the neighbours like?" Dot asked. "The couple next door are real nice. They're preppers as well. They persuaded Vicki and I to buy loads of storable food, water, bottled gas, that sort of thing. Jesse suggested I get a rifle. I managed to get my address sorted out and bought an AR. He and I went deer stalking and I got a decent size stag. So, we had some venison." "Are they pro-independence?" Kirk asked. "Ha! You bet! They got us to join the Idexit Party and we went leafleting with them a bunch of times." "So, you did your bit for them movement." Dot said. "Well, I like to think so. But, I wonder how all this Capitol business will play out." "It'll be fine." Kirk said. "Like that guy in Texas said, if they want to secure an empty building, let them." He added.

*

Saturday afternoon, mid December. Cliff washed the trailer and the Sierra, with his pressure washer, on the driveway. There had been snow on and off, for weeks. The vehicles were covered in salt and mud, from the treated roads. He carefully washed inside the wheel arches, the wheels and tires and the whole of the body. After he was done with the truck and trailer, he washed Vicki's Monte Carlo. Hers was not so dirty, as it was mostly used to go to the supermarket and other errands around town. He repeated the procedure that he used on his: washed with hot water and cleaning fluid, then turned to cold water and rinsed.

The house door opened and Vicki appeared. "Hey, come and see this!" She shouted. "OK, be a minute." He called back. He packed the washer away, into the garage and closed the garage door. He locked the truck and car and went inside. He slipped his rigger boots off and went into the living room. Vicki was waiting for him, holding the TV remote. "You missed it." She said. The news was on. "What?" Cliff asked, taking of his overalls. "The Army International took a ship, to Juneau, Alaska, to secure the State Capitol. But, the Alaskan Navy blocked the Thane Inlet, with several warships.

There is a stand-off now." "Oh em gee!" Cliff said, watching the TV. He went to the laundry room and put his overalls in the wash-basket, then went back to the living room and sat on the sofa, next to Vicki. The news had gone onto other stories, but soon went back to Alaska. The reporter spoke about the situation in Alaska, then handed over to a news helicopter. It showed the Thane Inlet, a narrow sea-lake, with pine forest covered mountains on either side. In the inlet, was a large merchant ship, used to transport the Army International to Juneau. Further up the inlet, about a mile South of the village of Thane, were two Navy Frigates and one Navy Destroyer. The helicopter went as close as it safely could to the ships, circling at a few hundred feet above them. The ships Gatling Cannons were trained on the AI ship, a mile or so South, from their position. The reporters continued to speak, over the video feed. The Captain of the Naval ships was talking to the Captain of the merchant ship, over an encrypted radio channel. He was not letting the AI into the city of Juneau.

The news went back to the studio. Vicki turned down the volume on the TV. "I'm gonna call my folks." She said, grabbing her laptop from the coffee table. It was Cliff's night to cook, so he got up and went to the kitchen. He looked in the fridge. He starred at various items. He realized that he was distracted, by what was going on. But, they needed to eat, so he got his brain into gear and found hamburgers and cheese. He took some potatoes from the cupboard and cut them into fries. He put them and the burgers in the air fryer and turned it on. He took a bag of peas from the freezer and poured some into a pan, then added water and put it on the hob. He could hear Vicki, speaking to her folks on a video call, but did not hear well enough to follow the conversation. He watched the cooking and looked at news on his phone. All news sources were talking about the Thane Inlet stand-off. A little later, he took dinner into the living room and set it on the table. Cliff said 'Hi' to Larry and Amy, then they ended the call and ate. "What were they saying?" Cliff asked. "Dad reckons that this is a much worse situation than Texas or Idaho. If it goes wrong, it could lead to civil war. He didn't actually say that, but I think that is what he was thinking."

Chapter 6

Stand Off

West State Street, Boise, Idaho, late December. Cliff slowed to a stop, in his Sierra. A soldier in an OCP uniform, holding a M4 rifle, approached his window. Cliff rolled the window down. "What's your business Sir?" The soldier asked. "Delivering goods to site." Cliff replied. "What goods?" He asked. "For the AI troops. Food, water, blankets, that sort of thing." Cliff replied. "Can I see ID?" The soldier asked. Cliff took his drivers license from his pocket and handed it over. The soldier looked at it, then handed it back. "We'll need to have a look." He said. "No problem." Cliff replied. Several other soldiers loosened the ratchet straps and lifted the tarpaulin. They found bundles of blankets, crates of food, bottled water and electronics. They put the tarp back and re-tightened the straps. The soldier raised the barrier and waved Cliff through. Cliff drove on, towards the Capitol building.

After a block or so, he arrived at another road block. An Asian soldier in an AI uniform, with a tactical rifle, approached his window. Cliff rolled the window down. "Err… Yes Sir?" The soldier asked. "Delivering goods to site." Cliff replied. "What goods?" He asked. "For the AI troops. Food, water, blankets, that sort of thing." Cliff replied. "Can I see ID?" The soldier asked. Cliff took his drivers license from his pocket and handed it over. The soldier looked at it, then handed it back. "We'll need to have a look." He said. "No problem." Cliff replied. Several other soldiers loosened the ratchet straps and lifted the tarpaulin. They found bundles of blankets, crates of food, bottled water and electronics. "That's fine." The soldier said. "Turn right on Eight Street, then left on Jefferson Street and report to canton office." He said.

Cliff turned right on 8th Street and left on Jefferson Street. He arrived at the canton office and stopped at the side of the road, in front of the Capitol Building. He turned off the engine and got out. He crossed the street and arrived at the door of the office, which was a port-a-building. He pressed the buzzer. Footsteps came his way. The door opened. A middle aged man in an AI uniform appeared. "Yes?" "I have goods to deliver." Cliff said. The man stepped out of the office and closed the door behind him. He and Cliff walked to the trailer. Cliff loosened a ratchet strap and unhooked it. He lifted the tarp and showed the officer the goods. "OK. Wait here." The man turned and went back to the office. Cliff sat in the truck and waited. A few minutes later, a number of soldiers, without rifles, appeared. Cliff got out and unhitched the ratchet straps. The officer appeared again and directed the troops. They lifted the tarp and started to take the bundles and crates. They carried them to other buildings and tents on the camp, on the lawns around the Capitol. A short while later, the flat bed was clear. Cliff folded his tarp and strapped it onto the flat bed, near the front. He stashed the other straps in the tool box. He turned left and left again and headed back up West State Street. The soldier raised the barrier and waved him through. The soldier raised the barrier and waved him through.

*

Later that day, Cliff arrived home. He parked the trailer and unhitched the truck. He parked the truck next to Vicki's Monte Carlo and set the trailer alarm. Vicki appeared at the door. "Hey! Come see this!" She said. "I'll be there in a mo. I need to speak to Jesse." He went to Jesse's door and knocked. Jesse came to the door. "Come in." Cliff came in. "How'd it go?" He asked. "The troops took the stuff off the trailer. No problems." Cliff said. "OK.

What did they do with it?" Jesse asked. "They carried it off, to tents and portable buildings. They just disappeared inside with it." Cliff replied. Pause. "OK. Fair enough." Jesse said. "I'll try to connect and see what I get. Thanks for your help with this." "No sweat. Any time." Cliff replied.

Cliff left and walked back to his house. He went inside. He slipped his boots off, in the hallway, then went into the living room. Vicki greeted him with tea and cookies. He sat on the sofa and looked at the TV. "That's the Auke Bay Ferry Terminal!" She said. A reporter was speaking over a video stream, showing a ferry terminal in Alaska. The stream was from a news helicopter, flying over Auke Bay. Cliff spotted the merchant ship, used by the Army International, in the bay. "The Alaskan Guard has blocked the terminal." Vicki said. The helicopter circled over the terminal. Tanks and armoured cars were parked on the quay. "The AI circled around Douglas Island and tried to land at the terminal earlier today, but the Alaskan Guard blocked them." Vicki relayed. "Another stand off." Cliff said. "How long had that been going on?" "Since early this morning. It was on the news when I turned the radio on, just after you left." "Is there a road from Canada to Juneau?" Cliff asked, as he opened the maps app on his laptop. "No. My folks took me there when I was a kid, a few times. The only way to get there is by ferry, from Haines or other ports on the coast." "I wonder how many ferry terminals there are at Juneau." He said, zooming in on the city. "Two." Vicki answered. "The one in the

Thane Inlet, in the city and the one further up the coast, North of the airport." She added. "So, the Alaskan Guard and the Navy only have to secure one terminal each, I guess." Cliff said. "The Captain of the ship has been talking to one of the officers of the Guard, but we don't know what had been said." Vicki added.

*

Mid January, mid morning. Cliff drove East bound, along the I90, towards Moses Lake. The mountains were behind him and the interstate was arrow-straight, across a large flood plain. The ground was covered with snow and the road was wet and slushy, from gritters and traffic. Most of the traffic was semi trucks, with few car drivers braving the weather. Behind him, an old AMC Pacer restomod project, strapped to the trailer. The customer was moving from Central District, Seattle, to a small town in Montana. Another couple, whose kids had left home and they had decided to get away from the city of riots and crime. Their other personal possessions were on a semi-trailer, somewhere on the same road as Cliff. The couple were in their daily driver, somewhere on the same road, also.

Cliff's mind wondered from this to that, as he drove along the lonely road. Vicki had been talking about getting into freight forwarding, to increase their income, from the $40-50k that the hot-shot business currently made them. She had been poking about on the internet, setting up accounts on various sites and taking advice from her Dad, here and there. Cliff encouraged her, although he was a little worried about the new side to the business. He made sure that she got their insurance to cover any issues, that may arise.

The truck radio played the news, but he cold not be bothered with it. He turned it off, pulled into a rest stop, logged into his phone and put on a news program from an independent media site. The sound came over the trucks speakers and he set off again.

The conversation was about Texas. They confirmed what Kirk had told him, weeks earlier. The Army International had left the State Capitol. The TV news had said nothing about that, turning their attention to Boise and Juneau. The Texas Government had moved back into the Capitol building. They had set a date in February, for an election. The Texit Party, Constitutional Party, Libertarian Party and Green Party were all putting up candidates. The Plebiscite Party had said nothing about the election, so far. The TV news was not covering the Texas election at all.

The election would be carried out the same way as the referendum – paper ballots and a hand count.

He stopped in Spokane, for diesel and lunch, then hit the road again. He arrived at the Idaho border, crossed the Spokane River and joined the rear of the queue, near State Line. The queue edged forward. After ten minutes he arrived at the barrier. He showed the guard his US passport and proof of his Idaho address. The guard raised the barrier and he drove on. He drove through Coeur d'Arlene and the road took him up into the mountains of Northern

Idaho. The road twisted and turned, through snow-covered pine forest. Mid-afternoon, he approached Lookout Pass. He expected to find a queue at border control, but there was none. He drove straight into Montana. Across the central reservation, on the other carriageway, was a border control hut, barrier, guards and a queue of traffic. Idaho was controlling it's border with the USA, but the USA was not controlling it's border with Idaho, the same as at Ontario, on the I84, when he was driving to Seattle, the day before.

He drove on, through the mountains. Late afternoon, it got dark. He arrived in Missoula and found a motel, just off the interstate. He found a truck parking area with enough space to park the truck and trailer, without unhitching, which was a bonus. He took his hold all, locked up and set the alarm. He went inside, paid and went to his room. He showered and ordered dinner from a local take out. His burger and fries arrived. He sat, ate and watched the news.

The AI ship was still in Auke Bay. The Alaska Guard tanks were still on the quay. Neither side had moved. The reporter said that the AI were considering various options. Cliff wondered what 'various options' were. After dinner, he booted his laptop and connected to the motel Wi-Fi. He opened a browser and went to cog dot com. He found the page on Alaska and read the latest. It told him the same as the news, but also that the AI had approached the Marines and asked for the use of amphibious landing craft. Cliff opened the maps app and navigated to Juneau. There was a coast road, around the North side of Douglas Island, with beaches nearby. Fritz Cove was just South of Auke Bay, so it was not far from the AI ship. But, according to the article on cog dot com, the amphibious craft would have to come from elsewhere. That would give the Alaskan Guard some time to secure the beach, or the road, or both. So far, neither side had fired a shot. Neither the State Governments, nor the DC Government wanted a shooting war on American soil, each for their own reasons. So, each side manoeuvred and circumvented the other's manoeuvres. And so far, the States were wining at that game. Cliff had another beer, then went to bed.

*

Next day, early. Cliff drove down the I90, towards Butte. It was a clear, sunny day. Blue sky met the horizon, in the distance. It was true, Montana had big skies. And mountains. The morning wore on. He passed Butte, Belgrade and Bozeman. Around mid-day, he stopped in Livingston for gas and lunch. Then, he hit the road again and continued through Montana. It followed the Yellowstone River, twisting and turning through the lightly wooded mountains. He passed Billings and took the I94, North-East. Late afternoon, he arrived in Miles City. It was dusk. The GPS guided him to the customer's address. It was a bungalow in a residential street, with a chain link fence, driveway and a double garage. Cliff parked outside and dialled Ron's number. "Hi, Cliff here. I'm outside, with your car." The door opened and Ron came down the path. Cliff got out and started to unhitch the ratchet straps. "Ah, the old girl looks fine." Ron said, looking at his work-in-progress classic. Cliff lowered the ramp, at the rear and reversed the car off, onto the damp and slushy road. Ron had a better look around it, while Cliff put the ramps back and the straps in the tool box. Ron paid Cliff in cash and parked the car on his drive. "Normally, I'd ask you in, but all we have is packing cases all over the house." Ron said. "Hey, no worries, I will need to find a motel for the night anyway." Cliff replied. "OK. Safe drive, back to Twin Falls." Ron said. Cliff went on his way and found a motel. He parked in the large, gravel area at the rear.

It was Friday evening and Cliff fancied eating out. There was a bar and grill, next door to the motel, so after a shower and fresh clothes, he went out. He wore dark green cargo pants and his black fleece, against the cold Montana air. The waitress seated him. He ordered and called Vicki, while he waited. She was fine, busy with admin and trying to get the new business going. His steak dinner arrived and he let her go.

After dinner, he sat at the bar and had a beer. Another guy sat down, near him. "Howdy." Cliff said. "Howdy." The man echoed. He was a middle aged man, about twenty years older than Cliff, wearing blue denims and a wool jacket. The man ordered a beer. "You local?" He asked Cliff. "No, I'm from Idaho, just here the night." Cliff replied.

"You?" "No. Fargo, North Dakota. You a trucker?" The man asked. "Sure." Cliff replied. "Malcolm." "Cliff." Fist pump. "And you?" Cliff asked. "Sure." Malcolm replied. "What do you haul?" He asked Cliff. "All sorts. Cars, bikes, lumber, sheds. Whatever comes my way." "You're a hot-shot?" "Sure. GMC Sierra and a goose-neck. You?" "Peterbilt 389." "OK. What do you haul?" "I haul ISO containers, from the rail terminal in Salt Lake City, to towns all across the West." Malcolm said. "Ah, OK. Including Idaho?" Cliff asked. "Sure. Including the 'Peoples Republic of Idaho'." Malcolm quipped. "Ha! I don't think we are … that ...exactly. But, there are border controls now." Cliff replied. "I know. I had to show my passport, on the way to Pocatello, the other day. And Montana is going the same way." Malcolm said. "Really?" "Sure. And Wyoming. They have a referendum, next month. They want to separate from the USA and join Idaho."

*

Cliff arrived home, around 8:00pm, after taking another small load, from Billings to Idaho Falls, on his way home. Vicki had cooked a rack of lamb and Idaho potatoes. They tucked in, then sat on the sofa with bottles of beer and caught up with each others news. "What have you been up to, the last few days?" Cliff asked. "I have got us an account with the rail terminal, in Salt Lake City. I can now organize containers, from LA to Salt Lake City and hire drivers to take them from there to wherever. We get a cut of the delivery charge for every container that we ship." "Awesome. How about I haul some of the containers … oh wait …" "You need a commercial license, remember." Vicki reminded him. "I met a guy, in Montana, who said that he hauls containers from that terminal and he is always busy." "Then he probably has his own forwarder and won't need us. But there will be plenty of others out there." Vicki replied. "Sure. And you know what else he told me?" "What?" "Montana and Wyoming are having an independence referendum, next month. They want to join with Idaho." Cliff told her. "Cool. That would make us a bigger country." She replied. "That would boost the Idaho Dollar to US Dollar exchange rate." Cliff pointed out. "Then again, we are actually better off with the exchange rate the way it is." He added. "True. But nearly two Idaho Dollars, to one US Dollar, is making everything expensive here. I spent nearly a hundred bucks, at the supermarket, earlier today." "For one week?" "Well, I filled the freezer right up." She answered. Cliff thought about offering to do a supermarket shop, in the US, on his way back from jobs. But, then he decided he couldn't be bothered. That was Vicki's department. "You could go to Brigham City, to a supermarket there." He suggested. "That's a five hour round trip. And I don't want to be a groceries bootlegger." Vicki replied.

She put the TV on. He grabbed his laptop, from his holdall and booted it. He went onto cog dot com and looked around. He found a page on Montana and Wyoming. It was true, they were having a referendum on February 22. Both on the same day. He skimmed through the article, reading the paragraphs that most interested him. The referendum would have a 3-way question. He clicked on an image of the ballot.

Please read the following question carefully and mark your choice clearly, with an X, in the box.

Should Montana;

A. Remain a member of the United States of America, governed by the Federal Government, in Washington, District of Columbia.

B. Secede from the United States of America, become an independent country, governed by the State Government, in Helena, Montana.

C. Secede from the United States of America and join with Idaho and Wyoming, forming a new country, called Mountainland.

He showed Vicki, then closed the image and read on. Some counties in Eastern Oregon were also having a referendum, with A and C options. Idaho maybe going to grow, both East and West. The independence movement was growing. The article went on, but he was tired. He shut the laptop down and went to bed. He was asleep when Vicki turned in for the night.

*

Saturday afternoon, late January. Cliff had finished pressure-washing the truck and trailer and giving them their weekly check. Jesse walked up the driveway. "Howdy!" He used the greeting that Cliff had helped spread, all over the West. "Howdy!" Cliff echoed. "How's it going?" Jesse asked. "Awesome, thanks, you?" "Yeah, man, good. You got some time to spare?" "Sure. Give me a few minutes to get changed and I'll come over." Cliff went inside and took off his boots and overalls. A few minutes later, he was on Jesse's door step in denims, trainers and fleece. Jesse answered the door. "Come in." Cliff followed Jesse inside and closed the door behind him. "Take a seat." Jesse and Cliff sat down on swivel chairs, in front of Jesse's large office desk, in the corner of Jesse's large living room. "What's up?" Cliff asked. "Remember your delivery, to the Army International camp, at the Boise State capitol?" "How could I forget? It's the only time in my life that I have been through a DMZ, about a hundred yards wide." Pause. "OK. I've been listening in to the bugs in the TVs." Jesse said. "Cool. Anything interesting?" Cliff asked. "Most of the recordings are useless. Most of the troops are Asian and speak in languages that none of us understand. I have played bits of it to other people in the ... Idexit Party, but no one can understand it. One of the ladies has a friend who is a translator, she is going to try to translate some of it." "OK. Maybe we will get something interesting." Cliff replied. "Actually, there are some AI troops that speak English." Jesse said. "The sound is not great, there is TV sound in the foreground and speaking in the background, but I have tweaked it a bit in AudioGeek, wana have a listen?" Jesse asked as he woke his PC, logged on and hit play. White noise came over the speakers on his desk.

Sounds. "Sapnin, bruh?" Bruh 1. Sounds. "S' nippy out." Bruh 2. Sounds. "...w choo got?" Bruh 1. "..stew from the cookhou... You?" Bruh 2. "Same." Bruh 1. Sounds. Television. Long pause. Indistinct speech. "..How long're we here?" Bruh 1. Pause. "Few months, I heard." Bruh 2. Pause. "...S not much .... deployment, ... guard... we .... " Bruh 1. "No chance, there's a fence around our fence! We ain't gonna do shit!" Bruh 2. Sounds. Television. Long pause. Indistinct speech. "Uh, Montana, or Wyoming, I think .... maybe .... dunno." Bruh 2. "Then Utah, in the summer ..." Bruh 1. "Huh? Utah?" Bruh 2. "...S what I heard." Bruh 1. Pause. Door slam. "Sup fuckwits?" Bruh 3. "Hey, Dodge, bruh, broken any ... today?" Bruh 2. "...Sure. Three." Bruh 3. "They gonna knock them outta your wages?" Bruh 2. "Nah ... Told the Skipper it was you ... get knocked outta your wages." Bruh 3. Sounds. Television. Long pause. Indistinct speech. "...Donkey says we're .... Utah in the

summer?!" Pause. "Yeah. Toad says so." Bruh 3.
"Why the fuck Utah?" Bruh 2. "Same deal.
They're goin' independent."

Jesse turned the recording off and turned to Cliff.
"What do you think?" He asked. Pause. "Did he say
Utah?" Cliff asked. "Yeah. Well, that's what it
sounds like. The sound quality is not great, I'm sure
you'll agree." "Why are they talking about Utah
independence, is that a thing?" Cliff asked. "Yeah,
pretty sure it is. They have a referendum in about
two months." Jesse replied. "Holy shit man, I can't
keep up with this!" Cliff exclaimed. Jesse laughed.
"Don't you get it?" Long pause. "The whole country
is going to break up." Pause. "Almost every State
wants independence from DC." Jesse explained. "A
bunch of magical kingdoms on a large continent."
Cliff posited. "And what happens when the
kingdoms join again to form one huge empire?"
Pause. "DC loses?"

*

Tuesday, late February. Cliff pulled over and
stopped in a gas station, in the tiny hamlet of Oasis,
in Northern Nevada. He brimmed the Sierra with
diesel, bought lunch, then hit the road again. It was a
grey and overcast day. Snow lay on the ground, but
the I80 was clear. He was on a two day haul, from
Sacramento, California, to Mountain View,
Wyoming. Behind him, his nearly new, Cargo
Metro, twin axle, goose-neck box trailer. Vicki was

growing her side of the business and so was he. Miles-Wisconsin Transport LLC was going from strength to strength.

In the box trailer, furniture and boxes of personal possessions, belonging to a couple, who were retiring to Wyoming. They were on the same road, somewhere ahead, Norm in his Dodge Nitro, Betty in her Chrysler Voyager, their valuables piled in the trunks of their vehicles. He had set out around mid-day, after they had loaded the trailer, with some help from friends. Cliff stipulated that he would not help load the trailer, as he did not want to tire himself out, before a long drive. He did not like to use his leg as an excuse, to do less than other people, but he also had to be realistic. Carrying boxes and moving furniture was hard going for him, as he had discovered during he and Vicki's move to Twin Falls. Norm and Betty had departed after him, in order to hand keys to their realtor and tie up other loose ends. An SUV and a mini van could drive a bit faster than a truck and trailer, so they caught up and went past, after Reno. He had stayed the night in the small town of Lovelock, in Western Nevada.

Cliff continued along the interstate and crossed the state line, into Utah, at West Wendover. The road took him across the Utah Salt Flats. It was the flattest area, on the North American continent, adjacent to Great Salt Lake, a land-locked lake, with no outlet, hence the salt. It was seriously vast, the grey sky meeting mountains at the distant horizon.

The news came on. Various news stories. The last one, was that Wyoming and Montana were having their independence referendum, that day. So far, there was very low turn out, according to reporters at polling stations. The report was brief and the station went back to music. Cliff drove through Salt Lake City and into the mountains. He crossed the state line into Wyoming and arrived in Mountain View at around 6:00pm. It was dark, as he drove through the streets of the small town. A long queue caught his eye. A sign read 'Polling Station'. Some people in the queue glanced his way, as he drove past. The turnout seemed to be good, even in a very small town. He arrive at the address. Norm and Betty unloaded the trailer, with some help from a relative, who lived in Salt Lake City. Cliff helped, by shuffling boxes and furniture to the rear of the trailer, as they emptied it, into their new house. An hour and a bit later, it was empty.

Norm paid Cliff, in cash. He thanked Cliff for the service and they Cliff left. He drove back down the I80 and arrived in Evanston at around 8:30pm. It was dark, but the snow on the ground made it lighter than usual. He found a motel, parked at the rear of the car park, at the side of a large, snow covered gravel area, took his hold all, set the alarm and went inside. He asked for a ground floor room, as always. He ordered dinner from a local Mexican take out, showered and changed. His food arrived and he sat, watching news and eating. The referendum was the last article in the news program. The turnout had been low and the count had now started. It looked like it would be a 'No'. By then, Cliff knew the drill. After he finished eating, he turned the TV off and booted his laptop. He logged on, opened a browser and went to his usual independent news outlet. The turnout for the Montana, Wyoming and Counties referendum had been phenomenal. Estimates from independent estimators were that over 80% of those eligible to vote, had voted. That was a higher percentage than most presidential elections, for those states. The count was under way.

Cliff had a video call with Vicki. Then he took his leg off and went to bed. He turned off the light and drifted off to sleep. He slept well on long hauls. A day's driving tired him out.

.... Walking around streets ...... night time .... darkness, but with street lights .... a building .... going up the steps .... going through double doors ..... inside .... people milling around .... tables .... crates of papers .... people looking at papers .... working through piles of papers .... walking in-between the tables .... people talking .... through the building .... corridors .... rear entrance .... going outside again .... waiting .... van arriving .... driver gets out .... presses buzzer by the rear shutter .... waiting .... shutter opens .... woman appears .... talking to driver .... opens tail gate .... another woman comes out .... argument .... another two women come out .... more argument .... driver waits .... driver gets back in van .... drives away .... women go back inside .... shutter closes .... Cliff woke up. That was a vivid dream, wow. He lay awake a little, thinking about the dream, then drifted off to sleep again.

*

Next day, early. Cliff drove up the I84, through the Weber River Valley, near the small town of Morgan, in Eastern Utah. The snow was thawing, as it was a little milder. The mountains in the distance were still snow covered. The sky was blue, with patchy cloud. Farms, houses and trees were dotted about on the flood plains and hills. A rail road ran beside the interstate. On it, a train that stretched as far as the eye could see. Tankers, flat beds, hoppers and ISO containers moved South-West, towards Wyoming. Vicki had been growing the business in various sectors, sending containers all over the country, by road and rail. Some of the freight on that train might be 'his', which was cool. Then, he remembered his dream. He turned on the radio and listened to the news. Various news stories. The referendum was last, again. The count was still going and the result was not in, but it looked like a 'No'. He found a rest stop, pulled over and stopped. He logged onto his Android phone and opened the independent news app. The audio came over the Sierra's speakers and he drove off again. The referendum was the main story. The result was still not in. There were reports of some of the counting offices receiving deliveries, from vans, in the small hours of the morning. Some of the poll watchers had intercepted the deliveries and found that they were crates of ballots, of unknown origin. They had turned them away and sent out an email to other poll watchers, to look out for deliveries at the back door of the public buildings. But, there was a risk that some of the ballots had gotten past the poll watchers and been counted. The result of the referendum would now be in question.

Cliff arrived home at around mid day. He went through his parking and unhitching routine and went inside. Vicki greeted him with a cooked brunch of bacon, sausage, fried egg and pancakes. They sat at the kitchen table and ate. "Did you hear about Alaska?" Vicki asked. "No. I was listening to news about Montana and Wyoming. Why?" Cliff asked. "The Army International got a loan of some landing craft. They tried to land on the beach, on the North side of Douglas Island." "Oh em gee, what happened?" Cliff asked. "The Alaskan Guard put hedgehogs on the beach, I mean, big steel things, not ..." "Yeah, I know what a hedgehog is. I was in the military for over a decade, remember." Cliff interjected. "Did the AI manage to land anywhere?" He asked. "No. They sailed up and down the coast, looking for a way in, but anywhere with a landable beach was armoured." She relayed. "Where did you head that?" He asked. "On the news?" "No. The news said nothing about it. I looked on cog dot com." Cliff finished his brunch and booted his laptop. He found the article on cog dot com and read it. It had taken the AI weeks to get the amphibious craft, which was enough time for the Alaskan Guard to prepare. They had hired a contractor in Anchorage to build several thousand steel hedgehogs – spiky steel frames, made from scrap girders, welded together at angles. They had them shipped to the island and dropped them all over the beaches, wherever the beach came close to Highway 31. When the AI arrived, the Captain of the ship spotted the armour on the beach and stopped the amphibious craft, from attempting to go ashore. He had the crew lookout, while he sailed around the coast of the island. The hedgehogs lined the entire beach, anywhere that there was highway, nearby. They only ran out, when the road ran out and the slope from the water was steep, rocky and densely wooded. Landing craft could not traverse such terrain. The ship had anchored, over night. The crew got some rest and the Captain discussed the situation, with his seniors, the article suggested. The next morning, Alaskan Guard scouts, using quad bikes, who had observed the ship the day before, saw it weigh anchor and leave. The AI had given up, at least for the time being. It looked like Juneau would not need a fence around a fence, after all.

*

Saturday, mid March, early morning. Vicki drove up the I84, in her Monte Carlo. Cliff was in the passenger seat, beside her. The Sun was out and the snow was thawing. They had been working hard, through a hard winter and decided to have a weekend of leisure. The cars V6 engine purred, under the hood. Vicki had the radio tuned to a station which played liquid drum 'n' bass. Cliff dipped into news articles, on his phone. They arrived in Boise at around 10:00am. "Wana check out the fences?"

Vicki asked. "Or, do you think they might recognize you?" She asked. "I'll put a phlu mask on." Cliff quipped. "Why not just cruise around the Capitol and see if anything has changed?" He suggested. They drove around the roundabout at Fort Boise Park and headed up West State Street, expecting to come to an Idaho Guard road block. One block, nothing. Two blocks, nothing. Three blocks, nothing. Four blocks, still nothing. "There's the Capitol." Cliff said. They drove past the Capitol building. Still nothing. "Strange." Vicki said. She turned left, down 9th street, then left again, down West Jefferson Street. They past the Capitol, going the other way. Still nothing. "The building that I delivered to was right there." Cliff said. There were no portable buildings or tents. The Army International had gone.

Chapter 7

Theocracy?

East 6th Street, Helena, Montana, early April. Cliff slowed to a stop, in his truck. A soldier in uniform, holding an AR15 rifle, approached his window. Cliff rolled the window down. "What are you shipping, Sir?" The soldier asked. "Goods to site, for the AI troops. Food, water, blankets, that sort of thing." Cliff replied. "Can I see ID?" The soldier asked. Cliff took his drivers license from his pocket and handed it over. The soldier looked at it, then handed it back. "Park at the side, just there, please." He said. "No problem." Cliff replied. He turned in, to the side of the road and parked. Several other soldiers loosened the ratchet straps and lifted the tarpaulin. They found bundles of blankets, crates of food, bottled water and electronics. They put the tarp back and re-tightened the straps. "Good to go." The soldier said and waved Cliff on. Cliff continued down the residential street.

After another block, he arrived at another road block. A soldier in an AI uniform, with a foreign bull-pup rifle, approached his window. Cliff rolled the window down. "Yes Sir?" The soldier asked. "Delivering goods to site." Cliff replied. "What goods?" He asked. "For the AI troops. Food, water, blankets, that sort of thing." Cliff replied. "Can I see ID?" The soldier asked. Cliff took his drivers license from his pocket and handed it over. The soldier looked at it, then handed it back. "We'll need to have a look." He said. "No problem." Cliff replied. Several other soldiers loosened the ratchet straps and lifted the tarpaulin. They found bundles of blankets, crates of food, bottled water and electronics. "Turn right on North Montana Avenue, then left on Lockey Avenue and report to the canton office." The soldier said.

Cliff turned right on North Montana Avenue, then left on Lockey Avenue. He arrived at the canton office and stopped at the side of the road, in front of the Capitol Building. He turned off the engine and got out. He crossed the street and arrived at the door of the office, which was a port-a-building. He pressed the buzzer. Footsteps came his way. The door opened. A middle aged man in an AI uniform appeared. "Yes?" "I have goods to deliver." Cliff said. The man stepped out of the office and closed the door behind him. He and Cliff walked to the trailer. Cliff loosened a ratchet strap and unhooked it. He lifted the tarp and showed the officer the goods. "OK. Wait here." The man turned and went back to the office. Cliff sat in the truck and waited. A few minutes later, a number of soldiers, unarmed but in uniform, appeared. Cliff got out and unhitched the ratchet straps. The officer appeared again and directed the troops. They lifted the tarp and started to take the bundles and crates. They carried them to other buildings and tents on the camp, on the lawns around the Capitol. A short while later, the flat bed was clear. Cliff folded his tarp and strapped it onto the flat bed, near the front. He stashed the other straps in the tool box. He turned left and left again and headed back up East 6th Street. A few minutes later, he was through the DMZ.

It was late afternoon and he had been driving all day, from Salt Lake City. He found a motel, near the I15. He reversed the trailer into an angled parking space, in the corner of the lot, unhitched the truck and parked it next to the trailer. He went through his usual routine and half an hour later was in his room, eating a burger and fries and watching news, on his laptop. Montana, Wyoming and the counties of Eastern Oregon had voted to secede from the USA and join Idaho. The referendum had gone their way, but only by a whisker. Wyoming was around 41% for joining Idaho, 38% for remaining in the USA, 21% for full independence. Montana was even closer, at 40%, 39% and 21%. The counties, with their simpler two-way question, won, at around 52% to leave and join Idaho. There was endless talk, on the internet, about ballots of dubious origin, finding their way into the system. Both sides claimed that the other had tried to hack it. The New York media claimed that the result was not valid and said that the referendum was not legal, anyhow. So, the AI had turned up at the State Capitols. Anyone watching only TV news would think that the AI was guarding about six Capitols, as the TV news always hailed their arrival and hushed their departure. None of that had deterred Utah, which was the latest to hold a referendum. Theirs was a few weeks away.

Cliff had video calls with his Mom, Nancy and Step-Dad, Chuck from time to time. They lived in Tallahassee, Florida and he only saw them occasionally. Flying was difficult for him and it was a long way to drive. Nancy and Chuck had flown out to Idaho, to visit Cliff and Vicki, a couple of times, but mostly, they kept in touch by tech. They had a call arranged for that evening, so Cliff closed out of the news and opened the soft phone. "Hi, darling." Nancy said. "Hi, Mom." "Hi Cliff, hows it going?" "I'm fine, you?" "Yeah, we're good. Where are you today, in a motel somewhere?" Nancy asked. "Sure. In Helena, Montana." "Not too far from home, this time." Chuck said. "Yeah and still in Mountainland!" Cliff replied. Pause. Nancy and Chuck watched more TV than internet, so they were not really up to speed on the independence movement. "Just took a load from Salt Lake City." He added. "Ah, OK." Nancy replied. "Business still going well?" She asked. "Sure. I'm on the road, most days." "How's Vicki?" She asked. "She's busy with her side of the business. She has a training course, in about a week, so she'll be away for a few days." "Oh, OK. Where is the course?" Nancy asked. "It's in Salt Lake City. To learn how to use some new software, for the logistics business." Cliff replied. "That will give her a change of scene. She works from home, most of the time, doesn't she?" "Well, since the new side to the business, yeah. She used to come with me on hauls, but not so much, now." Pause. "How are you guys doing? Retirement in Florida still good?" "I'm only semi-retired. I still do the tours, over the summer." Chuck reminded Cliff. Chuck had been a helicopter pilot, in the Army and now flew tours, in the summer months, for tourists. "I'm just getting back into it now, the season is starting." He added. "How about you, Mom?" Cliff asked. "I'm keeping busy in the garden, doing things for the church, at the weekend." Nancy replied.

*

Monday morning, mid April. Vicki's yellow Monte Carlo drove down a street, in Glendale industrial estate, Salt Lake City. She had left her motel ten minutes earlier and the GPS was guiding her to the Logistics Solutions office. She arrived, turned into the parking lot and parked. Wearing smart black denims, navy blue jacket and mid heeled boots, she got out and walked to the front door. She pressed the buzzer and the receptionist let her in. She took the lift and went to the 3rd floor. The receptionist checked her in and asked her to take a seat. She sat on one of the firm, cloth-covered seats. A number of other people, roughly half and half, men and women, in business casual dress, were waiting there. A few minutes went by, then a middle aged lady, in a gray skirt suit, appeared. "Who is here, for the training? All of you? OK, follow me." She lead them through double doors and down a corridor, they turned right, into a classroom. They all took seats, behind the desks. Vicki sat near the rear, where she had been through most of school. The room was large, clean and modern. Floor to ceiling windows were covered with blinds.

"Welcome to Atlas Connect one oh one, I'm Calypso." The woman addressed the class. "I am going to give you a basic introduction to the company and Atlas Connect, this morning. This afternoon, and the rest of the week, we will do some exercises and there will be a test on Friday afternoon, for you to get your certificates." Calypso started by talking about the companies background, it's horizontal market growth, across numerous sectors of the logistics market. She explained how they used independent contractors, to grow the business, without needing much larger numbers of employees. She explained how the Atlas Connect software suite, developed in-house, helped them bring all the factors: contractors, shipping lines, rail operators and freight forwarders together, to form a logistics symbiosis. The software enabled the company to move millions of ISO containers per year, through hundreds of ports, around the globe, with one office, in Salt Lake City and a few dozen employees. They had large numbers of loyal contractors, across the North American continent, driving loads and forwarding the freight. The freight forwarders took ownership of ISO containers from hubs in the far East, such as Shenzhen, across oceans, through ports, onto rail roads, through hubs, onto trucks, to market. Once she had explained the basics, to the class, she went onto the software, giving them an overview of the way it worked.

Calypso looked at her watch. "That's mid day now. We'll break for lunch. Can you be back here for one PM, please?" The class broke up. Some went to their cars, others to the LS staff canteen. Vicki decided to give their canteen a try. She joined the queue and bought a ham salad and fries. She took a seat, near the window. There was a view, over the roofs of industrial buildings, of the Wasatch Range. The canteen was crowded. A late thirties woman, in a blue suit, with blonde hair, in a pony tail, came over to the the table that Vicki was sitting at. "Mind if I join you?" She asked. "Sure." Vicki replied. "Vicki." "Carol." Fist pump. The woman sat down and started her lunch. "How are you finding the course, so far?" Vicki asked. "That was a good introduction. I think it is more for the newbies, though." Carol said. "Newbies?" Vicki asked. "People who are new to the company, maybe new to FF." Carol replied. "Ah, like me, I guess." Vicki said. "How long have you been in the business?" Carol asked. "Just a few months." Vicki said. "How are you finding it?" Carol asked. "Well, I'm still learning, really. I did the online course, a few months back, just to understand the basics. How about you?" "I've been in the business over twelve years. I started after I had kids, because it was something that I could do from home." Carol replied. "Are you from around here?" Vicki asked. "No. I live in Cedar City. My husband works in Vegas." "Wow, that's a long commute." Vicki replied. "He's in security. He does a week on, week off rota. The hotel provides him a room, as part of the job." Carol said. "How about you?" "I live in

106

Twin Falls, Idaho. My partner drives a truck, so he is away from home a lot, as well." "You got kids?" "No. Just me and him." "You from Twin Falls?" "No. I'm from Wasilla, in Alaska, but I lived in San Bernardino for about a decade. Cliff is from Pomona." "What made you move to Twin Falls?" Pause. "We just wanted to move away from the big West Coast cities. To move inland, you know, away from all the crime and homelessness, that sort of thing."

They arrived back at the classroom, just before 1:00pm. A few people were there already. Calypso returned and the afternoon's class started. She asked them to log into their laptops. The class all logged in and Calypso gave them the URL for the training website. They logged in and found a training version of the Atlas Connect software. They spent the afternoon working through exercises. They created mock paperwork, using the wizards and uploaded it to databases. They learned about container sizes and weights, shipping costs, legalities, exchange rates and how it all went together, in the Atlas world.

4:30pm came and Calypso let them go. They filtered out of the building, into the mild April air. "What're you doing for dinner?" Carol asked. "I guess I'll go to one of the restaurants, near my hotel." Vicki said. "I know a good steakhouse, just a few blocks from here. Wana join me?" Carol asked. A few minutes later, Vicki's Monte Carlo and Carol's white, 2016 Lincoln MKZ parked next to each other, in a parking lot, at the rear of The Beehive Bar and Grill. They went inside. A waiter seated them. They ordered food and had soft drinks, while they waited. "What sort of trucking does your man do?" Carol asked. "He is a hot-shot trucker. He has a GMC Sierra and a goose-neck trailer. He does a lot of vehicle moves, cars, motorcycles, some agricultural work, there is a lot of that in our region. That sort of thing." "So, is that how you got into freight forwarding?" Carol asked. "Well, yeah. Kinda. I do the scheduling, for him, from home. I find jobs online, phone him and run them past him. So and so load from town A to town B. If he says yes, I bid on it. We try to have loads for most of his miles. Driving with an empty trailer, to get back home, is just wasting diesel." Vicki said. "Also, my Dad does FF. My folks live in Wasilla, he used to work in the port, in Anchorage." She added. "What do you think about your state going independent?" Carol asked. "Does it make it more complicated for you to move goods between states?" She added. Pause. "Well, it's an odd situation, at the moment. Goods that we bring into Idaho, are taxed, by the Idaho government, but goods going from Idaho to US states are not taxed. Likewise, with Texas. Still, the taxes are low and the paperwork is minimal, so not really a big deal." Vicki replied. "Sure. Because, there is still a question around whether the states have actually, legally, left the USA." Carol said. Pause. "Pretty sure we have left." Vicki replied. She got the impression that Carol was not in favor of the independence movement. Should she talk about Utah?" Maybe not. At least, not right now. See how it goes. "So, are you from Cedar City?" Vicki asked. "Sure. Born and raised. Pete is from Vegas. We lived in Vegas for some years. When we had the kids, we decided to move back to my home town. We felt it was a better place to raise kids, than a big city." Carol said. "Now, we're a bit uncertain about the future. If Utah goes independent, he will be doing his weekly commute across an international border." Pause. "True. But, Cliff goes across borders all the time." "Sure. I mean, life will go on. But, the exchange rate, between Utah dollars and US dollars might affect our income, from his work. I guess that could be a plus or a minus." Carol said. "Sure. Our income has been affected a little, by the exchange rate, but usually to our advantage. The Idaho dollar is weaker than the US dollar, in general." Their food arrived and they ate.

*

Thursday evening. Vicki swiped her motel card on the pad by the door and went into her room. She closed the door behind her, showered and changed. She booted her laptop and opened the soft-phone. She clicked on Cliff's icon. Cliff answered. "Hey Babe. How's it going?" He asked. "I'm fine. You?" "Yeah. Good." "Have you had your dinner?" "Sure." "What did you have?" "I had a coupla jacket potatoes and the last of the chilly beef and coleslaw. You?" "I had a Mexican with Carol." Vicki replied. "Who's Carol?" Cliff asked. "A lady on the course." "Ah, OK. You've got yourself a new friend?" "Sure. She's real nice. Lives in Southern Utah. Her man works in Vegas." "You got plenty to talk about?" "Sure. She's been in the FF business for over a decade, she's given me some pointers." "Have you talked about independence?" Cliff asked. "Hahaa! Er, yeah." Pause. "She's not keen on Utah independence. Worried about the exchange rate effecting her husbands pay packet." "Well, the exchange rate has given our income a boost, overall." "I know. But, I don't wana give her the hard sell. I don't think she would appreciate that. She has her own point of view. And we did our bit for Idaho independence, huh?" "Sure. How's the course?" "It's awesome. Learned loads." "Confident about tomorrow?" Cliff asked. "Sure. One hundred multiple choice questions in two and a half hours. Eighty per cent to pass. I can do it." Vicki replied. "Of course you can. And then you get a pay rise." "Well, I get to do end-to-end. Shenzhen to Chicago. Hong Kong to Houston." "Sounds sexy when you say it like that." Cliff said. Vicki giggled.

*

Friday, 4:30pm. Vicki and Carol went into a fast food restaurant, for dinner, before going home. They sat at a table, outside and ate burgers and fries. "How did you do?" Carol asked. "Eighty nine percent." Vicki said. "OK." Carol replied. "You got a pass. That's the main thing." "How about you?" Vicki asked. Pause. "Ninety nine percent." Carol said. "Wow! Well done! Champagne when you get home." "Haha! Yeah, I'll probably have a drink, when I get home." How long does it take to Cedar City, from here?" "Hmm, about three and a half hours. Nearly all the way down the Dominion of Utah." "Dominion?" Vicki asked. Pause. "One of my friends has been talking about the relationship, between the Church of Utah and the Utah Government, if we go independent." Carol said. Pause. "Concerned?" Vicki asked. "Sure. It...might not be good for those of us with other religions." Pause. "You really think Utah will become a ...theocracy?" Vicki asked. Pause. "I don't know. Maybe. Maybe not. I'm a Mom. I work full time, near enough. I have a husband that lives away, fifty percent of the time. I don't have time to get up to speed on all the latest geopolitical stuff." "Uh. OK. Sorry." Vicki replied, awkwardly. "Well, I don't know how things will turn out, for Utah, but...life goes on." She added. "I sure hope so." Carol replied.

*

About 9:00pm, Vicki turned onto her driveway and parked, next to Cliff's Sierra. She got out, took her case from the trunk and went inside. Cliff was in the living room. "Hi Babe." He greeted her with a hug. "Hungry? Lamb stew in the oven." Vicki unpacked her case and Cliff set the table and dished out his stew. They sat and ate and caught up on news. "How has your week been?" She asked. "Mostly local stuff. A load of animal feed to the farm in Pendleton. Other stuff, within the state. I mean, country. How about you?" "Well, I passed." "Yeah. I got your text. Eighty Nine percent is good, well done! You're gonna make us rich now, huh?" "Hahaa! Dunno. Maybe. Hey, listen. Perhaps you should learn FF as well. We could both do it. It would be less tiring for you, than driving." "Mmm. Not sure. I kinda like the road. I've never been a real big desk-guy. Plus, we don't wana put all our eggs in once basket, huh?" "Yeah. I guess." They finished dinner and loaded the dishwasher, then crashed on the sofa.

Vicki put the TV on and flicked around the channels. Cliff booted his laptop and scrolled through some news, on nulla-sepe.com. "How did your friend get on, with the test?" He asked. "Carol? She got ninety nine percent." "Wow, good result." "She's been doing FF for over a decade, she knows it inside out and back to front." "So, you hit it off with her?" "She's a nice lady. We had dinner at a few different restaurants, in the Crossroads. Talked about all sorts." "Even independence." Cliff said. "I mostly stayed off that, as she's a Unionist. We got back onto it, somehow, after the test, this afternoon. One of her friends thinks that the Church of Utah would influence the Utah Government, if the state gets independence." Pause. "I guess she is not a CoU member, in that case?" "No. She said she has a different religion, but did not say what." Pause. Cliff skimmed through a news article. "Some people say that the CoU already influences government." He said, his mind on two things at once. "Do you think they do?" Pause. "Dunno. Maybe." Vicki found a movie and started to watch it. Cliff left the news site and went to cog dot com. He found the page on Utah and started to read. "Hey!" He exclaimed, a few minutes later. Vicki grabbed the remote and paused the movie. She was used to interruptions, from Cliff, as his internet excavations uncovered information gems. "What?" She asked, glancing at the screen of his laptop. "Did you know, Utah had a war, with the United States, in eighteen fifty seven?" He asked. Pause. "No. History was never my subject, in school." She said. She went back to the movie. Cliff went back to reading. "The US Government, at the time, said that Utah was a theocracy, but the CoU did not agree." Cliff went on. Vicki ignored him and continued to watch the movie. Cliff continued to read. "There seems to have been a lot of friction, between Utah and DC, for most of the state's history." He mused. "The Utah Government tried to join the United States, for decades, through the nineteenth century, but the government in DC would not allow it, because of some of the Church's laws." Vicki continued to watch the movie and barely half listened to Cliff. Cliff continued to read. "Before it was a state, it was a territory." He mentioned. Vicki paused the movie. "Whats a territory?" She asked. Pause. "I guess ...a country with a lower status, like a colony." Cliff said. "Taxation without representation." Vicki suggested, then un-paused the movie. A few minutes later. "Oh wow. No way." Cliff exclaimed. Vicki paused the movie again. "What?" "The DC Government offered Utah statehood, on condition that members of the Church were not allowed to vote, in US presidential or mid term elections. The Church declined." "Sounds like discrimination ...by the DC Government, I mean." Vicki agreed, then went back to the movie. Cliff decided to let Vicki watch the movie and read on, in silence. Utah had joined the union in 1896, after the Church had changed some of its laws, he learned. Utah had been a state, for nearly 130 years, but the relationship with the Federal Government had been strained, on numerous occasions. Disputes between ranchers and government agencies had lead to armed stand-offs, in recent times. He neared the bottom of the article, on the cog dot com page. The final paragraph had the most interesting piece of information. The Church of Utah had released a statement, on the referendum. Their position was that Utah should *not* secede from the United States. Cliff had not expected that. He sat and digested the information.

He got another beer, from the fridge, then sat and watched the movie, with Vicki. The laptop went to sleep, but his mind was still on geopolitics. The movie came to an end. "Finished reading?" Vicki asked. "Sure." Cliff replied. "What else did you uncover?" Pause. "Bit of a shocker, actually. The Church of Utah is against independence." Pause. "Really?" Vicki asked. "That's what it says on cog dot com." "Hmm. I would have expected them to be for independence." Vicki said. "More than half of the population of Utah is CoU. If they all vote according to Church, it's likely Utah won't get independence at all." Cliff replied. "Why don't you speak to Jesse about that, get his take?" Vicki suggested.

*

Saturday afternoon. Cliff had done his weekly vehicle maintenance and had lunch. Vicki went to see a friend, across town. Cliff showered and put on fresh denims and polo, then went next door. Jesse had cut their lawn and Sophia was in the back yard, tending the vegetable plot. Cliff gave her a wave and said 'Hi', then knocked on the door. Jesse answered, in his usual check shirt and jeans. "Hey, Dude. Come in." Cliff followed him into the living room. The dining table was covered in newspaper, with several rifles, in bits. Rags, gun oil and cleaning rods lay among the rifle parts. "Busy, as usual?" Cliff asked. "Not too busy, for my neighbor. Wana beer?" "Is the Pope Catholic?" "Hahaa! Good answer." Jesse went into the kitchen and re-appeared with two bottles of beer, from a local craft brewery, in Boise. Cliff sat in an easy chair and Jesse on the sofa. "So, what's been happening in the world of Jesse?" Cliff asked. "Well, I just finished the project, that I have been working on, for the last six months, for a software house in

114

Sacramento. It's been pretty full on. Gonna take a few weeks off and have a break, catch up on a few things. How about you?" "Mostly local stuff, this week, deliveries to farms and what not." "You get enough work?" Jesse asked. "More than enough. I get a fair bit by word of mouth, nowadays." "Awesome. Glad your business is doing well, buddy." Sophia came in and joined them, in her gray leggings and green jumper. "How's Vicki?" She asked. "She's fine. She was away, in the Crossroads, for a week, doing a course." Cliff replied. "She told me about that. How did it go?" "She got eighty nine percent. She's now qualified to do what they call 'end-to-end', which is where the freight-forwarder organizes a container, all the way from a port on the other side of the Pacific, to a supermarket on the Eastern seaboard." Cliff said. "That sounds like a lot of responsibility." Jesse replied. "Sure. She suggested I do the same as her. But, I like the road and I'm not sure about us both working from home. I think we might fall out more often." "You and her are like the reverse of us. You work away from home, Vicki works from home." Sophia said. "Sure. It did her good to get a trip to Utah. I think she needs a change of scene. Most of the time, she's at home or around the town." "Utah's in the news at the mo." Jesse said. "Their referendum is only a few weeks away." He added. "Yeah, well. Vicki met a lady, on the course, who lives in Southern Utah. She told Vicki that she's not keen on Utah getting independence. She was worried about the usual things, exchange rate, whatever else. But, she also said something about the Church of Utah, being involved in the State Government, which worried her. When Vicki told me

115

about that, last night, I did a bit of reading on cog dot com. I was surprised to find that the CoU is against Utah independence." Cliff said. Jesse rested his bottle of beer on his knee and scratched his beard with his left hand, thinking. Cliff continued. "What I wonder, will Utah get independence, at all, if the Church is against it, because, according to the stats that I found, more than half of Utah residents are CoU." Pause. "That's all true." Jesse agreed. "But, I'm still confident that they will get independence." Pause. "You think some of the Church members will not vote the way the Church has told them to?" Cliff asked. "Well, the Church has not exactly *told* it's members to vote a certain way. It has just expressed it's own position. Also, look at the stats from the referendums, that have been done so far. Most of the votes to secede, come from incomers, like us. Of the people who are born and raised in the state, the percentage that vote to secede is usually about forty-five to fifty percent." Jesse explained. "I have not seen those stats. Why do you think that is the case?" Cliff asked. "Surely, the locals are more conservative, than the incomers, from big coastal cities, in general." He added. "Sure, they are, in general. But, they are less aware of how radical the cities have gone. They don't walk or drive through homeless camps everyday. Independence is less imperative, from their point of view." Jesse replied. "So, you reckon Utah will go independent? Are they having a three way question, like Montana and Wyoming?" Cliff asked. "No. Just a two way question. They have about three and a half million people, enough to go it alone. They might join Idaho at some point, or other states, that break away, who knows."

Late April, Tuesday, early morning. Cliff drove North, on the I15, out of Vegas. Industrial estates rolled by the truck windows. Arid mountains met blue sky, in the distance. Behind him, in the box trailer, was a very valuable, custom chopper. The seller had wrestled the chrome-plated, 600lb beast, with its raked out forks, massive 2,000cc v-twin motor and road-roller like 300 section rear tire, into the trailer and Cliff had strapped it down, very carefully, with soft cloth between the straps and the bike. The customer had paid mega-bucks for it and was in a hurry to get it, before the exchange rate doubled the price. Cliff was moving it from Sin City, to the Crossroads, aka, Salt Lake City, about six hours drive.

An hour and a bit later, he past Mesquite and crossed the border into Arizona. The radio played news. Various news stories. The radio signal broke up, as the interstate went into Virgin Canyon. Twenty minutes later, he left the canyon and neared the Utah border. The news had finished. He had not heard anything about the Utah referendum, which was taking place that day. Never mind, he knew the drill. Low turnout, likely to be a No. He stopped at St. George, for diesel and brunch, then hit the road again. The gas station was near the interstate junction, so he did not drive through the suburban areas of the town. He went on, driving through the semi-arid valleys of Utah, with bushes, trees, scrub, ranches and irrigated fields here and there.

He arrived in Salt Lake City, in the early afternoon and the GPS took him to the address, in Upper

Avenues. He texted Chad and waited. A late-fifties man, in blue jeans and a black t-shirt, with a long gray beard, came out. Cliff got out of the Sierra. "Cliff." "Chad." Fist pump. Cliff opened the rear doors of the trailer and pulled out the ramp. They went inside. Cliff unhitched the ratchet straps and took them off. Chad carefully rolled the large, heavy motorcycle out of the trailer, put the kickstand down and stood back. "Nice bike, huh?" Cliff said. "Man, I've wanted one of these for a long time." "Now's the time. Before the exchange rate is against you." Cliff said, closing the trailer doors. Chad paid Cliff his fee, in cash. Cliff printed a receipt, from his portable printer and handed it to Chad. Chad pocketed it and thumbed the bikes starter button. The big twin spun over a few times and came to life. The chrome-covered, air-cooled lump rumbled nicely, sounding healthy. Chad cracked the throttle and claps of thunder came from the open pipes. "You're neighbors are really gonna like you." Cliff quipped.

Cliff hit the I15 again and headed for home. He had stayed in a motel in Vegas, the previous night. It was a little after 2:00pm and Twin Falls was only a few hours away, so he would be home at about 5. Vicki usually had dinner ready, when he arrived home, as long as remembered to text her his ETA. The scenery rolled by. He was tired of the radio, so had started an independent news program, on his phone, before setting off. They mainly talked about Utah. They talked about the lack of coverage of the referendum, in the New York media. They talked about long lines at polling stations, in towns and suburbs across the state. They talked about the possibility that Xerox'd ballots might find their way into the system, as had happened in some other

118

referendums. The people behind the Xeroxing would now have a better idea how many ballots they needed, so this time they might actually change the result.

Cliff arrived home, parked, unhitched and went inside. Vicki had beef stew in the oven. He showered and changed, then they sat and ate. "How was your journey?" She asked. "It was fine. I was a bit nervous, transporting that bike. It was one of the most expensive things I have ever moved, but it went fine. How about you?" "I've been learning to use the Atlas Connect Artificial Intelligence Language Plug-in." "What does that do?" Cliff asked. "It translates English into any other modern language, on the fly, through their messaging app, so that we can talk to people at foreign ports." "Wow, sounds high tech." Cliff replied.

They finished dinner and sat on the sofa. Vicki flicked around TV channels and Cliff opened a browser on his laptop. He read a few news articles, then went to cog dot com, to see if there was an update on the Utah referendum. The page would not load. He tried again. Error 404. Strange. He tried another page on the site, from his bookmarks. Still nothing. He grabbed his phone and texted Jesse. Then he put the phone to one side and watched the TV with Vicki. A few minutes later, his phone pinged.

Hi Cliff, yeah, it's been down for most of the week. Someone hacked them. They have a temp site at cog dot biz. Try that. Jesse.

Cliff typed cog dot biz into the browser and found himself on their home page. "Everything OK?" Vicki asked, when the commercial break came on. "Cog dot com was down. They got hacked. Jesse gave me their new address." He found the Utah page and read the updates. The count had started and it looked promising, although it was still early in the night.

Chapter 8

Blucifer Country

Thursday, early morning, June. Cliff drove up Pena Boulevard, Colorado, Eastbound and turned off, onto East 75th Avenue. To the right, large warehouses. To the left, Denver International Airport, with Blucifer, the stallion, standing guard, at it's entrance. He arrived at the freight company, where the delivery was. He parked in one of the bays, alongside a semi truck and trailer. He got out and walked to the office. "Howdy." He said, to the woman behind the counter. "Howdy. How can I help?" "I have to collect a delivery." He handed her a sheet that Vicki had printed, at home, the day before. She scanned the QR code into her PC. "A Nissan Skyline?" She asked. "That's the one." He agreed. "Where's your truck?" "Parked at the front." "I will get someone to bring it out to you." She pressed the button and called someone to the front desk. Cliff went back out to his truck and put the ramps down at the rear of the trailer. A few minutes later, a car drove around the end of the building. He waved and the driver drove it up the ramps, onto his trailer. It was a showroom condition, Nissan Skyline GT-R R34, in metallic blue, with bronze alloys. The driver got out and handed Cliff papers to sign. He signed them, then carefully strapped the car onto the trailer and slid the ramps back in.

A few minutes later, he was back on the 470, heading for the I25. He drove very carefully. The car had come all the way from Japan. It had a six figure price tag and cost nearly as much to fly it to the USA. Cliff had called his insurance, to be sure that he was covered, for such a high value vehicle.
The customer was a wealthy young software developer, who lived in Boise. He knew Jesse, as they had worked together, on a project in Northern California, before moving to Idaho. He had made some serious money, trading crypto-currencies and decided to splash some of it on the model of car, of his favorite movie hero. Jesse had recommended Cliff, as a careful and experienced vehicle transporter.

Later that morning, Cliff arrived at the queue, to cross the border into Wyoming State, Mountainland. The queue edged forward, one vehicle length at a time. Cliff arrived at the barrier and rolled down his window. He handed the guard his passport and the car papers. The customer had pre-paid the import duty. The guard looked through the papers, then handed them back and raised the barrier. Cliff drove on. A few minutes later, he arrived at Cheyenne and stopped at the gas station. He brimmed the truck, then drove to the semi parking lot and stopped for lunch. He sat and ate his sub and listened to the radio. The news came on. Jesse had told him that Colorado and New Mexico were having a referendum, with a 3-way question, in a few weeks time, but the news said nothing about it. He changed to a local station and listened to local news. The last article on the news was about Colorado. There was to be a counter-independence protest, in downtown Denver, that weekend, which was expected to be peaceful. He hit the I80 and headed West.

Late that evening, he passed Twin Falls, on the I84. He did not stop at home, as he did not want to leave such a valuable car, sitting on his trailer, in his street, while having dinner. Instead, he carried on, up the interstate and arrived in Boise at around mid-night. The GPS took him to the workshop, in Meridian Industrial Estate, where the car was to be fitted with lights and speedo, suitable for North America. He stopped outside the business unit, which was closed for the night and sent a text message. The shop owner texted back that he would be down in ten minutes. Cliff rested his head on the headrest and closed his eyes, for a short power-snooze. Fifteen minutes later, a dark color Crown-Vic pulled up, in front of him. The driver, a large, middle age man in cargo shorts and a t-shirt, got out. Cliff got out. "Cliff." "Randy." Fist pump. "This is the beast, huh?" "Sure. All the way from Japan." Cliff pulled the ramps out and walked onto the trailer. He unhitched the ratchet straps, then reversed the car off the trailer. He got out and let Randy drive it into the workshop. The customer had already paid Cliff his fees in Solana crypto currency, so no money changed hands at the shop.

Cliff hit the road and headed back to Twin Falls. He arrived home at about 2:30am. He parked the Sierra and left the trailer hitched, as he was exhausted. He had driven for about eighteen hours, since leaving his motel in Puritan, North of Denver. Vicki had made him a burger. She knew he did not eat a full dinner, when arriving home very late, but a burger, in a bun, with onions and BBQ sauce went down well, followed by a beer. He sat on the sofa and ate. "I think that's your longest day, ever." She said. "Lucky hot-shots don't have tachographs." He replied. "You should have stopped part way." Vicki said. "No way. Not with a hundred-k-plus ride on the trailer. It's worth it for a pay day like that." He said. "Just be careful when you cash it in. You know how volatile cryptos can be." She replied. "I have a few days clear now." He pointed out. "Sure. You can have a long lie, tomorrow." "Today, actually." Cliff replied, glancing at his watch.

*

Saturday evening. Cliff had done his vehicle maintenance and Vicki her household chores. They sat at the dining table and ate jacket potatoes, salmon steaks and mushrooms. "I heard something on the radio, when I was in Wyoming, about a protest in Denver, against the independence movement." Cliff said. "Yeah. There was something about that in the TV news." Vicki replied. She grabbed the remote and turned the TV on. The news showed a large group of people, marching down Colfax Avenue, holding banners with anti-independence slogans.

They finished eating and sat on the sofa. Vicki had a glass of white wine and Cliff a bottle of beer. The news continued. The protesters were from the ARS, the Anti Reactionary Society. Cliff booted his laptop and opened cog dot biz. He found the Colorado and New Mexico page and started to read. It was a long article. It had been updated, with links to videos, of the protests in Denver. The full name of the organization, behind the protest, was 'Anti Reactionary Society, to End; Hate, Oligarchy & Laissez-faire Economics'. Cliff opened one of the links. It took him to a page on a video platform. He plugged in headphones and started the video. It was a montage of short video clips, taken through the day, edited and uploaded minutes earlier. It showed streets in the Denver downtown, filled with protesters in helmets and armor. The protests had become increasingly violent, as the day went on. ARS protesters clashed with riot police. The police held them back, with riot shields. ARS threw bricks and bottles at the police. The police threw tear gas canisters back, into the crowd. Some of the protesters kicked or batted the canisters back, towards the police. The gas filled the street, obscuring many of the people from the camera. It cut to other clips, from later in the day. The riot got worse. Protesters smashed the windows of stores and restaurants, went inside and looted goods. They set police cars on fire. A group of about 15 or 20 of them, rocked a police car to and fro, until they turned it right over, onto it's roof. Police re-enforcements arrived, in armored cars. Some of them had water cannon, which they used, against the protesters, knocking them off their feet and soaking them. As the evening wore on, the protest started to die down. ARS members started to leave the area. Cliff showed Vicki the video. "TV news did not show any of that." She said. "Well, maybe some of the riot police, but none of that violence, by the ARS." "What I don't get is, why does anyone need to protest against a referendum? If they don't want independence, just vote against it." Cliff said.

*

Several weeks later, in late June. Jesse's Impala cruised down the I80, Eastbound, through Wyoming, Mountainland. Cliff was in the front passenger seat, Kirk in the rear. Their luggage was in the trunk and piled next to Kirk, in the rear. "You don't often have a chauffeur, do you?" Jesse asked Cliff. "Only when Vicki and I go somewhere in her car, on the weekend. I do this road a lot, in the truck." Cliff replied. "You're lucky, I'm stuck in Portland, most of the time, nowadays." Kirk said, from the back. He had driven to Twin Falls and left his 300C parked on Jesse's driveway. Cliff was having a week off work, after several months of being very busy. Jesse had finished a contract, a few weeks back and had not yet started another. They all had some time on their hands. They had set off early, that morning and arrived at their motel, on Frontage Road, Fort Collins, at around 6:00pm. They checked in, showered and went to dinner in a steakhouse, nearby.

They ordered, drank beers and talked, in low tones, while they waited. "So, what exactly is it that the Colexit Party want us to do?" Kirk asked. "The CNM Party, actually. They changed their name, when the Colorado and New Mexico exit parties merged." Jesse replied. "Do they know that I'm not even a Mountainland Citizen?" Kirk asked. "It doesn't matter. You're with us. It'll be fine." "Mainly, what they want is vets and two of us tick that box." Cliff said. "Sure." Jesse agreed. "They have asked for volunteers, from all over the West, who are vets, or bikers, or both." He added. "You're not either." Kirk pointed out. "I can put on boots, cargo pants and look the part." Jesse replied.

They ate dinner, then returned to the motel. They crowded into Jesse's room for a more formal discussion and to check weapons and equipment. "OK." Jesse said. "Rules are, no rifles, handguns must be carried concealed. We must not do anything that might intimidate the voters, in any way. We'll wait in the car, near our polling station and watch for ARS members. CNM will track and monitor ARS buses and notify us, if there is one heading our way. Our job is to protect voters, if any ARS members show up and try to intimidate or assault anyone. We are to use the least amount of force necessary. The use of a firearm is a last resort."

They laid their weapons out, on the desk. Kirk had brought his Wilson Combat EDC X9 compact pistol and a sub-compact, as backup. Cliff had his Rock Island Armory 1911 and a Taurus snub-nose .357 revolver. Jesse had a pair of Heckler and Koch P30 9mm pistols. They all had holsters, spare magazines and lightweight jackets or shirts that would conceal them on a hot summer day. Jesse has also brought cans of bear spray, for each of them, to use in the first instance. "Good. Glad everyone is well prepared. We should not need to use a gun at any stage, only if things really go South." Jesse said.

*

Next morning, Tuesday, they arose early, had breakfast and headed out to the car. Jesse started the Impala's V6 and drove out of the parking lot. "Where are we going?" Cliff asked. "Thunder Lane, Fort Collins, is our post." Jesse replied. "Not Denver?" Kirk asked. "No. They have Denver covered, already." Jesse answered.

They arrived at Thunder Lane and parked at the side of the residential street. "The school is about a hundred yards ahead." Jesse said. "I can see playing fields, ahead on the right." Cliff replied. "Shall we take a walk?" Kirk said. They got out and walked up the side walk. As they neared the school, they saw a sign - 'Polling Place', outside the school entrance. A few people came and went, as they neared the entrance. "No queue yet." Cliff observed. Jesse looked at his watch. "Only just past eight. The polling station will just have opened." They walked past, turned around and headed back the way. Some people arrived on foot, from the local area, others in cars, from streets further away. As they walked past the entrance, back towards their car, a silver VW Beetle parked outside the school. Two middle-aged women got out and went inside. A black, lowered, GMC Syclone pick-up truck parked next to them. A young man with long hair, baggy t-shirt and ragged jeans got out and went in. They continued back, towards Jesse's car. "All sorts of people voting." Kirk observed. "Every demographic, old, young, male, female." Cliff agreed.

They got back into the car, Jesse in the driver's seat, Cliff in the front passenger seat, Kirk in the rear. "No sign of any ARS protesters." Kirk pointed out. "I don't think anything will happen here, TBH." Jesse said. Cliff took a book from his overnight bag and started to read. "What're you reading?" Kirk asked. "A History of Area 51" Cliff replied. "Ha, OK. You turned into an alien aficionado?" He asked. "No, not really. I've driven past the place once or twice, taking loads, between Northern California and other Western States. The book caught my eye, in a newsagent a while ago." Jesse booted his laptop and worked his way through some emails. Kirk plugged ear buds into his iPhone and watched a video. They could see the entrance of the school and kept an eye on it.

The day wore on. They took it in turns to walk up the road, for a closer look, every half hour. Nothing happened. They ate sandwiches and snacks in the car at lunch time. The afternoon wore on. Nothing happened. "Real hurry up and wait deal, huh?" Kirk said. They all laughed. Around 5:00pm, a queue started to form at the school. "People are on their way home from work." Jesse pointed out. "We need to watch carefully, this is when something could happen." He added. "Wana drive a bit closer?" Kirk suggested. "It's real busy around the school now, I don't think we'll get parked neared." Jesse replied. "Lets take another walk then." Cliff suggested. They got out and walked towards the school again. Both sides of the street were solid with cars. The queue was several dozen people long and edged forward, one person at a time. Jesse's Baofeng radio lit up. The co-coordinators were calling him. He pressed the PTT button and answered. "How are things at

Thunder Lane?" A woman's voice came over the radio. "All good, no issues." Jesse replied. They walked back to the car.

The evening wore on. Nothing happened. Cliff was nearly half way through his book. Jesse had run out of admin to do. Kirk had watched several long documentaries. "I'm starting to get peckish." Cliff said. It was 7:45pm. The queue was shorter now, with just a few people outside the door of the school. "OK. I'll check if we can go get dinner." Jesse pushed the PTT on the Baofeng. He told the coordinators that the queue was almost gone and nothing was happening. The woman on the other end said they could go get dinner and thanked them for their help.

Ten minutes later, they parked on College Avenue, near a bar and grill. They went inside. A waitress seated them. She brought them drinks, beer for Cliff and Kirk, alcohol free beer for Jesse. They ordered steaks with fries and salads and waited. "Well, that was an exciting day." Cliff said. "I was actually kinda looking forward to bear-spraying an ARS." They laughed. "Better luck next time." Jesse said. They ate dinner and talked about this and that. Then, the radio lit up again.

11:30pm. Jesse's Impala drove over a rail road track, then turned into an industrial estate. They drove through the estate and arrived at the address that Jesse had been given. It was a warehouse, built of gray box-profile sheeting. He parked the car outside. Various other cars were parked outside the building, unlike most of the other businesses, which were closed at that time of night. "This is where the count is being done?" Cliff asked. "That's what she told me." Jesse said. They got out of the car. It was a balmy Colorado night. They walked around the outside of the building. On one corner, they tripped an IR sensor and a light came on. No one inside noticed. They carried on and walked all the way around. "What are we actually looking for?" Kirk asked. "Deliveries of ballots." Jesse replied. "But, there is no-one here, other than the people inside, doing the count." They arrived back at the car and got in. "Mary said not to wait here all night, just take a look." Jesse said, starting the car. He drove away up the street. They stopped at the stop light. A Freightliner box van drove down the main road and turned into the industrial estate. "Hmm. Where's that going?" Jesse pondered. Kirk looked out of the rear window. "It's stopping at the building we were just at." He said. Jesse whirled the Impala around and drove back. He stopped in the street, nearby. The van had reversed up to a vehicle door, on the side of the warehouse. The driver, a young man in a track suit, got out and pressed a buzzer, next to the door. The door rolled up and a large woman appeared. They spoke to each other, briefly. He opened the rear door of the truck.

"Go!" Jesse said. They scrambled out of the car. Jesse and Kirk ran towards the truck. Cliff followed, walking as fast as he could. Jesse and Kirk arrived at the rear of the truck. The man was inside the truck, moving plastic totes toward the rear. The woman was joined, by several other women, lifting the totes from the tailgate. They looked surprised to see Cliff and Jesse. "CNMP" Jesse said, holding up the plastic ID card that he had been sent, for the job. "What's in these?" He asked. Pause. "Who are you?" One of the women asked. "Jesse Bailey. Volunteer Security Operative for the CNM Party." Jesse held up his plastic card again. "What are you doing here?" The woman asked. "We were asked to check in on this counting center. I assume these boxes contain ballots?" He asked. Cliff and Kirk stood behind him and let Jesse do the talking. There was a long pause as the woman tried to work out how to handle the situation. The driver stood still in the rear of the truck, unsure what to do. "We will need to have a look in some of these." Jesse said. He lifted one of the plastic totes from the tailgate and set it on the ground. He opened the lid and looked inside. It was full of ballots. He took a wad and handed some to each of Cliff and Kirk. They looked through them, the bright floodlights on in the yard, clearly illuminating them. "They are all 'A' votes." Kirk pointed out. "Same here. All to remain in the USA." Cliff agreed. "The signatures are identical on all of them." Jesse added. "These have been photocopied." Cliff said. Several women stood in the doorway of the warehouse, watching Jesse, Cliff and Kirk. The driver of the truck shifted about, uncomfortably. "I am going to have to call this in." Jesse said. He walked away from the door, a dozen yards or so and pressed the PTT button on the radio. He told Mary what they had found. She told him she would pass the message on and asked him to ask the driver, where the ballots had come from. He let her go and returned to the truck. "Where did you bring this load from?" He asked the driver. The driver looked at the woman in charge, with whom Jesse had been speaking. She said nothing. "I picked these up in a parking lot, on the freeway." The man said. Pause. "From another truck?" Jesse said. "Sure." "Where did the other truck come from?" Jesse asked. He saw the woman shaking her head, slightly, in his peripheral vision. The man looked at her, then back to Jesse. He shrugged and said no more. Kirk heard cars approaching and looked around. Several black and white Crown Vics headed down the road and turned into the parking lot. "Local PD." He said. They pulled up around the truck, blocking it in. Several officers got out and walked around the truck. "Who called this in?" One of them asked. "I radioed the CNM HQ and they called you." Jesse said. "And you are?" "Jesse Bailey. Volunteer Security Operative for the CNM Party." He held up his plastic card again. The officers opened some of the totes and looked at the ballots. "OK. And who are you guys?" He asked Cliff and Kirk. They gave their names and showed their cards. "OK. You guys can go. We'll take it from here." The officer said.

They drove back out of the industrial estate. "Hey, I hope those cops are not in on it." Kirk said. "Perhaps we should go back and see what's happening." Cliff suggested. "I don't want to drive right past them, on the road. If they see us, it'll be really obvious that we don't trust them." Jesse said. "Perhaps we can see them from a different road." Cliff suggested, logging into his phone. He found an adjacent road and directed Jesse to it. They drove into the industrial estate again, on a different road. They found a parking lot for some business units, that backed onto the warehouse. There was no gate on the entrance, so they drove in and parked. They got out and walked over to the boundary fence. There were some trees and bushes, between the fence and the warehouse. They peered through them and could see various people, including the police officers. They waited a while, then a recovery truck arrived. The officers moved their cars and the recovery truck hitched the box truck. "Looks like that's getting towed to a police compound." Kirk suggested. It was after 1:00pm when they arrived back at their motel. They went straight to bed, exhausted.

*

A few days later. Kirk had stayed one night, with Cliff and Vicki, then returned home. Jesse went back to business as usual, securing his next contract. Cliff had some local deliveries to do, on Thursday and Friday. He arrived home late on Friday, parked the truck and unhitched the trailer. He went inside. Vicki had cooked dinner and they sat at the dining table and ate. "How was your day?" Vicki asked. "Fine. Coupla deliveries to farms. You?" "Got a container stuck at Long Beach. Been flagged for inspection." "Shit. How did that happen?" "It's happened before. But it did not take so long, last time." "What are they looking for?" "Don't know. They don't tell us." "When does it get moving again." "When they say it gets moving again." "Oh well. Just gotta play the waiting game then. This is why I like the road. Cause I'm in control." "Perhaps I should jack in the FF and buy another GMC Sierra, then." Vicki replied. "Go on then. Become a hot-shot. Lets see you do that." "Lets see you become an FF and make some real money." Vicki came back. "I bring in more than you." Cliff said. "I'm catching you up." Vicki retorted. "Never mind that. Have you heard the result?" Cliff asked. "College football?" Vicki quipped. "No. CNM?" "Yeah, I heard. You guys rock." Vicki replied. "I don't think we can take the credit, for two whole states." "I dunno. It was dead close. Fifty point something to forty nine point something in Colorado. That steal that you stopped could have tipped the balance." "New Mexico was a large margin. Fifty five percent." Cliff said. "Yeah. I wonder why they are so keen on independence." Vicki mused. "I dunno. I'll consult 'the Jesse', sometime over the weekend, when I get time." Cliff replied. "Jesse's the oracle. He knows everything about independence." Vicki said. "I wonder if he is behind the whole thing? Perhaps the whole independence movement is being organized from a suburban house in Idaho." "Stranger things have happened at sea." Cliff replied.

They crashed on the sofa. Vicki put the TV on and looked for a movie. Cliff grabbed his laptop and booted it. He logged on and went to cog dot com. He skimmed through page after page, getting up to speed on everything independence. He decided to just let Vicki watch her movie and he just read. The AI had lost the battle and given up in Alaska. Texas was a lost cause. Idaho State Capitol was now the seat of the Idaho government. The boulder was almost at the top of the hill. Soon, they could stop pushing and it would roll, by itself. Maybe. Or maybe the summit was hidden. Cliff felt that the independence movement was on a roll, but there was a little doubt in his mind, about what lay ahead.

*

Friday, late September. Cliff drove along Highway 160, Eastbound. Behind him, the box trailer, full of

134

furniture and boxes of possessions, belonging to his customer. Eugene and Dawn were a couple from LA, retiring to Pagosa Springs, Colorado. It was a warm, sunny day. The sky was blue, with white cumulus clouds here and there. The road twisted and turned, through the Rockies. Pine forest covered slopes towered over the road and around every bend was a different view. LA to Pagosa Springs was too long a drive, to do in one day, so he had stopped for the night, at a motel, in Flagstaff. He had crossed the border, from Arizona, into New Mexico, passed the Four Corners Monument, then, in under a mile, crossed into Colorado. A sign, by the road, read 'Welcome to Colorful Colorado', but there was no border control. The state's independence day had been less than a week earlier. Cliff was not sure whether there would be border control on the 160. He usually drove on interstates, when doing long hauls, but there was no interstate to Pagosa Springs. Most of the states that had seceded so far had border controls in place immediately, but only on the major routes. The smaller highways would no doubt get border controls some time later. As he neared the town, the GPS took him off the highway, onto a dirt road. The road was wide and well surfaced, with stone chippings. It went uphill, twisting and turning, through forest. Houses and bungalows were dotted about, here and there, just visible, through the trees. He arrived at the customers house at 5:15pm. Eugene's dark gray, 2020, Malibu and Dawn's wine red, 2017 Chrysler 200 were parked outside. Eugene's bike trailer, with his Indian Scout was still hitched to the rear of the Malibu. The house was a large, modern bungalow, of brown painted clapboard and a terracotta color box-profile roof. Cliff parked and turned the Sierra's engine off. Eugene appeared at the door and walked over towards the trailer. Cliff got out. "Howdy." "Howdy." Fist pump. "Can you reverse the trailer, up to the front door?" Eugene asked. "Sure thing." He got back in and drove away from the house, over the large, gravel parking area. Then, he carefully reversed the trailer, towards the front door, making small corrections. Eugene waved him on, then put a hand up, to stop. Cliff got out again and opened the trail gate. Dawn appeared, with a hand trolley. They started to move boxes into the house, Cliff shuffling the boxes to the rear of the trailer, Eugene and Dawn going to and fro with hand trolleys. Cliff and Eugene carried sofas and other furniture inside. After an hour or so, everything was inside.

"Would you like a cup of coffee?" Dawn offered Cliff. "Thanks. Milk, no sugar." Cliff replied. "Have a seat." Eugene pushed a dining chair towards Cliff. Cliff sat down and rested. Eugene and Dawn sat down on dining chairs. "We can't off you a seat on the sofa." Dawn said. The sofa was piled up with boxes. "No worries. That is usually the case on these jobs." Cliff replied. "What am I due you?" Eugene asked. Cliff opened the calculator on his phone. "Let's see, eight hundred and thirty five miles at two dollars per mile, is one thousand, six hundred and seventy miles. You paid a six hundred deposit, so that is one thousand and seventy dollars." "Cool. Cash OK?" Eugene asked. "Sure, perfect." Cliff said. Eugene took a jiffy bag from his rucksack and took out a wad of US dollars. He counted out eleven Benjamins. "There you go, keep the change." Eugene said. "Thank you, kindly, Sir." Cliff replied.

"We would usually ask you to stay for dinner, but all the kitchen stuff is still boxed." Dawn said. "That's OK. That is usually the case, when people are moving." Cliff replied. "Mind if I ask, what gas mileage do you get from your Sierra?" Eugene asked. "I get about nineteen to the gallon, with a full load, twenty one with a small load, or empty trailer." "Ah, OK. I have been thinking about getting a truck, now that we are living out in the boon-docks." Eugene said. "And I had better get it sooner, rather than later, as the Rangeland dollar to US dollar might not be in my favor." He added. "I think the Rangeland dollar is likely to be one of the strongest of the independent states. Colorado alone has a population of nearly six million, add New Mexico and that is nearly eight million, more than twice the population of Mountainland, including Montana and Wyoming." Cliff said. "Well, the Texas dollar is strong, certainly. Yours is weak, more than two Mountainland dollars to one US." Eugene replied. "Yeah. It works well for my earnings. When I do work in the US states and get paid in US, I basically double my money, when I go home. But, the cost of living is high in Mountainland. Anything imported is expensive. Me and the missus used to joke about boot-legging groceries from Utah, but now they're independent, as well." "Well, I don't know your view of the independence movement, but I like the idea of being free from DC." Eugene said. "Oh, sure. I voted to secede, as did Vicki and our neighbors. Myself and a coupla other guys volunteered to do security, for the CNM, at a polling station in Fort Collins." Cliff replied. "How did that go?" Eugene asked. "Nothing happened at the polling station. But, the dispatch lady asked us to check out a counting center, late at night. We caught someone delivering a truck load of photocopied ballots, all no votes." Cliff replied. "Wow. Someone really does not want the US to break up." "Yeah. Someone in DC." Cliff agreed. "Same deal as the presidential race, fake ballots finding their way into the system." Eugene agreed.

Chapter 9

The Middle Pillar

The following January. Cliff drove up Highway 71, Nebraska, Northbound. Behind him, a load of lumber, for a customer who was building a house in Scottsbluff. Mountainland was selling plenty of lumber, to customers in US states, due to the exchange rate. Cliff was getting plenty of work, taking loads of lumber from a sawmill in Pocatello, to the Dakotas, Nebraska and sometimes further. He had set out early and driven all day, down the I80, through Wyoming and into Nebraska. There was no border control and no taxes, outbound, from Mountainland into the USA. He had crossed the border, at Pine Bluffs, without stopping. There was a queue, at the Nebraska-Mountainland border, on the Westbound carriageway. He sometimes took shortcuts, but when there was snow on the ground, he kept to interstates and divided highways, as they had more traffic and were more likely to be clear. It had gotten dark, but was a light night, due to the snow and a full moon, in the starry sky. He arrived at the customer's plot, just before 5:00pm. It was a large lot, on the South side of town, surrounded by other houses. He parked at the side of the road, alongside the plot. The customer was already there, working on the foundations. He brought his forklift over to Cliffs trailer and unloaded it, setting the pallets of clapboard down on the snow covered gravel. He paid Cliff and thanked him. Cliff hit the road, driving around town to a motel. The motel parking lot was rather small, so he found a residential street nearby and parked at the side of the road. He set the trailer alarm and walked back to the motel. He paid and went to his room. He went online and ordered dinner, then had a shower. Dinner arrived and he went to reception to get it. He sat, ate and watched news, on his laptop.

The hosts of the news program talked about various news, then went onto the latest events, relating to independence. Colorado and New Mexico had formed a new country, called 'Rangeland'. That had changed the geopolitical landscape, more than any other state's secession. Rangeland bordered Texas, to the South-East, Utah to the West and Wyoming State, Mountainland, to the North. Independent states now stretched from the Mexican border in the South, to the Canadian border in the North. It was no longer possible, to drive from New York, to LA, entirely within the USA. It was necessary to cross one or more foreign countries, to get from shining sea to shining sea. Goods were being taxed, by Mountainland, Utah, Rangeland or Texas governments, when being transported from the West coast, to cities and towns in the Mid-West and Eastern seaboard. The New York media were talking about that, constantly, while avoiding talking about the AI withdrawal from the State Capitols of Texas, Idaho, Montana and Wyoming. The AI were playing the same game in Salt Lake City, Denver and Santa Fe, but the media barely mentioned that. Most Americans followed independent media and knew that the state governments re-located elsewhere, shortly after a successful referendum and before their leave date. Anyone watching could see that secession had become formulaic.

*

Monday, late January. The Horizon Airlines Boeing 737 touched down at Sioux Falls Regional Airport. The pilot thanked the passengers for flying with Horizon. Passengers got up from their seats and took their luggage from the lockers overhead. Cliff and Jesse did likewise and filtered out of the airplane, with the other passengers. They went through immigration control, Jesse getting a tourist visa, Cliff using his work visa. They made their way to the car rental office to collect the keys to their ride. The lady behind the counter went through the paperwork and directed them to the pick up point. They went outside, to the pick up point. A minute or so later, a young man delivered their car, a Nissan Kicks SUV. They put their bags in the trunk and Jesse took the wheel. "Nice, er, big car." Cliff commented, from the front passenger seat. "The party would only pay for a compact, but it's only for a few days." Jesse replied. They drove to their hotel, in the down town, a few blocks from the I29. Jesse parked and they went inside. They checked in, went to their rooms and showered. There was a knock at Cliff's door. He answered and Jesse was there. "I'm going to pick up Eugene, his flight should be in now." He said. "OK. I'll head out and get a beer."

Cliff went to the restaurant next door and got a table.

Half an hour later, Jesse and Eugene arrived. "Hey dude, how you doing?" Eugene asked, sitting down at the table. "I'm good. How was your flight?" Cliff asked. "It was fine, thanks." Eugene replied. "Durango Airport is a lot smaller than LAX, which is what I'm used to. So that was a plus, but I needed my passport to fly to South Dakota, so that's different." He added. They drank beer, while they waited for dinner to arrive and talked about the next day. "It's the same deal as last time." Jesse said. "Use of a firearm is an absolute last resort. Only if we, or someone else, is threatened, would we use a gun. We'll have some bear spray, to use in the first instance. If we see suspicious people, we approach them and ask them what they are doing, first." "What guns did you guys bring?" Eugene asked. "I brought my Rock Island nineteen eleven and my Taurus revolver." Cliff said. "I had to buy a coupla hard cases, to put them in as checked luggage. I've not flown with firearms as a civilian, before." He added. "I have H and K pistols." Jesse said. "OK. I brought my Kel-Tec K9. I just brought one gun. We're not gonna encounter a real mob, right?" Cliff and Jesse laughed. "The last one of these that we went on, absolutely nothing happened." Jesse said. "Apart from catching a trucker, delivering fake ballots to a counting center." Cliff and Jesse told the story of that night. Their dinner arrived and they ate.

*

Next morning, early. After breakfast, the three men got into the little Nissan. Jesse took the wheel and they drove to the polling station that the Mid West Independence Party had allocated to them. It was in a large suburb, called Brandon, South of the I90. Jesse parked the car in a parking lot, next to the school. "Lets take a walk." He said. They got out of the car. All three looked the part, smart but practical. Cliff wore desert boots, khaki cargo pants, a black wool jacket and black ball cap. Jesse wore his usual black boots, blue jeans and red and black checkered jacket. Eugene wore biker boots, black jeans and a black leather jacket. They walked around the school. A school bus was dropping off children. At the other end of the building, a sign read 'Polling place this way'. A few people followed the sign, to the side entrance and went inside, to vote. "Dead quiet." Cliff observed. They went back to the car. "I'm gonna park where we can see the entrance." Jesse said. He drove to a different space, at the other end of the school, where they could see the entrance from the car. "Do we have to report to the staff, here?" Eugene asked. "No. I just call the dispatch." Jess said. "Can you pass my bag?" Eugene passed Jesse his overnight bag from the rear seat. Jesse took out the Baofeng radio, called in and confirmed that they were on site. "Who are we doing this for. I know you told me, but I forgot." Eugene asked, from the rear seat. "We are volunteers for MWIP, that reminds me ..." Jesse rummaged in his bag again. "Here's your ID card." He handed Eugene his plastic photo-ID card. "Wow, very professional." Eugene hung the lanyard around his neck. "Em-whip, huh?" "Mid-West Independence Party. They work with the State Governments, of North and South Dakota, Nebraska,

Kansas and Oklahoma, to organize the referenda, for those states." Jesse explained.

The morning wore on. Cliff read a book. Eugene surfed the web, on his Android tablet. Jesse dealt with work emails and admin, on his laptop. Cars, mini-vans and trucks came and went, a steady trickle of voters, going to the polling place. "Hey, check that out." Eugene said. Cliff and Jesse looked up. "See the sticker on that RAM?" They looked at a red, 2005 Dodge Ram double cab, parked nearby. On the rear bumper, was a sticker that read 'Brandon, Let's Go Vote!' They all laughed. "He's doing his bit." Jesse said. "As long as the unionists don't read it." Cliff suggested. "Nah. There are more of us. As long as the turn out is good, we win." Jesse said.

Nothing happened, that morning. Lunch time came and went. The afternoon wore on. They had a walk around the school grounds, just to get out of the car for a bit. Nothing happened that afternoon. Late afternoon, a queue formed, of voters on their way home from work. Nothing happened. 6:30pm, Jesse radioed dispatch and they got permission to leave, to go and get dinner.

"What did you do for a living, in LA, Eugene?" Cliff asked Eugene. "Hey, just call me Gene, dude." Gene replied. "OK, Gene it is." Cliff agreed. "I was a gaffer, for forty five years." Gene said. "I went to work for Outlaw Studios, when I was eighteen. They don't exist any longer. I worked for Marsh Productions, for over twenty years. They went out of business as well. I worked for Red Lip Movies, for the last ten years. They're still going." "Times change, huh?" Jesse agreed. Their dinner arrived and they ate, then had a few beers. "What do you do?" Gene asked Jesse. "I'm a software developer. I'm a contractor. I write software, build websites, develop data bases, whatever comes my way." Jesse replied. "Awesome. Computers are black magic, to me. I can power my laptop on and open a browser and my mail client, that's about it." Gene said. "That's just the generation gap." Jesse replied. "How long have you been a trucker?" Gene asked Cliff. "Three and a bit years." Cliff replied. "What did you do before that?" Gene asked. Pause. "I was in the Special Forces." Cliff replied. "What did you do in the Special Forces?" Pause. "I was a demolition specialist. I was only in the Special Forces for a few years. Before that, I was in the Army." "Afghanistan? Iraq?" Gene asked. "Yeah. And a load of other countries. One of the perks of the military. You get to travel a lot." "I've known a few people, who were in the military, over the years, you know. I knew a guy who had PTSD, after a tour of Iraq. Military service takes a toll." Gene said. "Not being political, just, you know, thinking aloud." Pause. "I didn't get PTSD, but I got to become a cyborg." Cliff replied. He swung his leg out of the booth and pulled up his pants leg a little. Gene glanced down, then raised his eyebrows. Cliff put his steel leg away again. "How did that happen?" Gene asked. "IED." Cliff replied. "Me and the crew, in a Humvee, in ...a Middle Eastern country, hit one. Wrecked the whole vehicle. We should have been air lifted out, but it was one of ...those missions. I was lucky." Pause. "The driver ...didn't make it. The two guys in the back had minor injuries. We got a ride to a field hospital in a neighboring country. They did what they could. I was flown back to a

144

hospital in the States. They had to take my leg off, just above the knee. I got a trans-tibial prosthesis." "Shit. Man, that's harsh. How do you get on with that?" Gene asked. "I manage OK. I had to learn to walk again. I was homeless, in LA, for about six months, that was a challenge. I can only drive auto, now, cause I don't have a clutch foot. But, I have done loads of stuff that I thought I couldn't. Moved furniture, been up ladders, all sorts." Cliff replied.

Thirty minutes later, they arrived in an industrial estate, just off the I229. Jesse drove to the address that they had been given and parked nearby. It was dusk. The radio had gone off, while they were at the diner. The dispatcher had asked them to go take a look at the counting center, in Sioux Falls. They got out of the car and walked down the sidewalk, to the building. A number of cars were parked in the parking lot. Lights were on, inside the building. They walked through the entrance and into the parking lot, then around the outside of the building. It was quiet, no one was around. They came to a high fence at the rear corner of the building and could not go any further. Cliff flexed the chain link fence a little, at head height and was able to see down the rear of the building. "Anything?" Jesse asked. "Nothing. Concrete yard. A few dumpsters." He replied. They went back to the car. "What do we do now?" Gene asked. "We wait." Jesse said. "Hurray up and wait, again." Cliff quipped. Jesse looked at his watch. 9.30pm. "We might have to wait a while. The last time fake ballots were delivered, it was late at night." They sat and watched the entrance to the building. They talked. They read books. They watched pod casts. Mid night came and went. Nothing happened.

145

Then, a light went on, at the rear of the building. Cliff looked up, from his book. "See that?" Jesse and Gene looked up. "Someone has tripped a PIR." Jesse said. "Probably just stepped outside for a smoke." Gene suggested. "We ought to check it out, just in case." Cliff suggested. "Kinda hard to access the rear of the building, cause of that fence." Gene said. "If we drive to the next street, we might be able to walk through another business's parking lot and see the rear of the building." Cliff suggested. Jesse started the Kicks and they drove around the block. He parked near the entrance to a building that backed onto the counting center warehouse. They got out and walked through the parking lot. As they neared the fence, at the boundary of the lots, they heard voices, coming through the trees and bushes. They reached the fence and peered through. A door, at the rear of the building, was open. Several people were going to a fro, from the door, into the yard. They watched a woman come out of the door and walk across the yard. She stopped, in the middle of the yard, then bent down. A plastic tote popped up, out of a man hole. She grabbed it, turned and went back inside. A young man took her place, by the man hole. Another tote popped up and he grabbed it. A pair of hands disappeared back in the man hole. Another woman took his place, grabbing the next tote and dashing back inside. So it went on. One tote after another and another and another. "I need to call this in." Jesse said. "Shit. I left my radio in the car." He turned and ran through the parking lot, out onto the road. He headed back to the Nissan, fifty or so yards away. As he ran, he saw an International Step Van, about a hundred yards further up the road. Someone seemed to be busy at the rear of the van. He pressed the button on the Kicks's fob. It unlocked. He opened the driver's door and grabbed the Baofeng from the center console. Standing next to the car, he looked up the street, hoping that the people at the van had not seen him. He pressed the PTT button on the radio. "Jesse, calling HQ. Over." "HQ to Jesse. Over." A woman's voice came back. "Bogus ballot delivery in progress. Over." "What location. Over?" Jesse gave her the address. "Can you remain on site until law enforcement arrives? Over." She asked. "Still on site. Over and out." Jesse looked up the road, towards the step van. He wondered if he should go and look, or go and see the other guys. He turned around to go back and saw Gene coming towards him. "Wassup?" Jesse asked. "They've stopped moving crates and put the man hole cover back." He said, a little breathless, after a brisk walk, back from the yard. Cliff appeared at the entrance and headed back towards the car.

Jesse did the math. The traffickers were done and about to leave. He had to act, right then. He turned back, towards the van and started walking. He took one of his P30s from it's holster, pulled the slide back and let it go, chambering a round. Better be prepared, in case the traffickers were armed. He glanced over his shoulder and saw Cliff and Gene following him. The boys had his six. Cliff had his 1911 drawn and a round chambered. As he approached the van, he saw several young men in hoodies, wrestle a man hole cover back into place, behind the van. They saw Jesse and the boys approaching and scrambled into the van. The driver started the engine and they peeled away from the kerb, nearly running over Jesse. He, Cliff and Gene

147

scrambled onto the grass verge, missing the van by inches. Jesse raised his pistol, towards the van, temped to take a shot, but stopped himself.

They had to play by the rules. Any wrong move and the media would never let it go. Jesse and Cliff holstered their hand guns, they all stood up and head back to the car. They got back into the car. "Too late this time." Gene said. "I got the license plate number." Jesse said. They drank some water and chilled. A few minutes later, a black and white Dodge Charger turned into the street. The police stopped in front of them. An officer got out and walked up to their car. Jesse put the window down.
"Got a call for ballot traffickers in this street." The officer said. Jesse gave him the license plate number and a brief account of what had happened.
"So, you saw people taking crates out of a man hole, into the warehouse?" The officer asked. "Sure. Into the counting center." Jesse replied. "Where did you see this?" The officer asked. "From the parking lot of that business, there." Jesse pointed to the premises where they had been. "When did this happen?" The office asked. "About half an hour ago, now I guess." Jesse replied. "What are you guys doing, out on an industrial estate, at night?" The office asked. "We are volunteer security guards for the Mid West Independence Party. We were sent to check out the counting center, to see if there was anything unusual. We saw a light go on, after mid night, at the rear of the building and went to check it out." Jesse said, holding up his ID card, for the office to see. "OK. We will take it from here. You guys go back to your motel." The officer said. He went back to the cruiser and got into it. Jesse started the Kicks and drove away. "Are we gonna

148

make sure that the cops go to the counting center?" Cliff asked. "No. He told us to go. If he catches us snooping around again, we'll be in trouble." Jesse said. "I'll hear, through the MWIP, what happens at that counting center." He added. "It was you guys that caught ballot traffickers, both times?" Gene asked, from the back seat. "There have been many cases of fake ballots being delivered to counting centers, in various States." Jesse said. "That's why the Independence Parties send people like us to check on them." He added. They returned to their motel and went to their rooms, exhausted after a long day.

*

Mid April. Cliff's Sierra drove Eastbound, on the I80, through Nebraska. Cliff sat in the passenger seat, Vicki behind the wheel. They had traded places at North Platte, after Cliff had driven them, from Rock Springs, Wyoming, where they had stayed the night. They had passed through the US States of California and Nevada, across the border into Utah, then back out of Utah, into Wyoming, Mountainland, then from Wyoming into Nebraska. They were moving a $70,000 Dodge Challenger SRT Hellcat, from the bay area, to it's new home in Des Moines, Iowa. The weather was fine, for Spring. Still cold, but dry and bright. The radio played funky beats, as it always did, when Vicki was on board. "That's about fifteen hundred miles done, three hundred to go." She spoke up, looking at the mileage counter. "Three international borders crossed, one to go." Cliff said. "Lucky I got the customer to pre-pay the taxes." He added. "Fancy, no AI at any of the State Capitols, in Westland." Vicki replied. "They have

149

given up on that game." Cliff said. "They've tried using the military, propaganda, fraudulent ballots, riots and just plain pretending independence isn't happening. I wonder what DC's next trick is gonna be?" Cliff mused.

A little later, they drove through Omaha, Nebraska. Shortly after the junction, with the I480, they saw a sign, on an overhead gantry, that read 'US Border Control Ahead'. "Did you see that?" Cliff said. "Sure, I saw it. There isn't usually US Border Control on the borders of independent States, is there?" She asked. "I never encountered that." Cliff replied. She braked to a stop, at the rear end of the queue and put the truck's 4 blinkers on, to alert any fast approaching traffic. A few sedans and a semi pulled up, behind them. The queue edged forward, one vehicle length at a time. After a while, they arrived at the barrier. "What's the purpose of your journey?" The border control office asked. "Transporting goods, for a customer." Vicki said. "What type of goods and what value?" He asked. "One automobile, valued at seventy thousand US dollars." Vicki replied. "That will be two thousand, one hundred US dollars." The officer replied. Pause. "You're telling us we have to pay import tax, to bring the car into the US?" Vicki replied. "Correct. We can take payment by credit card, or cash." The officer replied. Cliff handed Vicki the company credit card, that he used, when on the road. She put it into the Chip and PIN reader and keyed in the PIN. The payment went through and she handed the card back to Cliff and the reader back to the office. The barrier went up and they drove off, over the Missouri River Bridge.

"Was not expecting that." Cliff said. "No. Usually, there are notices on FF dot net, when import taxes change, but there was nothing about US imposing duty at the Westland border." Vicki replied. "They have only been independent for a few weeks, it must be a new thing." Cliff suggested. He took his laptop from his rucksack and booted it. He logged on and went to cog dot com. He found the page on Westland and read through the recent updates. "The Government in DC has not acknowledged Westland as a country and still considers North Dakota, South Dakota, Nebraska, Kansas and Oklahoma as US States, as has been the case with all the other independent States." He read from the site, for Vicki. "But, the house has past a bill, whereby the Federal Government can charge a three percent tax on goods, being moved across State lines." He added. "The new legislation gives the Federal Government the right to use their discretion, as to which State lines will attract the tax. It will not be applied to States in the Eastern half of the country, but will apply, in many cases, to Western States." "They are trying to claw back some of the tax money, that they would have been getting, from Western States." Vicki replied. "And to discourage other States from seceding." Cliff said. "And they are still trying to get other taxes, from the independent States. Taxation, without representation." He added.

They arrived at Des Moines in the early evening. They drove through the city on the I235 and turned off, into the suburb of Rising Sun. They arrived at the address. It was a large, 2-story house, down a long driveway, through large lawns, with mature trees dotted about. Vicki turned into the drive, drove up to the house and parked. They got out of the truck. Cliff took out his phone, to call the customer, but the house door opened. A tall man, in a check shirt and beige chinos, came out. "Hi Guys, you made it!" He said. "Sure did. I'm Cliff." "Rick." "Vicki." Fist pumps. "I'll take it off the trailer, for you." Cliff said. He pulled the ramps out of the rear. Vicki helped him undo the ratchet straps. A few minutes later, the white, wide-body muscle car was on the driveway. Rick checked it over. "All good." he confirmed. "What am I due you?" He asked. "Well, the price that we agreed, three thousand, six hundred, for our service, but, we also had to pay two thousand, one hundred US dollars, at the Iowa border." He handed the receipt, from the border control, to Rick. Rick looked at it. "Yeah, I heard about the State Line Tax. Not a problem. What does that make the total?" "Five thousand, seven hundred, minus the one thousand eight hundred deposit, is three thousand, nine hundred." Cliff replied. "Come inside." Rick said. He lead them through a side door, into his kitchen. "Take a seat, I will be back in a mo." He disappeared through another door, then appeared with a wad of cash. He counted out 39 $100 notes, onto the dining table, then handed them to Cliff.

*

After a night in a motel, in the small town of De Soto, near Des Moines, they hit the road again, heading West, on the I80, for home. Cliff drove in the morning, then they stopped at Big Springs, for lunch and diesel. They traded places and Vicki drove, through the afternoon. "Wana try a back road, to cross the border, into Wyoming?" Cliff suggested.

"We don't have a load now, so, what's the point?" Vicki asked. "I would be interesting to see if there is border control, on a country highway." Cliff replied. They turned off the interstate, at Kimball and headed West, on Highway 80. As they neared Pine Bluffs, they saw a sign at the side of the road. It read

'Road Closed

Local Traffic Only

Use Interstate 80'.

Up ahead, in the distance, was a barrier, across the road. They turned onto Highway 30 and re-joined the interstate, then stopped at the end of the queue.

*

Next day, Saturday afternoon. Cliff finished his bacon and eggs and washed the dishes. Vicki was out for the day, doing something, or seeing a girl friend, across town. He decided to see if Jesse was around. He put a pair of trainers on and went next door. Jesse came to the door. "Come in." Cliff followed Jesse inside. "Beer?" "Thanks." "Grab a seat." Cliff sat on the sofa and Jesse disappeared into the kitchen. He reappeared with two bottles of beer. They sat and drank. "What's happenin'?" Cliff asked. "Usual. Busy with work all week. Sophia is out shopping." "Vicki is out as well." "They went out, together, earlier on." "Ah, right. That's where Vicki is." "Doesn't she tell you where she's going?" "She shouted something, when she went out this morning, but I didn't hear what she said, because I was busy with the angel grinder, in the garage." "What were you grinding?" "I've fitted a new back box on the truck. The old one was rusty. Had to cut the bolts with the angle grinder and the hangers with a knife." "It didn't wana come off." "No. But, it's done now, a shiny new one in it's place." "Cool. Been anywhere interesting, this week?" Jesse asked. "Me and Vicki took a Dodge Hellcat, from the your neck of the woods, to Des Moines." "That's a long one." "Yeah, that's why Vicki came along, we shared the driving, drove about thirteen hours a day, between us." "Wow. What happens to her side of the business, when she comes along?" "She does not start any new containers, when she's on the road with me. She did odds and ends on her laptop, in the motel." "You guys must be raking it in." Jesse quipped. "Ha! Dunno about that. Well, we do alright, I guess. We had to shell out over two grand at the border, though." "Which border?" "In Omaha, going into Iowa. The US Border Control asked for three percent of the value of the car, which was seventy K." "Shit. You out of pocket?" "No. The customer paid it all and our fee, no problem. He was loaded. His house was a palace, in about two acres of lawn." "Cool. Yeah, I heard about the new tax. Just DC trying to stop the independence machine." "You think they will succeed?" Cliff asked. "No chance. The machine keeps moving. They can't stop us." "Where do you think will be the next State to secede?" "Arizona is having a referendum in about two weeks." "OK. Going it alone? There aren't any other States that border it, that haven't already left, except California and I can't see them joining Arizona." "Arizona is having a three way question. Full independence, remain in the USA, or join Rangeland." "Hmm. OK. Colorado, New Mexico and Arizona, making one country. I guess that makes sense." "Are you up for some more security work?" Jesse asked. "When?" "In about two weeks, early May. I don't know the exact date, or location, yet." "Text me when you know, I'll try to keep my calendar clear, for a few days."

Chapter 10

10-71

Monday, mid May, Mountain Home Air Force Base. Jesse's Impala pulled up and stopped, at a barrier, on the road. Jesse rolled his window down and swiped a plastic card on the card reader. The barrier raised and Jesse drove through. "Where did you get a card, that gets you into an AFB?" Cliff asked, from the front passenger seat. "The Idexit Party supplied it, during our vote, so that I could get access, for meetings and what not." He replied. "Wow. Access all areas, huh?" "No. Just the front gate and an office." Jesse replied. They turned right, down a long, straight road and drove for a few blocks. Jesse parked the car in a parking lot and they got out. They took their bags from the trunk and Jesse locked the car. Cliff put his rucksack on and they walked across the parking lot, to an aircraft hanger. They passed between two aircraft hangers and arrived at the edge of the taxiway. A Lockheed C130 Hercules was parked, in front of the hanger. It was dark gray, with 'Mountainland Air Force' stenciled on the side. On the tail, was an Idaho Flag. Jesse lead the way. They arrived at the steps, near the front of the plane and climbed on board. They turned left, into the cargo area of the plane. Down either side, were red canvas seats. At the rear, were a few shrink-wrapped pallets. They put their bags down, sat near the front and put seat belts on. Cliff unzipped one of the pockets on his rucksack and took out two pairs of ear plugs, handed one pair to Jesse and put his in his ears. "You've been on one of these before?" Jesse asked. "Sure. Many times. All over the world." Cliff replied. "Have you?" "No. Never." Jesse replied. "Well, they're really quiet and comfortable and you get a great view, from the windows." "Gotcha."

The pilot and co-pilot arrived, said 'Hi' and went into the cockpit. A little later, the engines started up. They taxi'd to the runway and took off. The plane climbed hard. They kept their feet firmly planted on the steel floor and held onto their rucksacks. A few minutes later, they were at cruising altitude. Cliff craned his neck, to look out of one of the small portholes, behind his seat. Below, were the irrigated circles of Snake Valley. He turned back and took out his book.

Later that day, they landed at Davis Monthan Air Force Base, in Tucson, Arizona. They thanked the pilot and disembarked. It was a balmy evening. They walked across the concrete, into the town of Davis Monthan. They stopped on Phoenix Street. "I'll give him a call." Jesse said. He took his phone from his pocket and called Gene. "Hey, we're at the base ... next to the plane ... OK, see you .... He's a few minutes away." A few minutes later, a gray Malibu drove down the road and stopped beside them. Cliff got into the front passenger seat and Jesse into the rear. "Good flight?" Gene asked, driving away. "Well, Cliff says C130s are quiet and comfortable, but I'm not sure what he is comparing them to." Jesse said. "How was your drive?" Cliff asked. "It was fine. Did it in about nine hours, including twenty minutes wait, at the border." Gene said. "Hey, where am I going? Where's our motel?" He asked, as they came to the bases exit. Jesse directed him and they arrived at their motel, a few minutes later. They went to their rooms, showered and went to find a restaurant. They drank beer and chatted, while they waited for food to arrive. "How did you guys get a ride on a C130, anyway?" Gene asked. "Someone in the Idexit Party is a USAF vet and knows people in the Mountainland Air Force. When I told him that Cliff and I were going to Tucson, as RSVs, he said he might be able to get us a ride on a cargo plane, to save a few bucks." Jesse explained. "What is the MAF doing, landing at a USAF base? Do the USAF trust our guys?" Cliff asked. "Sure. They are trading some gear, dunno what exactly, for some airplane parts, from the Airplane Boneyard." Jesse replied. "What's an 'RSV'?" Gene asked. "Referendum Security Volunteer. That's us." Jesse said. Diner arrived and they tucked into a good Mexican meal.

*

Tuesday morning, early. Cliff and Jesse left their motel rooms and walked across the parking lot, to Gene's Malibu. "How'd you sleep?" Jesse asked. "Fine. You." "Sure. Fine." "What's the plan?" Cliff asked. "Wait for Gene, then go get breakfast." Gene arrived and let them into the car, Cliff in the front, as usual, as rear seating was award for him, Jesse in the rear. "Where to?" Gene asked, starting the engine. "There's a cafe a coupla blocks from here that does breakfast. Turn left outa here." They arrived at the cafe a few minutes later and went inside. They ordered ham and eggs and talked while they waited. "What do we reckon? Another quiet day?" Gene asked. "Probably." Cliff replied. "Although, there was something on cog dot com about traffickers trying to disrupt the referendum." He added. "I've discussed that with the RIP, already. They've assessed the situation and think that there is no more risk of any trouble than at the polling stations that we have watched, previously." "RIP?" Gene asked. Pause. "Rangeland Independence Party." Cliff got in, before Jesse could answer. "Same crowd that organized the Colorado and New Mexico referendums." He added. Jesse looked at him, eyebrows raised a little. Breakfast arrived and they ate. After breakfast, they left the cafe and walked to the parking lot, Northwards, on Windsor Avenue. Jesse and Gene were in front, Jesse nearer to the road, Gene on the inside. Cliff followed behind.

The following took place in less than a minute, this is a slow motion paragraph

Traffic went to and fro on the road. Cliff's Special Forces Sixth Sense kicked in. He sensed trouble, approaching from the rear and looked over his left shoulder. He spotted a blue Toyota Camry, heading their way. The front passenger window was down. The rear passenger window was down. It was early morning and still quite cool. The barrel shroud of an Intratec TEC-9 pistol appeared in the front window. The barrel of an AK47 rifle appeared in the rear window. "Get down!" Cliff shouted at the other two. He sounded like he meant it. Jesse and Gene stooped. "DOWN!" Cliff shouted. They hit the ground. The TEC-9 pistol rattled. The AK47 breathed fire. 9mm hollow points pinged off the front of the building. 7.62mm slugs ripped through bushes and kicked gravel into the air. Cliff landed in the bushes and rolled on his side. He pulled his 1911 from it's holster, pulled the slide and sat up. The Camry was at the stop light, behind another car, boxed in. A balaclava'd head glanced his way, from the rear passenger window. Cliff aimed his pistol at the head, ready to fire. The head disappeared. The Camry bumped onto the side walk and drove into the intersection. Cars and trucks swerved and skidded. Horns blared.

Cliff scrambled to his feet. The Camry was gone. He popped the magazine, so as not to chamber another round, then pulled the slide. The .45ACP round rolled on the sidewalk. He stopped it with his foot, then picked it up and pocketed it. Gene got to his feet and brushed himself off. Jesse tried to sit up, but his head span. "You OK buddy?" Gene asked. He and Cliff helped him sit up. Jesse looked pale and his shirt sleeve was soaked in blood. "Shit man, you're hit." Gene said. Cliff pulled up Jesse's shirt sleeve and found the bullet wound. He quickly took his belt off and used it as a tourniquet, on Jesse's arm, a few inches above the wound. He took his shirt off and wrapped it around Jesse's arm. He applied firm pressure to the wound. Meanwhile, Gene took his phone from his pocket and dialed 911. He gave details to the dispatcher and heard sirens approaching as he did so. Red and blue lights appeared. Police. Ambulance. Paramedics carefully helped Jesse into the ambulance. Officers asked Cliff and Gene about what had happened.

Neither of them had gotten the license plate number of the Camry. The officers took notes. Cliff noticed that the glass in the floor-to-ceiling window, of the cafe, was cracked.

The paramedics took Jesse away in the ambulance. Gene and Cliff got into the Malibu. "Shit, man, that was intense." Gene said. "You OK? 're you a bit shaken up?" "I'm alright. I hope Jesse is alright." "He'll be fine. I've seen people survive worse bullet wounds." Cliff replied. "Hey, you need a shirt." Gene said. "And a belt." Cliff added. "I can lend you them, that'll save us going back to the motel." He got out and took a shirt and belt from the trunk. "Thanks. I owe you." Cliff put on the beige polo. It was a little too large, as Gene was a stocky build, Cliff athletic, but it did. "OK. Let's go to work. The polling station is in Keeling." They hit the road and drove to Keeling. They arrived at the school and parked. "Usual deal?" Gene said. "Let me call Jesse." Cliff replied. He tapped on 'Jesse' in his contacts. He had a brief conversation with Jesse, then let him go. "What's the prognosis?" Gene asked. "They've stopped the bleeding and he's waiting to be examined, by a doctor." Cliff said. "Does he have travel insurance?" Gene asked. "Uh, I dunno, I guess he does." "His medical insurance might not cover him, in the US, if he's a Mountainland citizen." Gene said. "Perhaps I should ask Sophia what insurance he has." Cliff said. "Shit. How do I tell Sophia that her partner was just shot?" He added. Pause. "Just tell her straight." Gene said. Cliff called Sophia. It went to voice mail. He left her a voice mail, asking her to call back as soon as she got the message.

160

Cliff and Gene got out of the car and walked around the school. It was the usual deal. A sign read 'Polling Place This Way'. A few people went to vote. All else was quiet and normal. They headed back to the Malibu and got in. Cliff's phone rang and he answered. It was Sophia. She was between classes and had a minute or so. "Jesse was shot this morning. He was taken to hospital in an ambulance. He'll be OK." Cliff did not sugar coat it. Sophia said she would call Jesse herself and hung up. Cliff called the RIP contact, that Jesse had given him, before the trip and advised what had happened. They took note and thanked Cliff and Gene for attending site, in the circumstances.

The morning went by. They had parked where they could see the entrance to the polling station and kept an eye on it. Cliff read a book. Gene read news articles on his tablet. They ate their lunch at half past mid day. The afternoon went by. Nothing else happened, that day. Late afternoon, the usual queue formed. It grew longer, until about 6.30pm, then started to reduce. "Are we gonna radio HQ, find out when we can go for dinner?" Gene asked. "The radio was on Jesse's belt. It went with him to hospital. I have a number for them, though." Cliff dialed the RIP contact again. She thanked them again for spending the day at site and said they could go. "I'll call Jesse again." Cliff said. "Hi Jesse, how you doing? .... Ah ... Cool .... We'll come and pick you up." Gene started the car and they drove a few miles East on Grant Road, then turned right and headed South. They arrived at St Joseph's Hospital. Jesse was waiting in a bus shelter, near the main entrance, his arm wrapped up in a large bandage. Gene pulled up and Jesse got into the rear seat. They drove off. "How you doin', Dude?" Cliff asked. "I'm OK. The bullet went right through my arm, cracked the bone, but luckily missed the artery. It stuck in my shoulder blade. They got it out and gave me stitches." "Are you in pain?" Gene asked, as they drove towards the motel. "I'm on co-codamol, so not too bad. But, there is other bad news." Jesse said. "What?" Cliff asked. "They said I should not fly, until the plaster cast is off, which will be some weeks." Pause. "Damn. How do we get home, then?" Cliff asked. "Well, Gene can drive, you can fly and I will have to take a train, I guess." Jesse said. "OK. I have some good news. We are off counting center duty, tonight. The RIP are sending someone else, after what happened to us." Cliff replied.

*

Wednesday morning, early. Gene's Malibu pulled up and stopped on North Toole Avenue. Cliff and Jesse got out and took their bags from the trunk. Gene bid them farewell and set off, on his day-long drive, to his home in Pagosa Springs, Colorado, Rangeland. Cliff and Jesse went into the Amtrak ticket office and bought tickets. "Keep the receipt." Jesse said. "The party will pay our fares, even thought we should've been getting a free ride on a military plane." They sat on a bench, on the platform. Jesse read a few emails on his phone. Shortly, they heard the train approaching. The silver and blue Texas Eagle appeared in the distance. It stopped in the station and passengers disembarked. Cliff and Jesse boarded and found seats on the lower deck. The train started to move, heading West, towards LA. "Real good of you to come with me." Jesse said. "I hope you are not missing any important work." "Mostly local stuff, this week. I have called the customers and re-arranged. I was not gonna abandon you in the field." Cliff replied.

The train track followed the I10, out of town. Jesse did odds and ends on his laptop, as much as he was able, with one hand not working well. Cliff could not be bothered with electronic devices, that morning, so instead, watched the arid mountains of Southern Arizona glide by. They bought coffee from the trolley. "Hey, remember you said the C130 was quiet and comfortable? This is *even more* quiet and comfortable." Jesse quipped. "That's just the co-codamol talking." Cliff replied. "There are some good things about being shot. You get a more comfortable ride home." "And you get co-codamol." Cliff said. "So, do you think those guys meant to shoot at us, or was that likely a case of mistaken identity?" "No. They would have been traffickers." Jesse replied. "Ballot traffickers have upped the ante." Cliff said. Pause. "Not ballot traffickers." Jesse replied. "Drug, or human traffickers." He added. Pause. "Seriously? Why would drug or human traffickers be interested in us?" Cliff asked. Pause. "Because, we were there to guard the referendum. Organized crime gangs, that routinely cross the Southern border, do not want Arizona to become independent, because they know that the Rangeland Government, or the Arizona Government, if it goes it alone, will finish President Arcana's border wall." Pause. "OK. I guess that makes sense. Still, what about California, or New Mexico, or Texas? There is a whole load of Southern border." Cliff asked. "Sure, but the Texas Government has mostly completed the wall and the

Rangeland Government is finishing it on the New Mexico border. If Arizona does it's bit, the whole border will be walled, from the Gulf Coast, to the Pacific." Jesse explained. "Wow. That's awesome. The Great Wall of America. Or whatever we are now."

Jesse went back to his work. Cliff took his laptop from his rucksack and booted it. He logged on and went to cog dot com. He navigated to the page on Texas. He scrolled down the page, looking at headings, to find something on the wall. Texas had been busy. The page went on and on. He tried a Ctrl+F and typed in 'border wall'. Immediately, it took him to the section on the wall. There were photos of the steel wall, stretching across plains and over mountains. The wall ran all the way from South Padre Island, on the Gulf of Mexico, to El Paso, on the New Mexico border. "You're right." Cliff said. "Texas has been independent for two and a half years and they have finished their stretch of the border. And their border is about fifty percent of the total. Amazing." He added. "That's the wonder of freedom." Jesse replied. "No more DC, to get in the way of solving the countries problems." He went back to his work. Cliff went back to reading the page on cog dot com. Texas was making progress in many areas and pulling out a lead, over the USA. It's GDP growth was in double digits. The Texas Government was using tax revenue, from imports, through Galveston and other ports, to finance projects, all over the country. Farmers in the West were getting subsidies to invest in irrigation, which increased the productivity of the arid region. Roads were being re-surfaced. Schools were being repaired. Thorium reactors were being installed, to generate electricity, for the grid.

Early afternoon. The train arrived at Union Station, in LA. They took their bags and disembarked. They left the platform and walked up the walkway, into the old, ornate station. They found a fast food restaurant and had lunch. They had a few hours to kill, before their train departed. "Wana come see some of my old haunts?" Cliff asked. "Sure. Are they walkable from here?" "Kinda. Maybe half an hour's walk." "We could get a ride." Jesse suggested. A few minutes later, they were in an Uber. Cliff directed the driver. The Mazda 6 cruised through the streets, taking them to Skid Row. They paid the driver, got out and wandered around. They had to walk in the street, down the outside of parked cars, because the side walks were filled with tents. Blue tarpaulins were tied over the top of multiple tents. Piles of garbage were piled up around the tents. Bicycles were propped against buildings and fences. Scruffy people approached Cliff and Jesse and asked for change. "Geez, man, you lived here?" Jesse asked. "Not for long, thankfully." Cliff replied. They walked on and turned down another street. "This is where I stayed." Cliff said. "There were some other vets, in this street." There were more tents, in rows, down the side walk. In some places, there were gazebos, with deck chairs and tables under them. A Stars and Stripes hung from the side of one of the gazebos. "Must be some vets, still here." Cliff said. An old, bearded man in a black t-shirt and jogging pants, sat in one of the deck chairs. "Hey, seen a guy called Grayson around?" Cliff asked. "Never heard of him." The old man replied, in a gravelly voice. The man glanced at Cliff's smart cargo pants and polo shirt. "Spare a few bucks?" He asked. Cliff took a ten dollar bill from his wallet and handed it to the man. The man thanked him and they walked on. "Shit man! You gave that guy ten bucks?" Jesse said. Pause. "A few years ago, I was here. By the grace of God, I have a business, a truck, a house, a wife ..." Cliff replied. They called an Uber and rode back to the station.

*

The Coast Starlight whisked them through the suburbs of Northern LA and into the mountains. They had diner in the dining car. The California scenery slipped by and it started to get dark outside. After they finished dinner, they went back to their seats. Jesse gave himself a break from work and watched a movie on his laptop. Cliff went on cog dot com and found the page on Arizona. He started to read. There was a section on the trafficking gangs hostility towards the independence movement. One senior member of the Arizona Independence Party had paint stripper thrown over the hood of his car. Another had a brick thrown at his living room window at 2:00am. There was nothing on the page about the drive by shooting, the day before. Cliff found the email address, for the editor, on the 'Contact Us' page. He wrote an email, detailing the events of the previous morning. "What do you think?" He asked Jesse. Jesse paused the movie and looked at Cliff's screen. "I thought I'd better run it by you, before sending it, as it concerns you." Cliff said. "I have not named any of us." He added. "Send it. The cog mods will decide whether to include it." Jesse replied. Cliff clicked send, then read on. The Arizona page was the usual cog dot com effort.

Economic stats, population stats, election stats, geographic information, political analysis. Multiple contributors, paragraph after paragraph. Cliff worked his way down the page, reading some, scanning some. "Wow." He said. Jesse paused his video again. "What?" "The Navajo Nation are holding a referendum." Pause. "They are going to vote on whether to get independence, from the Federal Government." He added. "Uh, yeah. That's right. Someone was speaking about it at one of the meetings." Jesse replied. "I don't know the details, to be honest." "They have a multiple choice ballot paper." Cliff said. He clicked on the image of the ballot, opening it to full screen. He and Jesse read it.

_____

_____

Referendum on the Navajo Nations Constitution

_____

_____

Section A

1. Navajo Nation should remain under the administration of the United States Federal Government.

2. Navajo Nation should gain independence from the United States Federal Government.

_____

_____

Section B

In the event that Navajo Nation gets independence, should it;

1. Become an Independent, self governed nation.

2. Become part of Arizona, or Rangeland.

_____

_____

"So, if Arizona votes to leave, but Navajo does not, there will be a large area of land, controlled by the Federal Government, in the middle of Independent Arizona, or Rangeland." Cliff pointed out. "Or, if Arizona votes to remain, but Navajo does not, there will be an independent Indian Nation, in the middle of a US State." He added. "Or, If they both vote to leave, but Navajo votes not to join Arizona, or Rangeland, Arizona, Rangeland, will have an independent Indian Nation in the middle of their country. Or, if they both leave and Navajo joins Arizona, or Rangeland, Navajo will not get a say in whether Arizona is independent, or part of Rangeland, because that referendum already happened." Cliff finished. Jesse chuckled and went back to his video.

*

The California Zephyr slowed to a stop in Salt Lake Central Station. Cliff and Jesse took their luggage and disembarked. They were weary, after a night 'sleeping' in train seats. The budget had not stretched to roomettes. They shuffled down the platform and found their way to the parking lot. It was 7:30am. "I don't think she's here yet." Jesse said. "It's about three hours from Twin Falls to the Crossroads." Cliff said. Jesse took out his phone and dialed his wife. They spoke for a few minutes, Jesse shuffling around the parking lot as he did so. They ended the call and Jesse came back to Cliff. "She's just passing Ogden." He said. "She must have set off at about five AM." Cliff said. About twenty minutes went by. Sophia's Chevy Cavalier turned into the parking lot and pulled up next to them. Sophia got out and hugged Jesse. Cliff

169

popped the trunk and put their luggage in. He opened the rear door and got into the rear seat. Jesse took the wheel, to give Sophia a break, after a three hour drive. They headed North, out of Salt Lake City, on the I15. "Thanks so much, for everything that you did, for Jesse." Sophia said, to Cliff. "And pass my thanks on to the other guy, what's his name?" "Gene." Cliff replied. "And you're welcome, any time." He added.

*

They arrived home at around 11:00am. Sophia parked on their driveway. Cliff got out and took his bag from the the trunk. He thanked them for the ride and went to his door. He went inside. Vicki was in her office, on her PC. Cliff put his head around the door. "Hey babe, hows it going?" "I'm good. Are you OK?" They hugged. "I'm OK." Cliff said. "Sophia told me you had a near miss, with a drive-by." "Yeah. Well, I'm fine, but Jesse was hit. Anyway, I'll tell you about it later. I need to go to bed, I'm exhausted." "Didn't you sleep on the train." "Not much. We were just in seats, not roomettes." Cliff went to bed a slept like a log. He awoke just before 5:00pm. He showered and dressed. Vicki had made dinner. They sat at the dining table and ate jacket potatoes, beef steak and salad. After dinner they drank beer and talked. "What happened in Tucson?" Vicki asked. "We had just had breakfast. We left the cafe and were walking up the side walk, back to the car. I got this feeling that someone was stalking us, so I looked over my shoulder. There was a Toyota sedan, driving towards us, with the windows down. There were pistol and rifle barrels out of the window. I shouted to the others to get down and dived into the bushes, myself. They strafed the area, but only Jesse was hit and only one round. Gene and I were not hit at all, but they cracked the glass in the front of the cafe. Gangsters can't shoot for shit." They crashed on the sofa. Vicki turned on the TV and changed the channel to Canida News. The count had finished and Arizona had voted to leave the United States and join Rangeland, by a good margin. Navajo Nation had also voted for independence from the Federal Government and to join Rangeland. Cliff booted his laptop and went to cog dot com. He went back to the Arizona page and scrolled down to where he had left off, on the train. The leaders of Navajo Nation had been in discussions with the governments of Arizona and Rangeland, before the referendum and agreed that they would join them, on certain conditions. These included, that all land currently in the Reservation would belong to the tribes, all mineral resources on their land would also be theirs and they would form local governments, to manage their affairs. They would pay taxes to the Rangeland Government, at the same rate as other citizens of Rangeland and get the same services in return – roads, refuse disposal, schools, police, etc. Cliff looked up from the laptop and thought about updating Vicki. She was engrossed in a documentary. He waited until the documentary finished and told her about Navajo Nation. "Hmm. I wonder if that will be better for them than their current set up?" She pondered. "Well, they will be dealing with a state government. I mean, the governments of the new country of Rangeland. That has to be better than dealing with an agency in DC, I guess." Cliff replied. "I wonder about all the other

Indian Reservations. What will their situation be, when the states that they are located in get independent?" She mooted. "Not sure, but I know who will know."

*

Saturday afternoon. It was another balmy, late spring day. Dressed for the weekend in a black t-shirt, blue denims and trainers, Cliff walked up the Bailey's drive and knocked on their door. Jesse answered in similar attire. "Come in." Cliff followed him inside, closing the door behind him. "Take a seat. Beer?" "Thanks." Cliff sat on the sofa. Jesse brought beer from the fridge. "You wana pick my brains again? Every time you knock on my door, you are full of questions." Jesse quipped. Cliff looked offended. "Only kidding." Jesse replied. "How are you doing? Wound healing?" Cliff asked. "I'm alright. I'm taking C60, to reduce the inflammation." "You gonna see a doctor about it?" Cliff asked. "Only if it gets worse, in any way. Sophia and I are quite good at looking after ourselves." "Cool. Here's something from me and Vicki." Cliff handed Jesse a 'Get Well Soon' card. "Thanks, Dude. That's real nice. How is Vicki?" "She's fine. Native American's are her latest thing." "Huh?" "Yeah. I told her about the Navajo Nation, voting for independence, from the feds. The last few days, she had spent every spare minute, on the internet, digging into Native American things." "Vicki loves to dig into the internet, doesn't she?" "Sure. She caught it from me, I think." Cliff said. "Internet addiction is contagious." Jesse replied. "She reckons that the rest of the Reservations will join the states that they are located within." Cliff said. Pause. "Yeah, likely they will."

172

Jesse said, stroking his beard, pensively. "DC is losing tax revenue, every time a state gets independence. They don't want to continue administering Reservations, within the newly independent states." Pause. "You mean, Reservations are net recipients, of federal funds?" Cliff asked. "Not necessarily. But, the feds are cutting back wherever they can. An empire never likes to lose ground, but if it is losing ground, it will do whatever it can to shore up what it still has." "Retreat and regroup." Cliff summarized. "Vicki is more interested in whether tribal independence is in the interests of the tribes." He added. "Well, yeah, it is, or they wouldn't vote for it. For example, in the current situation, taxes from individuals, living on Reservations, are collected by the federal government. You know how your SALT are deductible from your fed taxes? Tribal taxes are deductible in the same way. Independence will enable tribes to negotiate better deals with the newly formed governments, than they currently get from the feds." "So, the tribes get a bigger slice of the tax pie." Cliff said. "Sure. And the new governments don't care, because by going independent, they are already saving tons of money, that currently goes into the DC black hole." Jesse replied. "Which reminds me, we need to talk money." He added.

Chapter 11

11-54

"How so?" Cliff asked. "How much do you make, per day, on average, from your driving business?"

Jesse asked. Pause. "That's classified." Cliff came back. Pause. "OK. I'll take a guess. About two hundred bucks per day." Pause. "You wana hire me?" Cliff asked. "Well, not me *personally*. The next referendum is Florida. The FLIP have decided to hire professional security contractors, to protect the polling stations and counting centers, instead of using volunteers, like the Western states." Jesse said. Pause. "Interested?" He asked. "What makes you think that I'm qualified as a security contractor?" Cliff asked. "You're a Special Forces vet. You have experience of providing security for previous referenda. You're ideally qualified. They're paying three hundred US dollars, per day, including travel to and from Florida and a day's pay to check out the counting center, after mid night. So, that's twelve hundred bucks, for a coupla days in the Sunshine State."

*

Late June, Tallahassee International Airport. Cliff put his passport back into it's wallet and slipped it back into a pocket, on his rucksack. Kirk caught up with him. "Car rentals this way." Cliff said. They went to the car rental desk. Half an hour later, they put their bags into the trunk of the Kia Soul, which was theirs for a few days. Kirk took the wheel and Cliff put his Mom's ZIP code into the GPS. They headed out of the airport and went South on the 363. A quarter of an hour later, they arrived in Woodville. They followed the GPS to Chuck and Nancy's street and found their house. They turned onto the drive and parked. They got out and took their bags from the trunk. The house was a red-brick bungalow, with a concrete drive and lawn around about. The suburb was low-density, more like a forest with houses than houses with trees. Nancy's Red Ford Kuga and Chuck's Red, 2019 Bronco were parked on the drive. They went to the door and it opened before they reached it. "Hey darling!" Nancy appeared, in blue jeans and a white blouse. "Hi, Mom!" Cliff replied. "This is Kirk." "Nice to meet you, Kirk, come in, both of you." They followed her inside. "This is Kirk. Kirk, this is Chuck." "Nice to meet you, Sir." Kirk said. Fist pump. "Let me show you to your rooms." They followed Nancy, through the large bungalow, to the rear of the property. They had a large single room, each. They showered and unpacked, then went to the living room.

"Take a seat." Chuck said, putting aside his newspaper. "Would you guys like a drink, before dinner?" He asked. "Beer?" He added. "Sure thing, thanks." Kirk replied. Chuck disappeared into the kitchen and returned with bottles of beer. They sat on the sofas and drank. Nancy drank a glass of wine. "So, what are you guys up to, in our State of Florida?" Chuck asked. "We're here as Security Contractors." Cliff said. "For the Florida Independence Referendum." "Did you say contractors?" Nancy asked. "Sure." Cliff replied. "That sounds grand. Are they paying you well?" She asked. "Yeah, it's a decent day rate and all expenses." Cliff replied. "Perhaps you can explain this independence thing to us old people." Chuck said. "See, every week, it seems, another state or two, in the West, votes for independence. But the newspaper tells me that they are not really independent. They are still part of the USA, and some rogue politicians and military are pretending that the states are now independent countries." Cliff glanced at Kirk. He wished that Jesse was there. Jesse knew the whole thing, inside out and back to front. Cliff ...kinda knew. "Well, I'm pretty sure that the states that voted our are now independent countries. I drive across their borders every day, near enough and pay taxes on the goods that I transport." He said. "Hmm. Last thing I heard, there were Army International troops controlling the State Capitols in Texas and all the rest of them." Chuck said. "The AI have gone from the Boise Capitol, I know that, for sure. Vicki and I had a day trip to Boise on a weekend, about a year ago. We drove all around the Capitol, all the AI were away. The fences were down. The Capitol is used by the Mountainland Government, now." Cliff said. "Mountainland?" Chuck asked. "Sure. Idaho, Montana, Wyoming and some counties of Oregon, formed Mountainland. Colorado, New Mexico and some time soon, Arizona, make up Rangeland. The Dakotas, Nebraska, Kansas and Oklahoma are now Westland. Texas, Alaska and Utah are independent and have not joined other states, so far." Cliff summarized the situation. "OK. But, what is the point of all this?" Chuck asked. Cliff glanced at Kirk again. "I mean, what do these states *gain* by being independent from the USA?" Chuck added. "Freedom from DC, I guess." Kirk threw into the mix. "But, is DC really that bad?" Chuck mooted. "I guess it is about the way the USA is going. It's not so much about where we are, but where we are headed." Cliff replied, then went on. "Federal Government is becoming more influenced by international interests. Many US politicians have connections to organizations in other countries. They are not necessarily working for the American people. America is all about freedom, right? Our country was founded on the idea of independence. But, the DC government is eroding them, all the time. Economic freedoms, religious liberty, free speech, the second amendment. All are slowly being chipped away." Chuck and Nancy looked at each other. "Well, ain't that something. Pomona does produce conservatives, after all." Chuck said. "I'm a libertarian, actually." Cliff said. "OK, libertarians, then."

Nancy had cooked battered alligator and fries, with salad, followed by Key Lime pie. They all left clean plates. "I've never had gator before." Kirk said. "It's real nice. Kinda like chicken." Nancy loaded the dishwasher and they all went back to the living room. "Where do you live?" Nancy asked Kirk. "I live in Portland, Oregon." Kirk replied. "OK. How do you know Cliff?" She asked. "We were in the Army. We did a tour of Afghanistan, together." "Ah, I see. So, what do you do now?" "Dot and I have a guest house and also do estate maintenance." Kirk replied. "Ah. What's estate maintenance?" Nancy asked. "Minor repairs to houses, tidying yards, clearing out foreclosed houses, that sort of thing." Cliff nearly said 'What you guys would call an odd jobs man.' But he stopped himself. Banter did not come off the same in an inter-generational conversation, somehow. "Ah, I see. That's useful. So, do you think that Oregon will go independent, as well?" Nancy asked. Pause. "Not real sure, to be honest. Many people in our state kinda like the Seb Frank administration. I am not sure that we would vote for independence." Kirk replied. "Jesse reckons that Oregon, Washington, California and Hawaii will go independent in a year or two, if Arcana

177

is back in office." Cliff said. "Do you think that Derek Arcana will get back in, at the next presidential election?" Chuck asked. Pause. "Well, I'm not sure. Maybe. Many of the states that voted for him have now left the USA, so I guess we don't get to vote in a US presidential race. We'll see."

"What does referendum security actually involve?" Chuck asked. "Just being present at a polling station. Just in case the ARS show up and make trouble." Cliff said. "Hmm. I heard about the ARS. What does it stand for, er..." "Anti-Reactionary Society." Kirk said. "Ah, yes. They were the ones that tore up the Denver down town." Chuck replied. "They've torn up a lot of cities." Cliff added. "Young people, nowadays, I don't know." Chuck said. "They're not organic. They are paid and organized by ....some organization, I forget what. Jesse would know." Cliff said. "Jesse is your neighbor, in Twin Falls, right?" Nancy asked. "Yeah. You met him and Sophia, when you visited, about two years ago." Cliff answered. "Does he do referendum security, as well?" Chuck asked. "Sure. He's in Miami, now with Gene." Cliff replied. "Gene is one of my customers, who got involved in security." He added. "You guys all have time for voluntary work. I dunno." Chuck said. "Well, Gene is retired. Jesse is a software developer and Sophia is a teacher. They do alright. Anyway, we are not volunteering any longer. They're paying us now." Cliff replied.

*

Kirk drove through the streets of St, Augustine, in Tallahassee. Cliff was in the front passenger seat. The area was a mixture of apartments, condos and town houses. Old cars, scooters and motorcycles were parked here and there. Frat house flags hung from windows. "You can tell that we're near a university." Kirk said. "Sure. This is a real student area." Cliff replied. "Arriving at destination." The GPS said. Kirk pulled the car up, at the side of the road. "Where are we?" He asked. "We're right outside a stadium." Cliff said. "One sec." He logged onto this laptop and opened the email client. He clicked on the email, which Jesse had forwarded, from the FLIP. He skimmed through the text. "Ah. The polling station is in the stadium, in one of the conference rooms." He said. Kirk started the car. "The road does not go all the way around the stadium." Cliff added, looking at the GPS. Kirk turned into a parking lot and parked. "Better go for a walk, I guess." He said. They got out and walked around the stadium. It was the middle of the summer holidays and the campus was quiet. They found the polling place, in one of the faculty buildings. They were dressed in smart, black cargo pants and the FLIP branded polo shirts, that Jesse had given them, as per the instructions on the email. They had FLIP photo ID cards, on lanyards. They went into the building and introduced themselves to the head referendum clerk. She told them the location of the staff canteen and facilities. They thanked her and went back outside. They walked back to the car. "Better move to where we can see the door." Kirk said. They went back out onto the public road and drove around the outside of the stadium. They stopped in another car park, with a view of the door, to the polling station.

"Perfect." Cliff said. "Have you got the regulation ammo?" He asked. "Sure. I bought a Springfield

1911, 'cause I didn't wana put the conversion kit in my X9." Kirk said. "And you?" "I could not find plastic ammo in forty five, so I bought a Charter Arms Pitbull in nine mil." Cliff replied. "Good thinking. A revolver doesn't need a kit to work with different ammo. I tried a round in the X9, it wouldn't cycle the action." Kirk said. "You must've spent nearly as much on the gun as you're getting paid." Cliff quipped. "Nah, man. It's an ex store demo. I got a good deal on it." "Cool. I'm gonna call Jesse and see how him and Gene are getting on." Cliff logged onto his phone and tapped on Jesse, in his contacts. "Dude, how's it going?" Jesse asked. "We're at the polling place." Cliff said. "On the University Campus, right?" "In the offices at the stadium, actually. How about you?" "Yeah. We're outside the school, in Homestead. All quiet, so far." "Cool. I'll call you again later."

They sat and kept an eye on the door, to the polling station. Small numbers of cars parked in the parking lot and people went inside, to vote. "Just a steady trickle." Kirk said. "Sure. Usual deal. It'll get busy in the late afternoon, when people finish work." Cliff replied, then went back to his book. Kirk read news and watched videos on his laptop. The morning wore on. Nothing happened. Around mid day, they went for a break, in turns, then had lunch, in the car. "How many more of these do you think there will be?" Kirk asked. "Dunno. Fourteen states have seceded, so far. So, thirty six still to go." Cliff replied. "But many of them will go in blocks, like the Mid-West, I guess." Kirk asked. "Yeah, I guess. Jesse'll know." Cliff replied. "Jesse is the independence expert." Kirk said. 'I get the feeling that he knows some people in high places.' Cliff nearly said, but stopped himself. "He's a really clued up guy. He knows the whole independence deal inside out." Cliff said, instead.

The afternoon went on. Cliff read a few more chapters. Kirk watched a few more videos. Nothing happened. Late afternoon, a queue started to form, a little way out of the door. "People voting, on the way home from work." Kirk offered. "Not as long as the queue in Arizona. Or South Dakota, actually." Cliff replied. "People in Florida are not as keen on independence?" Kirk mooted. Pause. "I think this polling place is mainly for the campus and it is right in the middle of the summer holiday, so most of the students are away." "Ah. That makes sense. Just some residents, from around about and one or two students, maybe." Pause. "Hey, three o'clock." Kirk said. Cliff looked at his watch. "Six thirty, nearly." "No, man! Over to the right!" Kirk replied. A dozen spaces down, a mini bus reversed into a parking space. It was white, with blacked out windows. They watched it. The side door slid back and some young men got out. They were wearing trainers, shorts and t-shirts. They closed the bus's door and walked to a door in the main building, about 30 yards from the entrance to the polling station. "Just a sports team." Cliff said.

They arrived back at Chuck and Nancy's house, just before 8:00pm. Kirk parked the Kia on the drive and they went inside. They took their guns off, stashed them in their rooms and went to dinner. "How was your day?" Nancy asked. "Quiet." Cliff said. "No altercations with hoodlums?" Chuck asked. "Nope. Nothing at all." Kirk replied. "So, there are guys like you at every polling place, through all of Florida?"

Chuck asked. "No. Just the urban ones, where there might be trouble." Cliff said. "Must still cost a fortune, hundreds of you, times hundreds of dollars. Who pays for all this, the Florida State Government ?" Chuck asked, as Nancy served dinner. Pause. "The FLIP, I mean, the Florida Independence Party...I think." Cliff replied. "How's your day been?" Kirk asked, changing the subject. "I did a few rides, earlier. Bit slow, this year." Chuck said. "What do you do?" Kirk asked. "I'm a helicopter pilot. I fly tours over Tallahassee and the Pan Handle." Chuck said. "Cool. Where did you learn to fly?" Kirk asked. "In the Army. I was a pilot in the Florida National Guard for nearly twenty years. Then I was in the Counter Drug for about ten years. Then I left and bought my own 'copter. I've been doing tours for about the past ten." "Sounds good, what chopper do you have?" Kirk asked. "I've got a Robinson R66." Chuck replied. "You get plenty of business?" Kirk asked. "Summers are good, kept busy most days. Winters, just one here and there." Chuck replied. They finished dinner and sat on the sofas, in the living room. "Wana beer?" Chuck asked. "Actually, we'll need to go back out." Cliff said. Chuck's eyebrows raised. "We have to check the counting center. Sorry, forgot to tell you, earlier." He added.

*

Pensacola Industrial Estate, West Tallahassee, 11:00pm. Kirk had parked the Kia, at the side of the road, under a row of large trees. The street was lit, but their car was in shadows. About 50 yards down the road, was a warehouse, with box-profile walls and roof. They had been there since about 10:00pm and had seen several GMC Savana Cargo vans come and go. Cliff had called the first one in, on the Baofeng radio, that Jesse had loaned him. The dispatcher had replied that there were a fleet of such vans, delivering ballots, from polling places, in the area. They sat and watched a number of the vans deliver their loads. "Different one." Kirk said. Cliff looked up and saw a Freightliner Sprinter Cargo van turn into the parking lot of the warehouse. "Might be just a different model, still part of the fleet." Kirk suggested. "I'd better call it in, just in case." Cliff said. He pressed the PTT button, on the radio and called the dispatch. "Cliff Miles calling base, over." "Come in, Cliff, over." The woman's voice came back. "Freightliner van seen, entering Charlie Charlie 2, over." Cliff replied. "Stand by." She replied. They waited a minute or so. "Calling Cliff Miles, over." She said. "Cliff, speaking, over." "Can you get the license number of the van? Over." She asked. "Sure. Stand by." Kirk started the engine and drove the Kia forward, past the corner of the adjacent building, slowly, until the front of the Freightliner came into view. He pulled up and stopped. "Cliff to base, over." "Come in, Cliff, over." "Van license is; Papa, Lima, Echo, Eight, One, Five, Seven. Over." "Stand by." She replied. Several minutes went by. "Shit. They're getting ready to go." Kirk said. Cliff looked at the van. The driver was shutting the rear doors. "Cliff Miles to base, over." "Come in, Cliff, over." "Van is about to leave. What is your instruction? Over." "Cliff. No local PD in the area. Can you follow the van? Over." Cliff and Kirk looked at each other. "Affirmative?" Cliff asked. "Affirmative." Kirk replied. Cliff pressed the PTT button again. "Affirmative. Over and out."

The Freightliner drove through the Tallahassee down town at nearly twice the speed limit. It was nearly midnight and the streets were almost empty. Kirk kept about a block behind it, so as not to alert the driver, to the fact that he was being followed. They hit the Apalachee Parkway and headed out of town, Eastbound. The Van driver put his foot down and the van started to pull away. Kirk dropped a gear and floored the pedal. They kept up with the van. Up ahead, was a green light. The van went through. As they neared, it changed to amber, then red. "Damn!" Kirk said, slowing to a stop at the light. "There's no traffic. Just go!" Cliff said, looking both ways. Kirk checked both ways and accelerated across the intersection. He accelerated as hard as the car would, changing up near the red line in every gear. The tail lights of the van disappeared, over the brow of the hill. They reached the brow, just in time to see it turn left, into a side road. Kirk slowed and turned into the road after it, the Kia's tires squealing, on the tarmac. They drove up the road, through a residential area. The road was densely wooded and dimly lit. The van's tail lights were not to be seen. Cliff checked the driveways, as Kirk drove. "We lost him." Kirk said. They could not see the van. After a few minutes of driving around residential streets, they gave up and went home.

*

"What do you guys wana see, then?" Chuck asked, as the rotors spun up. "Lafayette." Cliff said. "What's in Lafayette?" Chuck asked. "A white Sprinter van, hopefully." Cliff said. Chuck shook his head. He figured that they were up to something and did not like to get involved, but Cliff and Kirk had gone halves on an hour's flight, so they were paying customers, like anyone else. The R66 rose into the air, over the helipad. Cliff sat in the front left, Kirk in the rear right. Both had binoculars ready. They flew around the outskirts of the city, at about 1,000 feet, following the route on a FAA chart. Buildings, trees and vehicles appeared miniature, below them. They flew over the Apalachee Parkway. "We need to look at this area, South of the lake." Cliff said, over the sound of the helicopters engine. Chuck descended to about 500 feet. They flew up and down residential streets, Cliff looking left, Kirk right. "There's something." Kirk said. "Oh no, it's a white truck, sorry." They had several more false positives. After a while, Cliff spotted a white van, of about the right size and shape, parked on a driveway, in a cul-de-sac. "Let's check that one out." Cliff said. "OK, but this will need to be the last one, unless you wana pay more." Chuck replied. They flew towards the van. Cliff trained the binoculars on it. The movement of the helicopter made it hard to read the number, through the lenses. "Can we get a bit closer?" He asked. Chuck flew a little nearer and hovered. "Yeah, the license starts P-L-E. Pretty sure that is it." He said. "OK. Are we done?" Chuck asked. "Sure, lets go." Cliff replied. He could not see the number on the house, but made a mental note of it's physical position on the estate. They flew back to the helipad and landed. Kirk helped Chuck fit the ground handling wheels and roll the 'copter back into it's hanger. Cliff sat in the front passenger seat, of the Kia and sketched an aerial view of the residential street, showing the position of the house, where the van was parked. After he had given the helicopter a check over, Chuck locked the unit and set the alarm. Kirk drove them back to Chuck and Nancy's house. "You got what you wanted, then?" Chuck asked. "I was able to read the license and I have notes of it's location. So, yeah, we got what we wanted, thanks." Cliff said, as he emailed a photo of his sketch to Jesse, from his Android phone.

An hour later, they arrived at the airport. Their wallets were a little lighter, after paying Chuck's fee of a few hundred dollars. Kirk handed the Kia's key back to the rental company and got their deposit back. Cliff phoned Jesse. "Hey, how's it going? ...yeah, fine. Did you get my email? ...Good. Any good? ....Awesome. See you back home." "That Jesse?" Kirk asked. "Sure. He has some mapping software on his laptop that can tell him the house number, from my diagram. He will pass that onto local PD." Cliff said. "I wonder what the Police will do." Kirk mooted. "Dunno. We don't really have evidence that the driver was up to anything, last night, but they can at least knock on his door and ask what he was doing at the CC." Cliff replied.

*

A few weeks later, early July, Saturday morning. Cliff reversed his Sierra up the driveway. Unusually, his trailer was not attached. The goose-neck hitch was removed, temporarily. In the load bed, was a stack of 8x4 dry wall and some dressed lumber. He stopped, near the door and got out. "Another load?" Vicki said, from the door way. "This is the last one." Cliff replied. Jesse walked up the drive. "Want a hand?" "Sure. If you don't mind." Cliff and Jesse carried the dry wall inside and down the stairs, into the basement. Vicki and Sophia carried some of the lumber. After a half hour, the GMC's load bed was empty and the stack of building materials in the basement had grown. Vicki made lunch and they sat and the dining table, eating ham and eggs. "You've got your work cut out." Jesse said. "Sure. But, I'll just do a bit each weekend, for the next few weeks, or months." Cliff said. "What's the extra room for?" Sophia asked. "Storage." Vicki replied. "We're going to copy you guys and fill the basement with store-able food and other supplies." She added. "Good idea." Jesse said. "I hear that we are going to have a real bad winter, this winter." "I bought some ladder-rack shelving on eBay, which is in Seattle. It was a bargain and luckily, I have a small car to collect, for a customer in Pocatello, this week, so I can collect the shelving at the same time." "It's handy, having a haulage business." Sophia said. "Sure thing. We've had all sorts of stuff brought back on Cliff's trailer." Vicki said. "The customer does not know, or care, as long as they get their load delivered on time and at the price I quote." Cliff added.

Sunday, late morning. The sound of a nail gun came from the Miles-Wisconsin residence. Vicki held battens in place, while Cliff put nails in the top and bottom of each one, fastening them to the battens, that he had screwed to the concrete floor and ceiling joists, the previous afternoon. They worked their way around the walls of the basement and had all the lumber in place, by lunch time. Vicki made lunch while Cliff tidied up. After lunch, they started on the insulation. Vicki held the strips of glass-fiber in place, while Cliff stapled them at the top and bottom. They worked their way around the outside walls and filled the inside wall, which separated the HVAC and meters, from the storage area. By late afternoon, the insulation was done. "So, far, so good." Vicki said. "Just the drywall, floor underlay, carpet tiles, emulsion and shelving to do." She added. "That's for next weekend." Cliff replied.

Chapter 12

FF

About 8 months later, Tuesday, late morning, March. Cliff drove his Sierra, Southbound, down a rural highway, through the Ozark hills, of Southern Missouri. The trees were still bare and the snow on the ground was just starting to thaw. There was patchy cloud and some Sun, as he drove. He drove at a steady pace, as the road was narrow and twisted and turned, through the hills. On the trailer, several portable latrines, fastened down, with nylon mesh and ratchet straps. The client was paying serious cash, to have what was essentially, some large plastic boxes with a plastic toilet and plastic sink, inside, transported from a manufacturer in Denver, to a remote location, South of Springfield. He was usually suspicious of clients that payed over the odds, but this job was fixed by Jesse, who knew the client. Jesse had not given Cliff much detail, but said that it was for a training camp, in the hills. He had asked Cliff if he would like to stay at the camp, for a few days, after the delivery. Cliff had a load, of several quad bikes, to go from Kansas City, to Salt Lake City at the end of that week. Perfect.

He rounded a corner and saw a car, parked at the entrance to a dirt road, on the right. He braked and turned into the road, stopping near the car. Jesse got out of the passenger side and Cliff put his window down. "You found us." Jesse said. "Sure. Pretty remote, huh?" "It's about two miles up this road." "Is it clear of snow, do you know?" Cliff asked. "Sure, we just drove down it, you'll get through, easily." Jesse replied. He got back into the passenger side of the car and they set off, heading West. Cliff followed the white, 2015, Buick Regal GS AWD, up the dirt road. Patches of snow lay here and there, but the car and the truck both passed, easily. They went around one corner after another, deeper and deeper into the woods. They passed several forks in the road. After about 10 minutes, they arrived at the camp. It was in a large, more-or-less rectangular clearing. Several military, rapid deployment tents stood around a large gravel yard. The rest of the ground, in the clearing, looked like it was used to grow crops, during the summer months. At the other end of the clearing, hundreds of yards away, was a backdrop, for a target range.

The Buick parked, next to a row of other cars and trucks, on the South side of the yard. Cliff parked, on the East side and got out. Jesse and the driver got out of the Buick. "Cliff, this is Ben, Ben, Cliff." "Hey, man, nice to meet you." Ben said. "Good to meet you." Fist pump. Ben was a short, stocky forty-something, clean shaven, with glasses and short hair. He wore boots, blue denims and an olive, mole-skin jacket. "Want a tour of the camp?" Ben asked Cliff. "Uh, yeah, I guess. But maybe we need to unload the latrines, first?" Cliff suggested. "The boys'll get them." Ben replied, nodding at the tent, behind Cliff. Cliff looked around and saw Jesse lead a dozen or so men from the tent. They were all thirty or forty something, mostly with short hair. "Let's get these off the trailer. I need a dump." One of them said. Jesse pulled the ramps out at the rear of the trailer and the guys unhooked the ratchet straps. "OK. Lets have a tour." Cliff replied. Ben lead him around the tents.

On the East side of the yard, right of the road, there were barracks, with steel frame beds. On the West side, was a chow hall, which had a kitchen, at the rear, with all sorts of cooking facilities. On the North side a classroom and an armory. In the North West corner of the yard, a caravan, between the classroom and the chow hall. "Wow, this all takes me back to my Army days. Where did you get all this gear?" Cliff asked. "It's all Army surplus. I was in the Army myself, for twenty years. I know who to speak to, to get the best deals. The rifles are part of my stock. I have a gun shop in Springfield." Ben replied. "Who organizes this place, if you don't mind my asking?" Cliff asked. "Myself and a few other guys I know are putting the place together. Militias all over the country and from Mountainland and Rangeland are sending their best guys here, to train in gun smithing, sniping, survival skills and so on." Ben replied. They went back to the chow hall, where they were served soup and rolls on trays. About two dozen men sat around a table, on benches, eating and talking. All were dressed for the outdoors, in boots, cargo pants, jackets and fleeces. Jesse, Cliff and Ben sat at one end of the table. "How long can you stay?" Jesse asked. "I have a load to pick up, in Kansas City, on Friday, so I can stay a few days." Cliff said. "By the way, am I paying to be here?" He asked, in a low voice." "No. I got us both in, courtesy of the party." Jesse said. Cliff wondered how Jesse got so much work, travel and other stuff paid for by a small political party, in Mountainland, but did not ask.

After lunch, they all headed out onto the range. There was a concrete pad with 8 lanes. A sturdy, wooden bench rest ran the length of the pad. A wood-framed structure, with a corrugated PVC roof, covered the pad. Ben and a few assistants laid out rifles, boxes of ammo and ear defenders. The rifles were mostly target rifles, that Cliff did not recognize, but there was a Barrett semi auto, in .50BMG and an Accuracy International, Arctic Warfare rifle. One of the guys handed out single-spot, black and white targets. They took one each and walked up a long, gravel path, which was mostly clear of snow, having been walked several times before. "Want me to take yours?" Jesse offered Cliff. "Thanks, but I can manage." He replied and followed the group up the slight incline. They arrived at the target frames, a few minutes later and clipped their targets to the plywood. They went back down the hill, to the pad. "OK, eight of you pick a lane." Ben, who was the range officer, said. "Ten rounds in each target." He instructed. Cliff looked at Jesse. "I had a go yesterday, you go ahead." He said. Cliff picked the lane at the left hand end of the pad. He sat down, on the stool. The rifle was a traditional Winchester, bolt action, with a wooden stock. It had a bi-pod and a telescopic sight. Cliff removed the breech flag and opened the box of Black Hills 30-06. The rifles magazine was not detachable, so he loaded 5 rounds into the mag, through the breech. "All ready?" Ben asked. "Detail starts now." He blew a whistle. Cliff put on the ear defenders, closed the bolt and shouldered his rifle. He looked through the scope at the wind flags, near the targets. Shots rang out, from the other lanes, echoing around the valley. Cliff slowed his breathing, waited for the breeze to slow and squeezed the trigger. The rifle fired. After the shot, he looked at his target. It had printed a few rings high and right. He adjusted the wind-age and elevation on the scope, then cycled the action. He squeezed the trigger again. A few minutes later, he emptied 2 magazines, as had everyone else on the pad. "End of detail." Ben said. They walked back up the hill and collected their targets. "How did you do?" Jesse asked. Cliff showed him the target. "That's a much tighter group than mine. You're the pro." Cliff had 8 of his 10 rounds in one group, on the bulls-eye and a little into the first concentric ring. "The first two were to zero the scope." He said. Jesse showed Cliff his target. "Well, at least you got them all on the target and a few in a group." Cliff said. They stood back and watched, while another group had a go.

"That's top notch." Cliff said, with a nod towards the Accuracy International, at the far end of the pad. "That's Ben's fave. The best shooters get to try that. You'll probably get a go on it." Jesse replied. Ben looked at each shooter's target. "You can have a go on the AW, if you like." He said to Cliff. A few details later, Cliff was on the right end of the pad. He took the magazine out and loaded it, with .338 Lapua, then put it back in the rifle. He put the ear defenders on, carefully. "All ready? Detail starts now." He closed the bolt and shouldered the rifle, then looked through the scope, at the wind flag and the target. He remembered 338 from his time in the

Special Forces and braced himself. He squeezed the trigger. The rifle made a 'crack', that rang out for miles. It kicked him in the shoulder, as the massive round went off. A few minutes later, the mag was empty. "End of detail." Ben said. They put the breech flags back in and walked up the hill, to collect their targets. "Another tight group?" Jesse asked. Cliff showed him. "Not quite as tight. It's a few years since I fired anything like that." Cliff replied. "Still not bad. All within three rings." Jesse replied.

*

Wednesday, 6:00pm. The men at the camp had gone through several days of intensive training. Target rifle, stripping and cleaning weapons, talks on ballistics and so on. Ben dismissed the class. They filtered out of the classroom. Some went straight to the chow hall, others hung about and talked. Cliff called Vicki. He wondered around the yard, talking on his phone. As they talked, he heard a vehicle approaching, on the dirt road. He looked towards the end of the yard. A black, late model Mercedes-Benz GLC Class SUV appeared. It drove to one side of the yard and parked, next to Ben's Buick. Two men got out. The driver was a middle aged man, wearing a black jacket and blue denims. The passenger was younger, in similar attire. They glanced at Cliff, then went to Ben's caravan, which was on one corner of the gravel yard. They knocked on the door. It opened, they climbed the steps and went inside. Cliff let Vicki go. He was hungry and headed for the chow hall. He went to the counter, collected his bowl of stew and dumplings on a tray and returned to the table. He sat down next to Jesse. "You OK?" Jesse asked, as Cliff tucked in.

"Sure. Just called Vicki." "Ah. Sounded like someone else arrived." Jesse said. "Yeah. Two guys in an SUV." Cliff replied.

They finished dinner and left the chow hall. It was dark outside. "Where's that SUV?" Jesse asked. "Over there." Cliff replied softly, shining his Mini-Maglite at it. They wondered over to it, for a closer look. "That's nearly new. Must have cost six figures." Jesse said. "Not your typical camp guys." Cliff agreed. The rest of the cars included a rough looking Subaru Legacy, a Jeep Wrangler and various trucks. "Where did they go?" Jesse asked. "They went to Ben's caravan." Cliff said. Pause. "Find a long stick." Jesse asked. "Huh?" "Go and find me a long stick, from the woods, please." Jesse insisted. "Uh, OK." Cliff agreed. He turned on his Maglite and walked past the row of cars, onto the grass. He played the beam this way and that. Various twigs lay in the grass, but nothing long. Anyway, how long was long? Nearer the trees, he spotted a branch, about 8' long. He picked it up. It was covered in snow, mud and leaves. He dragged it through the grass, to clean it off, then returned to the yard. Jesse was waiting, outside the barracks. Cliff handed him the branch. "That do?" "Sure." Jesse took a small, electronic device from his pocket and zip-tied it, loosely, to the thin end of the branch. Cliff followed him across the yard, to the North side. The yard was flood-lit, but the edges were in the shade of the tents. There was no one around, as the rest of the men were in the chow hall, drinking beer and socializing. They arrived at Ben's caravan. "Wait." Jesse whispered. He crept up the 2' wide gap, between the caravan and the classroom tent. About half way along the side of the old caravan, he stopped. He could hear voices inside. He lifted the branch, being very careful, not to touch the side of he caravan. He lowered the device onto the roof. Cliff held his breath. If this went wrong, they would be shot and buried, in the woods and never seen again. The tiny device sat on the roof of the caravan, next to the vent, which was open a little. Jesse and Cliff retreated, as quietly as possible. "Come sit in my truck." Cliff whispered. His truck was parked next to the road, in the opposite corner, with the trailer on the grass.

Cliff got into the driver's sear, Jesse in the front passenger seat. Jesse opened an app on his Android phone. He plugged in ear buds and handed one to Cliff. They both listened.

Hiss and crackle. Inaudible male voice. Asking a question. Pause. "Like I said, I have never heard of your militia. I really need to know more about where you are going with this, before I give any information about my guys." Ben. Inaudible male voice. "The Florida vote was predictable. There has been fraud apparatus there for decades." Ben. Inaudible male voice. "No. I talk to Southern Party officials all the time. We have the situation in the other Southern States under control." Ben. Inaudible male voice. "Sure, there are always Fed operatives involved in the elections, but ...our guys have it all under control." Inaudible male voice. "What do you mean 'key people'?" Ben. Inaudible male voice. "Seriously? You want to tap one of my guys for hit job? Uh ...let me think ...no ...definitely not." Inaudible male voice. "Yeah, well, if your head guy doesn't like the idea, then neither do I." Ben. Inaudible male voice. Long pause. "OK. Cliff Miles is the best shot, he shot real tight groups, yesterday and today." Inaudible male voice. Movement, door opening.

Seconds later, the two men appeared at the corner of Ben's caravan. Cliff and Jesse pulled the ear buds out. The men walked back to their car, got in and drove away. "Shit, you heard that?" Cliff asked. "They're gonna tap you for a hit job." Pause. "Lets get the fuck out of here, we're in too deep." Cliff said. Pause. "Wait. If we let them tap you, we might find out more about them. This could be a breakthrough." Jesse suggested. Pause. "I dunno. It sounded like they threatened Ben. He sounded shaken, when he named me, just before they left." "I don't think Ben threatens. He's hard as nails." Jesse said. "Maybe they threatened his family. I have Vicki to think about. She's alone a lot of the time, when I'm on the road." "OK, Dude. No sweat. You get going. I'll stay here and talk to Ben, see if I can glean anything." Jesse said. "What? I thought you wanted a lift home? How are you gonna get out of here?" Same way I got here. Ben'll give me a lift, to the airport." Pause. "I dunno whether I want to leave you here. This is all getting too serious." Pause. "Well, make your mind up. I ain't leaving till I know what that was all about." Jesse replied.

*

Thursday, early doors. Cliff awoke, after sleeping in his truck bed, in his Special Forces all weather sleeping bag. He was too old for barracks. Jesse slept in the rear seats of Cliff's truck, in his own sleeping bag. They got up and went to the chow hall, for breakfast. After breakfast, they went to the range. It was the final day and they were to shoot 1,000 yard targets, which were further up the hill. Ben loaned one of the guys a quad bike. He rode up the hill, to the furthest back drop and installed the targets. "Hey." Jesse said in a low tone. "Don't look now, but they are here." The quads noisy exhaust had drowned out the arrival of the Benz. The quad guy came back down the hill and the detail started. Cliff shot a tight group, relative to the longer range, with the AW. The quad buzzed back up the hill to change the targets. "Hey, Buddy, you look like a pro." The man from the Benz said. He had changed his smart, black jacket, for a cammo one, obviously trying to blend in a little. The younger man loitered nearby, also in a cammo jacket. "I was in the Army, for a decade, then the Special Forces, for a few years." Cliff replied, pretending to take the bait. "You shoot a good group." The guy said. "Thanks. I've known better guys, but, yeah, I do OK." "Cool. I'm Rus." "Cliff." Fist pump.

The morning went on. Everyone shot at least one 1,000 yard detail, except for Rus and his colleague, who never touched a rifle. They all went for lunch, in the chow hall. Rus and the other guy sat next to Cliff and Jesse. Rus talked a lot, but did not give much away, about himself. He asked Cliff and Jesse about themselves, but when they asked about him, his answers were mono-syllabic. After lunch, it was time to leave. Cliff and Jesse went and found Ben and thanked him for everything, then headed for Cliff's truck. Rus intercepted them, half way across the yard. "Hey, Bud, could I have a word?" He said. "Sure." Cliff replied. Jesse took the hint and got into Cliff's truck. The other guy stood at a distance,

197

saying nothing, looking nervous, as usual. "Wassup?" Cliff asked. "How would you like to make some money, my friend?" Pause. "Doing what?" Cliff asked. "We need a few people taken care of." Rus said, in a low tone. "Seriously? You wana hire a hit man?" Rus looked at Cliff's black beanie hat, tired looking, brown wool jacket, his khaki cargo pants, crumpled from a night in a sleeping bag and his muddy desert boots. "Eight figures." Rus said, simply. Cliff breathed in, his belly pushing against his cross-draw holster. The shiny, black, back strap of his Rock Island 1911 was just visible, through a gap between buttons of his jacket. The mag was loaded with .45ACP hollow points. It caught Rus's eye. "No chance, Buddy." Cliff said. "I make enough money and I'm not a criminal." "Alright. Your loss is someone else's gain." Rus replied. "Good luck with that. By the way, you're the most obvious spook, ever." Cliff replied, evenly.

*

That evening, Cliff and Jesse sat in a steak house, in Springfield, eating dinner and drinking beer. After a shower, a change of clothes and thirty minutes snooze, they both felt a bit better. It had been a cold, uncomfortable few days, at the camp. "I'm gettin' too old for that kind of thing." Cliff said. "Your, like, mid thirties? Same as me." Jesse said. "Don't care. I've grown accustomed to beds and hot showers." Cliff replied. "Were you tempted, when that guy offered you eight figures?" Jesse asked. "Didn't entertain it, even for a nano-second." Cliff replied. "He noticed that I was strapped. That helped me back him down." "What did he say, when you told him to get lost?" "He said 'Your loss is someone else's gain'." Pause. "He probably tapped one of the other guys, the next best." Jesse said.

*

A few weeks later, early April, Wednesday afternoon. Cliff had been busy with work, catching up after his week in Missouri. He had delivered a load of animal feed, to a farm near Jackson, Wyoming, that day. He listened to the radio, as he drove back down the I86. The independence referendum, for the Southern States, was only a few weeks away. It would be far and away the biggest referendum yet, a large number of States, all more populous than the already independent Western countries. Louisiana, Mississippi, Alabama, Georgia, South Carolina, North Carolina, Tennessee, Arkansas, Missouri, Kentucky, West Virginia, Virginia and Florida, were going to vote. It was Florida's second referendum, after the last one went DC's way. It would be a simple, two-way question: remain in the USA, or leave and become one, Southern nation. The New York media were arguing against it, every which way. The South trying again for independence, white supremacists, subversives trying to divide the USA, etc., etc. Cliff was not surprised. He knew that the South going for independence would be a big deal, as did many people, across the North American continent. He read articles on cog dot com most evenings and Jesse explained the finer points, on Saturday afternoons. Feds of every kind were trying every trick in the book to shut the referendum down. Lobbying, threatening and bribing officials in State Governments, to make their State drop out of the vote. None of it was working. The citizens of the States were going to the, polls, like it or not.

He arrived home, reversed the trailer onto the drive, unhitched the truck and parked it, next to Vicki's Monte Carlo. He walked towards the house door. The door of Jesse's house opened and Jesse appeared, in a check shirt and denims. "Hey, come over!" He shouted. Cliff went over and followed Jesse inside. "Wassup?" Cliff asked. "Take a seat. Listen, I've got some stuff to talk about." "Make it quick, Vicki has dinner on the go." Cliff said, sitting on the sofa. "I've been speaking to Ben. Those guys did tap another guy, at the camp." Jesse sat on the other sofa and got straight to the point. "I got the name of the guy, from Ben. Chase Wilson, of Englewood, Chicago, Illinois. I spoke to one of my hacker buddies, from back home. He did some digging on the guy. Chase is mixed up in stuff, but good at covering his tracks." "What does this have to do with us?" Cliff interjected. "My guy did some more digging. Chase has booked a hotel room, in DC, for one week before the South's referendum." "Something's gonna go down." Cliff replied. "He'll be a patsy. He'll never see a penny of the eight figures they probably offered him." Jesse said. "After the job is done, he'll get whacked, himself. The story will be PD caught him and shot him, something like that." Cliff suggested. "One week before the referendum, the media and the Feds will use it to shut the referendum down, somehow." Jesse said. "Have you spoken to your contacts, in the party?" Cliff asked. "Sure. They said they will look into it. But I'm not sure they will be able to stop it, in time." Jesse replied. "One of us should email cog dot com. They could do an article on it. Maybe

200

someone who can stop it will read the article." Cliff suggested. "Maybe. But, I think this is too important to leave to chance." Jesse replied.

*

Thursday, early May. A Delta Airlines Boeing 737 touched down, at Dulles International Airport. It taxied to the terminal and stopped. The Pilot thanked the passengers for flying with Delta, over the intercom. Passengers arose from their seats and collected their hand luggage. Cliff and Jesse did likewise and filtered out or the plane, down the gangway, into the terminal. They passed through immigration and collected their checked luggage. They went to the car rental desk, did the paperwork and took the key. They went to the parking lot and found the car, a late model, blue, Honda Accord. A few minutes later, the car's 1.5 liter turbo engine whisked them down the 267, towards the down town. DC had countless hotels and motels, many of them quite pricey. It was not clear whether the party would finance their trip, as Jesse had been draining their coffers, for one thing and another. Also, the senior members were not sure about the mission, or whether he and Cliff were right for the job. So, he booked the cheapest hotel he could find, in Arlington. They arrived, parked in the parking lot and checked in, at the front desk. They went to their rooms, showered and changed. When he was ready, Cliff went downstairs and waited a minute or two, in the lobby. The elevator doors opened and Jesse appeared "I've found a restaurant, about one block away." Cliff said, looking at his phone. It was dark and raining outside. They walked a block and went into the restaurant. A waitress seated them and they ordered. "What's the plan?" Cliff asked, as they waited for dinner to arrive.

*

Chase Wilson drove down the George Washington Memorial Parkway. It was evening, Thursday. It was dark and raining, heavily. His rough, tired-looking, blue, Subaru Legacy station wagon had done Chicago to DC, in about 10 hours. Good old car, it had not let him down. It wore fake license plates, that his friend, who specialized in fake stuff, had made for him. The traffic was moderate and he made good time. The Potomac was off to the left, bright lights of the city, reflected in the water's surface. He passed under some grand, arched, bridges, as he neared his destination. He took the ramp off the Parkway and arrived at a set of lights. He turned left at the lights and headed South, parallel to the parkway, on a surface street. He drove around the outside of Arlington National Cemetery. A few blocks later, he arrived at his hotel. He found a parking space, next to a Honda Accord and parked. He went to the front desk and checked in. He had used fake ID countless times before and barely even worried about it. His friend had found a similar-looking, early twenties guy, in some database and punked his ID. The lady behind the counter found his booking and gave him his room card. He went back out to the car, collected his overnight bag and his other case, from the trunk. A few minutes later he was in his room. He showered and changed, then ordered a take out, on his laptop. He sat and watched TV, while he waited for dinner to arrive.

He did not think about tomorrow's job. 'Don't think about it, just do it' one of his early mentors, in his dark world, had told him. He did not like the idea of whacking someone, even if they were a politician. But, with $10,000,000, he would be made for life. He could retire to Latin America, somewhere with no extradition, in case the Feds tracked him down. His folks, brothers and sisters would get SD cards, containing wallets, loaded with crypto currencies, in the mail. In the weeks since Rus had tapped him, he had worked it all out. The app on his phone pinged. Dinner was at reception.

*

Next day. Chase arose, dressed and went to get breakfast. He had most of the day, before his job. Plenty of time, to prepare. After breakfast, he went back upstairs. He took a few things from his room, then walked down the corridor. He found the fire escape door and checked it out. In the top left hand corner, were two, white-plastic coated magnets, one on the door, one on the frame. He checked over his shoulder. No one was around. He took his 'magic-card' from his wallet and slipped it between the two magnets. Slowly and carefully, he opened the door. He left the card in place and closed the door, behind him. The steel fire escape took him down the rear side of the building, almost to ground level. For security reasons, it did not go all the way to the ground, but there was a ladder, for the last bit. He checked the catches on the ladder. They were a little stuck, so he sprayed them with some GT85 and worked them loose. He left his rope, tucked in, next to the wall, out of site of the windows. In this situation, it was all about belt and braces. He nipped back up the chequer-plate steps, hoping that no one had seen him. He closed the door and retrieved his card. Back in his room, he looked out of the window. The roof-top restaurant was less than a block away. It was on a four story building. He was on the fifth floor of the old, red-brick hotel, so it was more-or-less a level shot. He checked out the window. It was a casement window with a check strap that only allowed it to open a few inches. He broke out his tools and had a go at it, with a hacksaw. It was tough and it would take him a while to get through it. Luckily, he had another solution. He took out his Bloomoak, tungsten-carbide, self-oiling glass cutter and got to work. A few minutes later, he carefully lifted an approximately 10" circle out of the pane, with his car-dent sucker and put it on the desk. He taped up the edges with duck tape, then repeated the procedure on the outer pane. A little later, there was a hole, right through the window. Next, he moved the desk and chair to the window. Finally, he opened the hard, plastic case, that he had been given. Inside, was a Remington Arms Modular Sniper rifle. He took it from the case, folded out the stock and the bi-pod an set it on the desk. He took out the magazine and loaded it with .338 Norma Magnum, then put it back in the rifle. He put the bolt in the rifle, but did not close it, so as not to load a round, until he was ready. The scope and stock were already adjusted, after some time at a local range, the day before. It was late morning and he was ready.

There was a knock at the door. A firm, no-nonsense knock, like that of a Police Officer. Shit. He grabbed the rifle, opened the closet and put it inside, it's stock on the carpet, the barrel against the wall, then closed the door. He grabbed the case, lifted the comforter and shoved it into the bed. Another knock. He went to the door and quickly glanced through the spy hole. Two, tall, short-haired guys in casual dress. Plain clothes cops. Damn. He opened the door a little. One was really tall, with a shaved head and a beard, in a navy-blue jacket and green cargo pants. The other was a little shorter, in a black jacket and blue denims. He had seen them before somewhere, but could not think where. "Chase Wilson?" The shorter one asked. "No one by that name, here." Chase said and shut the door. They knocked again. He stood still. "Dude, listen. We're not cops. We're here to help you." The other one said, through the door. "You've been set up, let us in, we need to talk to you!" The first one added. Chase stood, mind going full speed. Who were these guys? What should he do? He opened the door. "Come in, but make it quick, I've got to ...go out." They came in. Cliff clocked the hole in the window, almost immediately. Shit was real. Jesse closed the door, behind him. "Who are you guys?" Chase demanded. "We were at the training camp, in Missouri. I dunno if you remember us? I think we exchanged a few words, at dinner." Jesse said. Suddenly, Chase remembered them. "I'm Jesse. This is Cliff." "Who do you work for?" Chase asked. "We're just regular guys, not Feds or anything." Jesse said. Chase was in a quandary. What was the deal with these guys?

While Jesse and Chase talked, Cliff moved over to the window and looked out. He clocked the roof-top restaurant and realized what the setup was. A perfect spot for a politician to have a Friday date, with a 'honey-trap' intern. He looked down, at the side-street, below. "Guys! We need to get out of here, now!" An armored car had stopped in the street. Officers in black uniforms and helmets, carrying AR15s, were entering the hotel, by a side door. "What?" Jesse asked. "SWAT! We need to go, NOW!" Chase snapped out of it. "I need to take the rifle." He said, opening the closet door. "Just leave that!" Jesse said. "I can't. My prints're all over it!"

Moments later, the three men scrambled down the fire escape, as quick as they could go. Jesse released the catches on the ladder and lowered it do the ground, as quickly and quietly as he could. Chase dropped his bag and rifle case and went first, carrying the rifle in one hand. Jesse followed. Cliff went last. The ladder was awkward for him, but he managed. They were on the ground, at the rear of the hotel. They hurried to the corner of the building, past dumpsters and air-con units. Jesse stopped, at the corner and signaled for the others to stop. He peeped around and saw the SWAT vehicle. It was in the side-street, between them and the parking lot. They turned around and went back, to the other end of the hotel. At the other end, was a small area of grass and ornamental bushes. A quarter-circle, chest height red brick wall stood on one side, with the hotels name and logo, facing the street. Behind the wall was a teenage boy, in a hoody and track-suit bottoms. He saw them, scrambled to his feet, jumped on a BMX bike, which had been propped against the wall and rode off, into the streets, as fast as he could. Cliff noticed that he had dropped something. He bent down and picked it up. It was a sub-compact pistol, of European manufacture. Cliff pocketed it. Meanwhile, Chase had taken down the rifle and put it in it's case. "This way!" Jesse hissed. They hurried across the street and headed down the rain-washed side-walk of a residential street.

A quarter hour later, an Uber dropped them at their hotel. Jesse paid the driver and Chase took his stuff, from the trunk. They went into the hotel. "Come up to my room and we'll figure things out." Jesse said. They took the elevator and went to Jesse's room. Chase dumped his bag and rifle in one corner and crashed into one of the tub chairs. Cliff sat in the other chair. Jesse handed them bottles of water, compliments of the hotel, then sat on the bed. "How do I get my ride back?" Chase asked. "I suggest you go back the next morning, when Law Enforcement is long gone." Cliff suggested. "This place is not too dear. About eighty bucks a night. You could get a room here." Jesse suggested. "And let us take care of that." He nodded at the rifle case. Chase hesitated. The rifle was worth thousands of dollars and money was tight. "Did you buy it or did the guys that hired you give it to you?" Jesse asked. "It was shipped to my house, by a courier." Jesse and Cliff looked at each other. Jesse looked back at Chase. "You don't know the history of it. You might be carrying around something that's already been used in a crime." "If you go back to collect your car, tomorrow and the police catch you with that, you could be in really hot water." Cliff added. "What are you guys gonna do with?" Chase asked. "I know people who can dispose of it." Jesse said.

*

Next day, Jesse drove the Accord to Chase's hotel. Cliff was in the front, Chase in the rear. They cruised past it, looking into the parking lot and the side street. "No cops." Cliff said. "My car is still in the parking lot." Chase said. Jesse turned around, in a side street and drove back. he pulled up, at the side of the road, near the hotel. "Hey guys, thanks for everything." Chase said, getting out of the car. "Good luck, Dude." Jesse replied. Chase slammed the door and headed for the parking lot.

Two hours later, Cliff and Jesse sat in the departure lounge, at Dulles International. They ate sandwiches for brunch. Jesse caught up on some work emails, on his laptop. Cliff read news, on his phone. "Hey!" Cliff exclaimed. Jesse looked up, from his laptop. "A politician died, in Arlington, yesterday." "Who?" "Dov Bernstein, a representative from Georgia." "Which party?" "The Plebiscite Party. He was one of the most vocal opponents of the independence movements." "What happened?" "He was at lunch, with a young female colleague. He collapsed, at the table and was taken away in a ambulance. He was pronounced dead, later, in hospital." "Shot?" "The article does not say." "Where did it happen?" "At Randy's Rooftop Restaurant." Pause. "The SWAT were going to arrest Chase, before he took his shot." Jesse connected the dots. "Then investigators would examine the scene and pass info to the media." Cliff added. "And the public would be told that Dov was shot." Jesse said. "That explains the kid, with the pistol." Cliff replied. "Huh?" "Remember that kid, that we scared off, from beside the hotel?" Cliff said. "Huh? Oh yeah. What about him?" "He dropped a sub-compact pistol on the ground, when he got on his bike. I picked it up and

208

took it. I took the magazine out, back at the hotel. It contained only nine mil blank cartridges, no live ammo." Pause. "He was right below Chase's window, now I think of it." Jesse said. "So people at the restaurant and around about would hear a shot."

Chapter 13

The Storm

About 3 months later. Audra, Michigan, was a town of about 5,000, on the coast of Lake Huron. It was a hot Saturday afternoon, in late August. People were going about their business. Cars and trucks drove to and fro, on the main street. People went in and out of small businesses, in the low-rise, one and two story, red-brick buildings. Moms played with their kids, in back yards. Men washed and worked on cars, on driveways. Everything was normal. The sky was mostly clear blue, with cumulus clouds here and there.

One cloud, some way out over the lake, was large and dark. It drifted, slowly, towards the town. As it neared the shore, a tail appeared, at the bottom. People outdoors watched and pointed. Some people took photos and video, on smart phones. The twister grew larger and nearer to the surface of the water. It touched the water and turned into a water spout. A vast quantity of water was sucked up into the cloud. It continued to grow and move towards the shore, touching the surface, all the while. The cloud grew larger and larger, darker and darker. The bright day became dark and overcast. The storm was heading towards the town. People from out of town got into their cars and left. People outside grabbed their kids and went inside. Phones rang and pinged with text messages, as people alerted their friends and family. All over town and in farms and houses around about, people closed shutters over windows, moved cars into garages and went inside. As the storm grew larger and nearer, people grabbed phones, keys, documents and kids, then hurried down stairs, into basements, closing hatches tight, after them.

Xavier Zachary, aka 'Zav', stood on his lawn, watching the twister come his way. He videoed it on his Blackmagic, 1080p, micro camera. He could not see the shore, as it was obscured by houses and trees, but he could tell when it reached land, as debris started to appear, swirling around the outside of the twister. He continued to video, as it came nearer. Winds picked up around him, whipping and tugging trees and bushes, this way and that. The Sun disappeared and it became very dark and overcast. Large drops of rain fell. The winds continued to rise. The roaring sound of the twister grew louder. Crashes and clatters came from the debris, as the tornado picked it up and dropped it down. A bright, blue and white flash came from a few blocks away, as the twister tore through power lines. A single-wide appeared, over the roofs of the houses. It was ripped from the ground and broken into pieces, as it disappeared again, into the dark cloud. Pieces of lumber, wheelie-bins and bushes whirled around the outside.

The first roof went up. A few blocks to the East, next to the shore, a large, white-clapboard house, was the first to go. Dormer windows and asphalt tiles were sucked up, into the deadly vortex, followed by the rest of the house, in a few seconds. Zav continued to video, moving about on his lawn, pointing the action cam through the gaps, between houses, on his street. Another roof went up. And another. And another. A whole street was being demolished. More flashes, blue, white, orange, yellow, as more power lines and transformers were brought down. It continued to come closer. Roofs in the next street went up. It was going through the down town. Red bricks and signage, from store fronts rose up and mixed with the other debris.

It continued to come closer. Zav continued to video. He would not go underground until he really had to, because he wanted to catch as much of the disaster as he could. A few blocks to the South, was a supermarket. The tornado reached it and peeled the box-profile sheets off the roof. They rose into the air and disappeared, into the blackness. Merchandise was sucked out of the building and swirled around. Then the walls went. Next, the canopy of the gas station, which was next to the supermarket, lifted off, broke up and rose into the air. Shit. The gas station was hit. There was another electric flash, followed by a bright orange explosion. The sound of the explosion reached Zav a fraction of a second after he saw it. It was followed by another and another. Zav got on the ground in an instant, then went back to filming. Then, the big one. The tanks under the gas station went up. The roar was deafening. The shock-wave went through town, adding to the destruction. Orange and black rose up, into the sky and mixed with the vicious, evil, black cloud.

The twister turned around and headed towards him. Debris started to fly around him, like food in a blender. It was time to go underground. He scrambled to his feet and dived towards the basement door. He pulled the handle and the door popped open. He scrambled inside, grabbed the handle and pulled the door closed. He latched it tight. "Damn! Zav! You should have come in sooner! I was worried sick!" Anna said. Zav's wife, Anna, sat on the sofa, in the living room, holding their 5 year old daughter, Annabelle, who had been crying. Zav grabbed the 'last resort', a door-sized grid of re-bar, from the cleaning cupboard and put it across the outside door. Even if the twister ripped the door off, it would still not be able to get them. "Hold on tight, it's about to get a bit wild." He said, peeling off his soaked waterproof and hanging it up in the hallway.

He checked his camera. It was still recording. He went to the kitchen-diner and looked out of the ceiling-level, 6" deep, double-glazed window. It was almost as dark as night. Trees at the back of the house were ripped from the ground, complete with the root ball and disappeared into the gloom. Mighty crashes and clatters came from overhead. People said he was eccentric, living underground, with his wife and kid. Now, he knew that he had made the right decision. He went to the living-room window, which was the same size and position. He peered out, into the street. Cars and trucks were being tossed about, like skittles. The property that he and his family lived in was a 'show-home', for his bunker building business. Now, it was going through the ultimate test.

Thirty minutes or so, later, the storm had past. Zav took the 'last-resort' from the door and went outside. Neighbors were starting to come out from their basements. People walked about, surveying the devastation, picking up some remaining possessions, which were strewn around the area. Virtually every house was gone. Cars were upside down, or on their sides. A semi truck and trailer lay on it's side, near the highway. Most of the trees were stripped bare, or gone altogether. Many of them lay across streets. Lumber and building materials of every kind lay in piles, like snow-drifts. The whole town had been razed.

*

Cliff drove across the Mackinac Bridge, Southbound. He had been driving two days, through Montana, North Dakota, Minnesota and Wisconsin and was nearly at his destination. The trailer was empty and he was on an unusual mission. The guy that had hired him sounded like a character. He ran his own business, building house-sized, underground bunkers, for people to live in. After a tornado had devastated his town, he started a crowd funding site, rebuild-audra dot org. It had already raised hundreds of thousands of dollars, within a few days of the storm. Cliff had priced his services as reasonably as possible.

He drove down the coast road and arrived at the town in the late afternoon. He had never seen anything like it. The GPS took him down a road that was blocked, by a huge oak. He stopped at the side of the road and called his client. A few minutes later, he was back out on the highway. He went in the other end of the town and followed the directions, that he had been given. Only one street, through the town, had been cleared. Cliff arrived at the address. It was a bunker house, built underground, with a flat, concrete roof, which was about a foot above ground level. Shallow windows peeped out, just above the grass. At one end was a concrete ramp, leading down to an underground garage. On the ramp, was a black Ford F350 Super Duty. He parked at the side of the road. A bearded, long-haired, thirty something man, in shorts, t-shirt and trainers, appeared and walked towards the Sierra. Cliff got out. "Hey man! Welcome to Audra! I'm Zav." "Cliff. Good to meet you." Fist pump. "So, this is the beast?" Zav checked out the Sierra and the trailer. Cliff had borrowed a goose-neck tipper trailer, which was more suitable than his flat-bed, for the task at hand. One of his farmer customers had obliged, when told that it was for a good cause. "Perfect. You've come a long way. Wana come in for something to eat?" Cliff followed Zav into his bunker house. They sat at the dining table, ate sandwiches and drank tea. "You have a family?" Cliff asked, when he noticed kid's clothes on the drier. "Sure, but Anna has taken her back to her Mom's house, in Pontiac, for a bit. Myself and other guys and some girls, from around town have started the clean up operation." "It looks like a massive task." Cliff said. "Yeah. Which is why we've hired a number of drivers, from out of town. How long can you stay?" Zav asked. "I've cleared my diary, for a few weeks." Cliff replied.

7:00am, the next day. Zav had let Cliff sleep in his spare room, in return for Cliff's reasonable fees. They went out to Cliff's truck. "Where to?" Cliff asked. "We'll start with the main street. You'll need to turn around, this street is blocked, further up." Cliff reversed the trailer onto a gravel side road and turned around. They drove to the main street. Insurance adjusters and assessors, in hi-viz vests, walked about, between the debris, surveying the damage. Residents and business owners sifted through the debris. Men cut up tree-trunks, with chain saws. Cliff parked the trailer at the side of the road, as directed by Zav. A Caterpillar 330 Log Loader, loaded the lumber onto the trailer. When it was full, they drove out of town. "Where are we going?" Cliff asked. "A farmer has loaned the town a bit of rough ground, to dump the debris." Zav directed him to the site, just outside the town, next to the highway. Cliff reversed the trailer onto the grass, stopped and tipped the load. They drove back into town and he dropped Zav off, on the main street, so that he could continue with other clean up tasks.

Cliff went to and fro, all day, for several days. Gradually, one street after another was cleared. Other contractors worked with skid-loaders, to clear the smaller debris. The electricity companies removed broken power lines. Residents, who stayed in motels, in towns around about, sorted useable lumber from broken lumber. The broken, splintered stuff went into Cliff's trailer and went out of town. Cliff and the other contractors worked all hours of daylight, starting around 7:00am and finishing around 7:00pm. They would take an hour's lunch break, around mid-day, to recuperate. Cliff would eat sandwiches and read news, on his laptop. Zav would cook dinner, for himself and Cliff, on a USA Propane stove, after the day's work was done.

*

Friday evening. Zav and Cliff sat in the living room, drinking beer, after a long, hard week. "How's the crowd fund going?" Cliff asked. "It's going good. We have plenty, to pay the contractors and some left over, to help anyone who does not have insurance." Zav replied. "Even for those that do." Cliff replied. "Insurance companies often find a way out." "True." Zav agreed. "The Federal Government has promised some assistance, but, we'll see whether that actually materializes." "The media is making a big deal out of the Federal funds, using it as an argument against independence." Cliff said. "Sure, they have said, over and over, if the tornado hit Southland, it would receive no Federal funds, which is true. But, Southland will not be paying any Federal taxes, going forward." Zav replied. "And when people pay less tax, they pay more to crowd funding." "Yeah. Did you notice, the tornado hit on Southland's independence day?" Cliff asked. "Sure." Zav agreed. "And DC had sent a delegation to Tallahassee, to try to persuade Southland to re-join the US." "Yeah. I like how the New York media says 'to remind the South that they are still part of the USA'." Cliff said. "Still using their old tricks." Zav replied. "At least they did not send the Army International, to the State Capitols, this time." He added. "I think they are getting to the point, where they realize that they have lost." Cliff said. "At this point, the United States is basically, just the North East, the West coast and about half the Mid-West." He added. "Sure. Until we vote to leave, as well."

Zav replied. "Yeah. I read something on cog dot com, about the states around the Great Lakes, having a referendum." Cliff said. "In two weeks, yes. We don't have anywhere, for a polling place. Ours will have to be in another town. Dunno if many people, from Audra, will vote. We have our own problems, to deal with." "Do you reckon Michigan will vote out?" Cliff asked. "It'll be the usual heat map." Zav replied. "Rural counties'll vote out, Detroit'll vote remain." "Reckon it'll be free and fair?" Cliff asked. Pause. "What do you think?"

*

One week later, 8:30pm. Bismark, North Dakota. Cliff took the ramp off the I94 and stopped at the lights. He turned left and headed towards the city. He found a motel, turned off the road and parked the truck and trailer, over a few car spaces, at one side of the parking lot. He took his hold all, set the alarm and went to the reception. A few minutes later, he was in a room. Too weary to go out, after a 15 hour drive, he ordered dinner on his laptop, showered and changed. He turned on the TV, ignored it and crashed on the bed for a bit. The app on his phone awoke him. Dinner was at reception. He went downstairs, paid the driver and took his food. He sat on the bed, eating burger and fries. After dinner, he booted his laptop and went to cog dot com. He read some of the Southland page, and a few updates on other countries. Then, he opened the page on Lakeland. He read some and skimmed some, working his way down the page. Ohio, Indiana, Illinois, Iowa, Michigan, Wisconsin and Minnesota were going to the polls in just over a week's time. They were using a simple, two-way question.

217

Secede and form a new country, 'Lakeland', or remain in the USA. Cliff came to a section on the Audra Tornado. It was an unusually long section, about a dozen, long paragraphs. He read some, skimmed some. Much of the information, he already knew, from having been in the town, for a fortnight. He reached the final paragraph and started to read. "Damn! No way!" He said to himself.

*

Two days later, Monday afternoon. Cliff sat on the sofa. He read some news on his laptop, then drifted off to sleep. Even after a good night's sleep, he was tired. He had worked long days, for two whole weeks, with a two day drive at each end. Vicki had cooked them a lunch of ham and egg, with fries, pineapple, peas and tomatoes. After lunch, she went back to her office, to continue her busy day. Cliff's profit, from the Audra job, was a little less than his usual day rate, especially when there were days of travel on either end. Still, he brought a good chunk home and they weren't broke. Her side of the business was doing well and she had nearly caught up with him, in the income competition. There was a knock at the door. Vicki jumped up and answered it. Jesse was there, in his usual work from home attire. "I see Cliff's truck in on the drive." He said. "Sure. Cliff's back. Wana see him?" Jesse followed Vicki inside. "Ah, doing what he does best, asleep on the sofa." She quipped. "Hey, Dude. How you doin'?" Jesse asked, as Cliff woke up. "Uh. Hi, Jesse. Good to see you." "I'll let you guys catch up." Vicki said and disappeared to her office again. "You got time for a beer?" Cliff asked, getting to his feet. "Well, it's the middle of Monday afternoon, so no, but

..." Cliff grabbed two bottles of beer, from the fridge. "This is my Friday and I earned it." He said.

They sat on the sofas and caught up. Jesse was in the middle of a major project and had been coding, all day, every day. He asked Cliff about the job, in Michigan. "I was basically working as part of a team. Local guys were cutting up fallen trees, with chainsaws. Myself and other contractors were carting the lumber away. It took us about a week, just to clear the streets. Then we started on the debris. Residents were sorting stuff, recovering usable things, bagging the rest. I took load after load, of bin bags and building materials. Then we started putting cars back on their wheels. I parked the trailer and someone put a chain on the towing eye of my truck. We went around town, hooking the chain onto the sub frame, or the opposite side suspension and turning them over." "Sounds full on. What did the town look like, after two weeks?" "Still real bad. The streets were passable, that was about it. Other than that, still much the same. Cleaning up is just the start. Rebuilding'll take years. Zav said he would get me back, to haul building materials, when they are at that stage." "Amazing. Is he paying for you out of his own pocket?" "No. He started a crowd funding website, the day after the storm. It took enough, to hire contractors from all over. Truckers, laborers, tree surgeons, all sorts." "Some guy. Was his house gone?" "No. He lives in a bunker-house, that he built himself. His flat, concrete roof was about a foot above the ground. It was untouched. He's a contractor, he builds houses like that for his customers." "Awesome. I was interested in going underground, before we moved here, but Sophia wanted a normal house."

"Another beer?" Cliff asked. They had another beer. "Michigan and the other states in the region are having their referendum in a week." Jesse said. "Yeah. Zav was talking about it." "What does he reckon?" "He reckons the rural counties will vote leave, Detroit will vote remain." Pause. "What do you reckon?" Cliff asked Jesse. Pause. "Lakeland will go ahead." Jesse said. Pause. "The tornado will not change the outcome, just like none of the other things that the deep-state have tried, have changed the outcome of the previous referenda." Long pause. "Seriously? You mean ...the tornado was ....artificial?" Cliff asked. "Wow. I read something on cog dot com, about weather warfare. But, I thought, surely that can't be real?"

Cliff and Jesse shuffled down the Miles-Wisconsin drive, around the end of the chain link fence, then back up the Bailey drive. The Bailey front door opened and closed. Jesse lead Cliff into the living room. The school term had started and Sophia was back at work. "Grab a seat." Jesse said, pulling a dining chair from the table and handing it to Cliff. Jesse sat on his swivel chair and tapped the mouse, to wake his PC. He logged onto the Kali Linux OS. "What are we looking at?" Cliff asked, curious as to where this was going. "Check this out." Jesse clicked on an app, on the XFCE task bar. The app opened, filling one of Jesse's three 27" monitors. "What's this?" Cliff asked. "Weather Radar Twenty Four." Jesse said. "Lets go back, a few weeks." He opened a dialogue box and typed in a date. The picture changed. Jesse tweaked a few other parameters, changing the picture again. "Check this out." Jesse grabbed a biro and pointed to areas of the picture. Cliff saw a big swirl of color, over the outlines of country and state boundaries. He recognized the state of Michigan and the Great Lakes. The center of the swirl of color was over Lake Huron, near the North end. "What's this?" Cliff asked. "An anomaly." Jesse replied. For several minutes, Jesse spoke about things that went over Cliff's head. Nikola Tesla, Ionospheric heaters, weather warfare ... After he finished, there was a long pause. "So, essentially, what you're saying, is .... the tornado was ....artificial?" "Yeah. Basically." "Why Audra?" Cliff asked. Pause. "Audra voted, like, seventy percent, for Arcana. They are the most Arcana town in Michigan." Jesse replied. "So, they would for sure, vote for independence." Cliff said. "Sure. Razing them sent a message, to the whole region. Vote correctly, or die."

*

Late afternoon, Cliff went home. Vicki was still busy, in her office. He cooked hamburgers, fries and peas, to give her a break from cooking. "Dinner's ready." He called, from the kitchen. They sat at the dining table and ate. "How's your day been?" He asked. "Good. Busy. I got another new customer this morning. An independent store in Albuquerque. They regularly import goods from the far East, so they'll likely be a regular customer." "Sounds good. How many borders does a container go across?" "Two. It leaves Shenzhen on a freighter, goes across the Pacific, goes through the container terminal in LA, which is the biggest bottle neck at the mo, then gets put on a train or a truck, goes through California and crosses the border into Rangeland at Ehrenberg." "So that's two lots of paperwork." "The Rangeland paperwork is minimal. Most of the headache is from LA." Vicki replied. "What were you and Jesse talking about?" She asked. "Mostly the tornado. He was asking all about it." Cliff replied. "No doubt he has his own take, on it." Vicki said. "Ha! You bet! Have you heard of a guy called 'Nikola Tesla?" "Uh, yeah, rings a bell." Vicki replied. "European dude, did experiments with lightening, in Colorado?" "Yeah, him. Jesse says that there are something called ...er...ionospheric heaters, in various locations, Alaska, Canada, Greenland. He went into some long explanation, all a bit above my pay grade. But, he basically told me that the tornado was artificial." Pause. "Seriously? You mean, someone wiped out that town on purpose?" Vicki asked. "Sure. There's a name for it, 'weather warfare', according to Jesse." "Wow! Perhaps you should email that site that you read, all the time, whats it called?" "Cog dot com. They already have an article on the Audra tornado. I read it, one evening, when I was in a motel, on the way back. I found it hard to believe. But, Jesse has a software app on his PC, which enables him to analyze weather systems. He says the tornado was an anomaly." "So, it's like someone nuked the town." Vicki said. "Sure. Someone pissed on them and told them it's raining. Literally."

Chapter 14

A Fence

About 4 months later, December, Mid-day, Tuesday. Cliff turned into a street, in an industrial estate, in Lincoln, Nebraska. He arrived at the rear end of a queue of trucks. A dozen or so semi trucks with flat bed trailers and a few pick-ups, with goose-neck trailers, like his, were parked at the side of the road. He parked behind them and turned off his engine. He had driven from Big Springs, Nebraska, where he had stayed in a motel. He had driven from Twin Falls, to Big Springs, on the I80, in one long day. He had acquired, for a small fee, one of the new 'North American Multi-Country Visas'. It was a plastic card that allowed him to use the fast lanes, at borders. He swiped the card on the barriers and they let him through. No border guard, no paperwork. It was the sort of thing that made him think 'New World Order', normally, but it was reducing his time at borders, so he opted for it.

He got out of the cab and walked up the queue, to the next truck. It was Malcolm. He put his window down. "Hey, man! How's it going?" Malcolm asked. "Awesome, thanks and you?" "Yeah. I'm doing good." "Is this the queue for the fence manufacturer?" Cliff asked. "Sure is. They're loading one truck at a time. It's gonna take a while to get into the yard, so you better get comfortable." Malcolm said. They talked a few more minutes, catching up on each others business and current affairs, then Cliff went back to his truck. The queue moved up, one truck length at a time, every few minutes. Cliff ate lunch, then booted his laptop and read news, watched videos and poked about on the internet. A little later, it was his turn. He drove into the yard. A man in a hi-viz vest waved him to the right spot. He parked the truck and trailer. An orange and black, Doosan 9 tonne forklift buzzed about, in the yard. It disappeared into the factory building and re-appeared with a stack of fence panels. It swung around and carefully loaded the stack onto the front end of Cliff's trailer. Then it went away for the next stack. The man in the hi-viz vest came to Cliff's window. "When he's done loading your trailer, can you drive out into the street and put your ratchet straps on there, so that we can get the next truck into the yard?" He asked. "Sure thing, no problem." Cliff agreed. The forklift filled his trailer with several more stacks. He drove slowly, out onto the road and stopped. He got out, took his ratchet straps from the rear of the truck and worked his way around the trailer, securing his load. When he was done, he hit the road.

It was a bright, chilly afternoon, as Cliff headed North-East, on the I80. He drove through Omaha and arrived at the border. Lakeland had only been independent for a few weeks and was not yet part of the NAMCV system, so he had to queue at the border. Up ahead, beyond a row of cars, he saw some of the trucks from the yard, with their stacks of fence panels. The queue moved forward, one vehicle at a time. He reached the barrier and put his window down. He handed his passport and goods documents, which Vicki had printed for him, to the border guard. A minute or so later, the barrier went up and he drove into Iowa, Lakeland, for the first time, since it had become an independent country. He continued East, on the I80, towards Des Moines. He turned on the radio. It picked up one of the local stations, which played country music, then news. The news was mainly about the formation of Lakeland and associated issues, especially the controversy over the location of the countries Capitol. The presenters discussed the issue, referring to conversations on various internet forums. Residents of each State generally advocated that the major city in their State, should be the Capitol, for one reason or another. People from Minnesota argued for Saint Paul, people from Michigan for Lansing, Ohio for Columbus and so on. Somehow, Springfield, Illinois, had picked up the baton and their State Capitol had become the Capitol of Lakeland. "...but, lets think ourselves lucky it wasn't Chicago ..." The presenter said, then went onto other topics.

It got dark, as he drove across the agricultural plains of Iowa. He passed through the suburbs of Southern Chicago, then joined the I90 toll road, at Lake Station. He drove a while longer, then exited the interstate and found a motel in Elkhart. The motel did not have any truck spaces or a gravel area at the rear, like many of the motels in the West, so he parked the truck and trailer over some car spaces, on the outer edge of the parking lot. The truck took 3 car spaces, the trailer another 4. It wasn't the first time he had parked like that. Motels welcomed all customers, including those that used more than their share of parking spaces. He took his alarm wire from the rear of the truck and weaved it through the stack of panels, pulling it tight, to the unit, so that the slightest movement would make the app on his phone ping. He went inside, paid and went to his room, exhausted. He went through his usual evening routine of shower and food, then crashed into bed. He put on a pod cast and lay back. The host and guests discussed various issues around Lakeland and Southland. The host was generally optimistic about the future of those nations, citing Texas as an example of a country that was doing very well. Cliff listened for a while and drifted off.

Next day, late afternoon. Cliff drove down the I70, through the hills and forest of Southern Pennsylvania. He had crossed the border, at Petersburg and was back in the USA again. He was now only about 60 miles away, from his destination. He had driven for 3 days, from Twin Falls, right across the North American continent. The radio played music and Cliff reflected on everything, that had happened, over the past few years. Six months ago, he had Jesse had been to DC, to stop an assassination. They had failed, but had stopped the false flag element of the plot. Now, he was heading back to the city again, for a very different, but perhaps not unrelated, purpose. It was dark, as he drove down the I270, turned off and headed South, through the up-market suburb off Chevy Chase. It was a densely wooded area, with large, red-brick and stone mansions. Apartment blocks loomed, at the side of the road, here and there. He continued, down Connecticut Avenue. He stopped at the lights, waited for green, then continued onto 17th Street. The car parking at the side of the street had been cordoned off. A man in a hi-viz vest signaled him to park on the rear end of the queue. He pulled in, parked and waited. The man in the hi-viz walked up to the Sierra. Cliff put the window down. "You might wana go get something to eat. The construction teams have just started." The man told him. He thanked the man, got out of the truck and went to find food. He found a grill, around the corner and bought a cheeseburger, fries and salad. He took it back to his truck to eat. DC still had phlu measures in place and his truck was warmer than the

226

restaurants' temporary shelter, on the sidewalk. He sat, with the heater and radio on, eating his dinner.

The evening wore on. About every half hour, the guy in the hi-viz got a call on his radio, then he waved one of the trucks on. It turned left and disappeared, down H Street. The queue moved forward, one truck and trailer length. Eventually, around mid-night, it was Cliff's turn. The man waved him on. He turned left and drove down H Street. Another man in a hi-viz, signaled for him to park on the left side, of the one-way street. He pulled up and stopped, opposite Lafayette Square. The road had been closed off. Everywhere, forklifts went to and fro. Construction workers lifted fence panels off pallets and linked them together. Flatbed trucks used HIAB cranes to lift concrete blocks into place, one every few panels, to secure the fence. It reminded Cliff of the fences around the State Capitols, in the early days of the independence movement. He sat and waited. Shortly, a fork lift started to unload the panels, from his flatbed. Once it was finished, the man directed him to turn left, onto 16th Street. It was half past mid night and he was tired, but he knew that he would not find a motel with enough space for his truck and trailer, in the center of DC, so he hit Massachusetts Avenue North West and headed out of town. He arrived at a motel in Clarksburg, at around 1:30am.

*

Thankfully, the other materials to be delivered to site came from nearer locations. Gates, barriers, posts, alarm systems, floodlights, cabins and so on were moved into DC, by Cliff and other truckers, from factories and workshops in Pennsylvania. After about a week, the White House, the Capitol and various other building were secured. After about 2 weeks and hundreds of gallons of diesel, for the whole trip, Cliff arrived home. His overheads for the long haul were substantial; diesel, expensive beltway motels, food and wear and tear on his truck and trailer. He had billed the client a good few grand, to cover his costs and make a reasonable income, for his time. It was late Friday afternoon, near Christmas. It was dark and there was snow on the ground, in Idaho. He parked the truck and trailer and went inside. Vicki had dinner ready. They sat and ate steak pie, mashed potato and mixed veg. "What was DC like?" Vicki asked. "Big. Busy. Expensive." Cliff replied. "Ha! Wana go there again?" Vicki asked. "Not really. I had to drive miles out of town to get a motel, every night. The motels in the city don't have enough parking space, for a forty-plus foot truck and trailer." "Well, I checked the business account earlier today. The money is in. Paid in full." "Cool. How's the FF business been?" "Crazy busy. So much stuff getting imported at this time of year. Been doing my head in a bit, to be honest. Still, nearly at an end, for this year." Vicki said.

They crashed on the sofa. Vicki turned on the TV and changed the channel to Canida News. They drank beer and watched news for a while. A reporter in DC stood in front of the fence and talked about securing the Capitol, from members of the independence movement. "Seriously?" Vicki said. "How many riots have there been, by independence people?" "I know." Cliff replied. "All the way back up the road, the news kept talking about protecting the DC government from us. I thought, if only they knew the truth." "Many people don't even know that the United States is a corporation." Vicki said. "Sure. I got into a conversation with two of the drivers, in a diner, one night. One was talking about eighteen seventy one, that the corporation was formed that year. The other said that was just the corporation of DC itself, essentially that the lines of the city were redrawn. They went to and fro a bit. They ended up agreeing that there are a number of corporations, the States themselves, DC and the United States." "Sure." Vicki agreed. "But, who owns the corporations?" Pause. "Well, I guess that is the sixty four thousand dollar question." Cliff replied. "Well, I'll tell you what I know. The liquidators that hired us are based it Basel, Switzerland." "Hmm. Strange. Surely that would mean that they don't have jurisdiction over the US?" Cliff mooted. "Dunno. All a bit above our pay grade, I think." Vicki replied.

*

The Christmas Holidays came. Vicki's parents, Larry and Amy, flew down from Anchorage, to Boise, for the holiday. Vicki picked them up, from Boise Airport, in the Monte Carlo, requiring Amy to squeeze into the rear seat of the 2+2, to give Cliff a break from driving. The airplane seat was more comfortable than the rear of Vicki's car, apparently. They slept in their spare room, next to Vicki's office. Vicki had cooked a full Christmas dinner, for the first time ever, with some of the laboring work by Cliff and some guidance from Amy. Larry stayed out of the way. The Wisconsins complimented Cliff and Vicki on the house improvements. Cliff showed off the basement, with all of their supplies. Cliff and Larry had talked business and trucks at every opportunity, on Christmas eve and Christmas day.

Boxing day. Jesse and Sophia had broken with tradition and invited the whole Miles-Wisconsin household to a buffet lunch, which comprised left over turkey, potatoes, veg and a multitude of other things that Sophia had conjured up. The Bailey kids, Chris, who was 9 years old and Luna, who was 8 years old, were well dressed and well behaved. Larry and Amy, who were in their sixties, were all-round impressed with the thirty-somethings houses, food and children. After lunch, the kids went upstairs, to play on the X-box, among other things, Mon and Dad had bought them. The adults sat and talked about everything that was going on, on the North American continent.

Larry: "So, what's your line of business?" Jesse: "I'm a software developer. I build websites, write HTML, CSS, php and so on." Larry: "OK. I understood the first few words, the rest went over my head. My generation struggles with sending an email, let alone writing whatsit?" Jesse: "Ha! OK. What do you do?" Larry: "I'm a freight forwarder, I organize shipping of goods to and from the USA, or what used to be the USA." Jesse: "Ah, same as Vicki. Did you inspire her to get into that business?" Larry: "Uh, I dunno that she takes much inspiration from her old man, or Amy, for that matter. She's always gone her own way." Jesse: "You and Cliff have some common interests, as well, I guess. Him being in the transport business?" "Oh sure. We were talking about all the places he has been, earlier on. I must say, he does get a lot of different types of work. Amazing what you can do, with a goose neck." Jesse: "He's the busiest man I have ever known. I get up at about seven thirty on a Monday morning and the trailer is away, already. Then I see him pull into the drive late on Friday. When I speak to him on the weekend, he's moved, like, three loads, between here, California and Colorado." Cliff: "Yeah and when I'm not working, you're taking me off to Arizona, or Florida, or DC on some mission to secure a referendum, or save the world, or whatever." Everyone laughed. Sophia: "I have to go to work and teach a class of teenagers, both sides of the independence debate, while being married to the biggest independence freak on the continent." Larry: "You're a big independence guy?" Jesse: "Sure. I got involved with the Idexit Party, about a year after we moved to Idaho. One of the prepper guys I know was a member and he asked me to go along." Larry: "I've been for Alaskan independence for, I dunno, maybe forty years. I was one of the earliest, in the movement. I always thought we would do well, we have vast natural resources." Cliff: "And do you think Alaska is doing well, three and a bit years after you cut ties with DC?" Larry: "Well, the sky did not fall, like a lot of people said it would. Economically, I'd say, pretty much business as usual. Anchorage is a busy city, but it always has been. And it's good to be free, from DC." Amy: "Some of the Moms that I know were worried about the end of the Oil Dividend, but that is organized within Alaska and is still going." Vicki: "I went on a course, in freight forwarding, in Salt Lake City, about a year and a half ago. Some of the people there were worried about being able to transport goods over State lines, after the States became independent. In fact, it is easier to move a container into or out of the new countries, than it is to move it through LA. The USA borders are the bottle neck, actually." Cliff: "Well, I'm not sure how much longer the USA will exist. The Federal Government is now in Chapter 7 bankruptcy." Larry: "Really? How do you know that?" Vicki: "MW Transport was hired by the liquidators, to transport security materials to DC." Pause. Larry: "Security materials?" Cliff: "Fence panels, gates, flood lighting, portable buildings. That sort of thing." Amy: "We saw the fence, on the news. So, you were one of the guys that shipped it there?" Cliff: "Sure. It was me." Larry: "Does the fence have something to do with the liquidation? I mean, the news tells us that the fence is to keep out independence protestors, whoever they are, but is that really what it's for?" Pause. Cliff: "Well, some of the other drivers thought so. But personally, I doubt it. The liquidators need to secure the assets of the corporation, I guess." Amy: "Haha! You mean, one of the White House staff might put an oil painting in the trunk of their car, when no one is looking?" Cliff: "Not so much that, although, that maybe part of it. But, I think the real reason, is to secure the data. Nowadays, it's all about the data, right?" Cliff glanced at Jesse. Larry: "I guess the White House is full of computers, that would figure." Cliff: "Actually, one of the drivers said that there is a gigantic data center, underground, under Lafayette Park." Larry: "Nothing works the way you think it does." Cliff: "Some of the other drivers were kept on, to move stuff out of Government buildings, to secure locations. I thought about asking Vicki to bid on the extra work, but I'd had enough at that point, so I headed home, for Christmas." Jesse: "Hey

man, you could've seen inside the underground!"
Cliff: "I used to be in the Special Forces, remember.
I've been in underground complexes all over the
globe. Mostly, all you see down there is more of the
same; offices, labs, equipment rooms, endless
corridors. I've never seen a lizard-being, eating a
baby-human." Everyone laughed. Vicki: "Hey, I tell
you what we do know, though. The company of
liquidators is based in Switzerland." Pause. Larry:
"That's where the New World Order is based, isn't
it?" Sophia: "Jesse is always talking about them.
They're in ...Grisons?" Jesse: "Leman, actually."
Vicki: "The company that hired us are in Basel."
Larry: "How about this for a question; who hired the
company of liquidators?"

*

A few days into the new year, it was time for Larry
and Amy to return home. Cliff drove them to the
airport in the Sierra. Vicki went with them, to say
farewell. They drove back down the I84, through the
snow covered Snake Valley. They arrived home in
the mid afternoon and tried to get back into work.
Vicki went to her office and got stuck in, as much as
she could, with a foggy post-Christmas head. Cliff
called a few local customers, to organize deliveries
for the coming week. He sat on the sofa, with his
laptop and phone, doing this and that, dealing with
emails and what not. The house seemed quiet and
empty, with the in-laws away.

After dinner, Cliff got a phone call, from a number
that he did not recognize. Must be a new customer.
He answered. "Hi, Cliff speaking." "Wassup, Cliff?"
"Who's this?" "It's Gray. Remember me? From the

camp." "Oh, yeah. Hi. How you doin'?" "I'm OK. I'm back in Abilene. What about you?" "Er, yeah. I'm in Twin Falls, Idaho." "Wow, what took you there?" "I live here, with my girlfriend, Vicki." "Oh, cool. What're you doing for a living?" "I work as a truck driver. Have been for about five years, now. What about you?" "I got a job at a radio store, in Abilene. Someone that I know, from the Army, asked if I wanted a job, just before Texas got independence." "Oh yeah, you were always on that radio set, in the camp." "I was a radio operator, in the Army. I've worked with radios all my life." "Good to be back in your home city?" "Well, I tell you what, I sure am glad I moved back when I did, 'cause this area is gettin' real expensive." "Did you buy a house?" "I bought a single wide, on the edge of town, on a city lot. Bit rough, but a good deal. How about you?" "We bought a house, in Twin Falls. Like you, we bought at just the right time. Independence seems to have accelerated the migration, from the West Coast, inland." "Man, hasn't the world gone crazy, these past few years?" Pause. "You don't think independence is a good thing?" "Well, I guess Texas is doin' pretty good. I dunno. It's just, like, the pace of change is different. It's hard to keep up, with everything goin' on." "OK. I agree with that." "Like, that fence around the White House. If someone told me about that, a few years ago, I'd have been like, no way, man!" Pause. "I was there. I got a contract, to haul fence material and other stuff, into DC." "Man, you're always where the action is!" "Haha! It wasn't that exciting, really. I just parked the trailer on a street, nearby and a forklift came and unloaded it. Then I had to go find a motel with space for a truck and trailer." "Sounds like fun. You must've picked up some stuff, about, you know, what the deal is?" "The drivers were all talking about it. Theories, observations of this and that. I dunno. Who knows? I mean, *really knows?*" "Well, I hear all sorts, on EchoLink. Someone that I talk to, in Maine, says that the State Governments in the North East are working on plans to become a separate country, called new England. So, that's pretty much the last part of the USA." "Are they having a referendum?" "Not as far as I know. They are just doing it." "That must be because of the liquidation." "Liquidation?" "Of the US Corporation. In DC." "Uh, right. So, that's what the fence is for. You heard that from one of the drivers?" "Er, yeah. Something like that."

Chapter 15

Sheep no more

About 4 months later, mid April, Saturday morning, Bountiful, Northern Utah. Vicki turned off the street and parked the Monte Carlo in a customer parking space. The Mountainland Dollar was unusually strong, the Utah Dollar not so much, making it an ideal time for a shopping trip, to Utah, even if it was 3 hours, each way. They got out of the car. Vicki was in low heels, tight black jeans and a purple top. Cliff wore his usual boots, khaki cargo pants and a black polo. Smart casual, for a day out, at the weekend. She locked the Chevy and they walked across the tarmac surface. It was 3 years, since Vicki had been to Salt Lake City, to train as a freight forwarder.

Since then, she had been saving hard and was ready for a big ticket purchase.

Cliff opened the large, glass door and they went inside. A tall, bearded salesman in a sharp, black suit greeted them. "Hi, can I help you?" He asked. "We were looking at two of your cars, online." Vicki said. "Could we have a look?" "Sure." Michael replied. "Which two?" A few minutes later, they were out on the lot. Vicki checked out the interior and sat in the driver's seat. Cliff looked under the bonnet, at hoses, drive belts and battery. He lay down on the tarmac, which was warmed slightly, by the Sun and checked out the under-body. Michael gave them the key and he gave the engine a rev. They stood back and looked at the white, 2017 Buick Regal. "What do you think? This was your preference, right?" "Well, that guy Ben, that ran the training course in Missouri really rated it and he seemed to use it pretty hard. But, its your car, so, your choice." "Can we have a look at the other one?" Vicki asked. Michael lead them across the lot, to the other car that she had found online. They repeated the procedure. Cliff got the feeling that the salesman was not used to customers looking, in detail, under the bonnet, or under the chassis, but he did anyway, because he knew that it would be him that serviced and repaired it. After that, they went inside, to do paperwork and a bank transfer. Vicki knew she would be sad to see 'Monte' go. She had owned the yellow Chevy for a number of years and was quite attached to it. But, it was time for a more practical car.

A few hours later, Vicki drove back up the I84, through the mountains, towards the Mountainland border. She was behind the wheel of a metallic gray, 2018 Cadillac CTS, 2.0 turbo. It had less than 30,000 miles on the clock, with full dealer service history and was a good deal, especially at the current exchange rate. Behind her was Cliff. She checked the rear view mirror, every so often, to make sure that he was OK. The yellow Monte Carlo was still there, keeping it's distance, on the interstate. Exchange rates could work both ways. What the dealer could offer her, for her cherished Chevy, was basically chump change, so she politely declined. Cliff reckoned he could get a better deal, selling it online, privately. Anyway, the Sun was out, she was pleased with her purchase and still had some money in the bank.

*

2 months later, mid June, Sunday afternoon. The Caddy cruised along the I84, Westbound. The radio played techno beats, with news now and again. Cliff was behind the wheel, as Vicki had added him to her insurance and kindly let him have a go in her new toy. They had decided to have a vacation, as they had not had one for a while. Kirk and Dot had offered them a room for free, for a few days, so they were heading to Portland. Vicki sat in the front passenger seat, watching the Oregon scenery slide by the windows of her luxury car. She was in a reflective mood. Her and Cliff had been through some rough stuff, Cliff especially. But, she couldn't help thinking, life was pretty damn good. "Thanks for letting me keep my maiden name." She said, out loud. She wasn't sure where that came from, it just came out. Cliff took his eyes off the road, for a second, to glance at her. They had married, a few

weeks earlier. A low key deal, in an office. Neither set of in-laws had attended, mainly because they had told their parents after the fact. "No problem. I told you, if we take the double-u out of MW Transport, I'll have to get Jesse to get his designer friend to re-do our logo." Vicki laughed. "Even so, thanks." She said. "How about if I let you name him, whatever you want?" She suggested. "Easy." Cliff said. "I figured out a name, already." "OK, go on then, wotcha got?" "Drum roll. Clifford Miles-Wisconsin, aka, Chip." Pause. "Very distinguished." Vicki laughed.

They arrived at the Wright residence. Cliff parked on their drive, next to Kirk's 300. Kirk and Dot were on the bench at the rear of the house and heard the crunch of gravel. Kirk came to greet them. They got out of the car. "Hey, Dude! Transport upgrade?" "Hey man, good to see you. Ah, it's Vicki's." "Wow, business is good! Come through, wana beer, before dinner?" They sat on benches, drank beer and caught up. "So, you traded in the Monte Carlo?" Kirk asked. "No, I was going to, but the price they offered was abysmal, so I said no. Cliff has been trying to sell it. Would you like to buy it?" Vicki replied. "What made you go buy a sedan? You need a four door car?" Dot asked, clocking Vicki's loose-fit top. Pause. "Four months." Vicki said, softly. "Cliff, your gonna be a dad?" Kirk asked. "Congrats, both of you." Dot said. "Thanks." Vicki replied. "You nervous?" Kirk asked Cliff. "Well, it's a big responsibility, but, I reckon I can handle it." "You can handle anything, dude." " 're you looking forward to being a mom?" Dot asked. "Sure. You bet." Vicki replied. She didn't sound so sure. Dot looked at her, with slightly raised eyebrows. "Well, it'd be nice if my folks were nearer, or Cliff's folks, but hey, we've got good neighbors and friends in town." Vicki replied. They talked a while longer, then went in for dinner. Dot had cooked her usual Oregon fare.

*

Vicki and Cliff spent the following few days around Portland. They went around museums and parks. They walked the streets, window shopping, sometimes shopping. They were enjoying being a DINKY couple, for the last time. On Friday, their last day there, they sat on a bench, near the Willamette River, eating half a foot long sub, each. "Shall we play a game?" Cliff asked. "A game?" Vicki asked. "How about, I spy, with my little eye?" Cliff suggested. "OK. I spy, with my little eye, something beginning with R." "River." "OK. Too easy." "OK. My turn. I spy, with my little eye, something beginning with B." "Bridge. Where are we going with this?" Vicki asked. "OK. What *don't* I spy, with my little eye? Something beginning with H." Cliff said. Pause. "What *don't* you spy? Huh? How am I supposed to get that?" "OK. Try, HP?" Pause. "Hewlett Packard." Vicki offered. "They're in Palo Alto. What did you used to see lots of, in Portland?" Pause. "Homeless People." "Good. One point for Vicki."

Back at the Wright residence, that evening, as a thank you, Cliff bought pizzas for all four of them and had them delivered to the door. They sat around the dining table, eating, drinking and talking. After dinner, they sat on the sofas, in the living room and continued their conversation around the current affairs of their ever changing continent. Cliff decided to bring up the subject of the homeless population. "Hey, are we gonna talk about the elephant in the living room?" Cliff asked. "I thought you were a libertarian?" Kirk quipped. Pause. "Where did all the homeless go?" Cliff asked. Kirk and Dot glanced at each other. "Well, it's funny you mention that, because everyone in town is talking about it." Kirk said. "Their numbers have been reducing, for, I dunno, six months, maybe?" Kirk said, glancing at Dot. "At least that." Dot chipped in. "Where are they going?" Vicki asked. "Well, officials are always talking about this solution and that, more shelters, more housing, blah, whatever, etcetera. But the city can afford, like, a few hundred beds, in a city with about ten thousand homeless." Kirk said. "So, it's not that." Cliff interjected. Pause. "People have been talking about it, a lot and it seems that most of them have gone home." Dot got to the point. "Gone home?" Vicki asked. "Many of the homeless people in Portland and I guess, most other West coast cities, are not actually from those cities. Some of them are from Latin America, but most are from all over the former USA." Kirk said. "One of my friends is a psychologist. She has a theory that the independence of the States has made many people return to their home State. People, in many cases, don't like having an international border, between them and their home town, or them and their parents, or whatever. So, they get a train ticket, or hitch a ride, or whatever." Dot said. "I know someone exactly like that." Cliff said. "One of the guys that I was in the homeless camp with, another vet, called me, a few months back. He moved back to Abilene, where he comes from, just before Texas went independent. He got a job in a radio shop. He invited me to stay with him, in his single wide, if I'm in his neck of the woods." "It's good to see homeless people get back on their feet." Dot said. "The city looks cleaner, as well." She added. "I've seen city trucks, all over the city, picking up tents, tarpaulins and other stuff, from homeless camps, over the past few months." Kirk added. "I wonder if the new Pacifica Government has different policies on homelessness?" Vicki mooted. "Ha! More controversy." Dot said. "A lot of people in Oregon and Washington don't like that the Capitol for the whole of Pacifica; California, Oregon, Washington and Hawaii, is located in Sacramento. And a lot of people are really angry that we did not get a referendum, like most other States did. I'm not saying that's my position, but I know people who are talking like that." She explained. "Our neighbor, Jesse, is really up to speed on all things independence. He says that there have not been referenda, in the West coast, or North East States, because the Federal Government has gone into liquidation. So, the States that had not already left, have to organize themselves, because there is no longer a Fed to do Fed stuff, like maintain Interstate Highways, or a host of other things." Cliff replied. "Gone into liquidation?" Kirk asked. "Well, I guess it has not been officially announced, but, you can, you know, connect the dots." Cliff said. "The company that hired MWT are a company of liquidators, based in Switzerland." Vicki added. Pause. "How come the Federal Government is being liquidated by a foreign company?" Kirk asked. "We don't know." Cliff replied. "But, I have heard, from various sources, that the USA, or rather the *US Government* is a corporation, owned by other foreign corporations." Cliff said. "Sure, I've heard that, also. The Vatican, the City of London and DC are all one corporation." Kirk replied. "So, I guess we've never been a Republic?" Dot mooted. "Maybe the USA was, after getting independence from Britain." Vicki suggested. "But then it was changed back to a corporate status in eighteen seventy one, according to what I've heard." Cliff added. "So, now we're in the Republic of Pacifica?" Dot asked. "I think State Governments are corporations, as well. So, the new Country Governments are likely also corporations." Kirk suggested. "I wonder who owns the corporations?" Dot asked. Pause. "According to Jesse, we do, we just don't know it yet." Cliff replied.

*

Next morning, Saturday. The Caddy cruised along the I84, Eastbound. The radio played techno beats, with news now and again. Vicki was behind the wheel, as Cliff had his turn, already. They had thanked Kirk and Dot for the stay and gave them a present of a pressure cooker. Pressure cookers always seemed to make a good present, somehow. "How are we gonna manage work and the kid?" Cliff said, out loud. "I mean, we both work full time. I work more than full time, much of the time." He added. "I'll have to reduce my work load. I've already started to reduce the number of bids that I put in." Vicki replied. "And you get a lot of local work, nowadays, don't you? Not like at the beginning, when you were away all the time, whole weeks at a time." She added. "True. I can maybe do more of my own bids and scheduling." Cliff

242

replied. "I have helped Sophia a lot, with Chris and Luna. They often come to ours, after school, before Sophia gets home, so she can maybe return the favor, here and there." Vicki suggested. "People say we're having kids really late, both of us being in our mid thirties, but hey, we have a house owned free and clear and no finance on my car or your truck, which is better than many people." She added. "We'll survive." Cliff replied.

*

About two weeks later, early July, Saturday afternoon. Cliff had given the Sierra another oil change and was inside, getting changed. His phone pinged. It was a text message from Jesse, inviting him over, for beer, that afternoon. He and Vicki had ham and eggs for brunch, then he went next door. Jesse was sitting outside, at the rear of the house, with his laptop. "Wana beer?" He asked. "Thanks, man." They sat on garden chairs, under the gazebo. "What's happening?" Jesse asked. "I've been doing some work for an oil company. They do drilling in the East, near Rexburg. They've been taking advantage of the strong Mountainland Dollar, using it to buy equipment and steel, for their rigs." Cliff said. "Makes sense. A lot of people, especially business people, have realized that Mountainland tends to have a strong Dollar in the late summer, because Idaho, Montana and Wyoming are all agricultural producers and most of the crops are harvested in the late summer. Particularly, Idaho potatoes and Montana wheat. In fact, the Mountainland Dollar gets stronger through the spring and summer, as traders buy Dollars, in order to buy produce, a few months later." Jesse said. "Hmm, interesting." Cliff said. "And countries like Utah, have relatively less agriculture, so their currencies don't fluctuate as much." He suggested. "Well, they fluctuate the opposite way, because of their close proximity to us. Their currency is a mirror of ours, to some extent." Jesse explained. "Amazing, that something as basic as food can have such an impact on finance." Cliff said. "Well, in my world, the world of IT, many people see computers, data, that sort of thing, as the be-all-and-end-all. Especially the younger generation. But, in reality, people still gotta eat." Jesse replied. "And use oil." Cliff added. "Sure. How are you finding the border crossings, nowadays?" Jesse asked. "It's a lot easier, since I got a NAMCV." Cliff replied. "Oh yeah, the North American Multi-Country Visas? Pretty cool huh? I guess you have a business one?" Jesse asked. "Sure. All I do is swipe it, at the border, then log into my account later, to log my load and pay my taxes."

"I've been thinking about getting one of the personal ones, for myself and Sophia. We go back to Frisco now and again, to see the folks and it would mean we can use the fast lane." Jesse said. "Funny how the country has been split up and now the governments are working on making things more joined up." Cliff said. "True. Kinda. But, the difference is that the control is less centralized. There are no Feds, just State Governments, I mean, Country Governments, doing deals with each other." Jesse replied. "Like a new kind of Federalism." Cliff mooted. "Actually, it's the old kind of Federalism. The DC kind was always part of the New World Order agenda."

Chapter 16

Texas Land is Born

The following January. Clifford Miles-Wisconsin Jr., aka 'Chip' had been born, in September and was now 4 months old. Cliff was not keen to leave them alone, but had an offer of some lucrative work, in Texas, which would plug the income gap from Vicki's maternity leave. Vicki said she would be fine. Jesse and Sophia were next door. Amy flew down from Alaska. She was retired and needed a change of scene, so she combined it with a trip to see her grand daughter. Sunday afternoon, Cliff hit the road. The Sierra was well serviced, with nearly new tires and was ready for the winter roads. Normally, when heading to Texas, he would cut through Utah and New Mexico, but that meant driving on rural highways, which would likely be treacherous. This time, he turned off the I84 at Coalville, Utah, onto the I80 and headed East, back into Mountainland. An army of yellow, Mack snowplows kept the interstate, through Wyoming, as clear as possible. A seed of a new business idea was planted in Cliffs mind. He drove on, carefully. The lonely road wove through the bleak, windswept plains of Wyoming. The sky was a white-gray color and snow came down, lightly. Local radio stations played music and news. Late afternoon, he crossed the Mountainland – Rangeland border, South of Cheyenne, on the I25, using his NAMCV card. He continued South and stopped at a motel, a little North of Denver. He parked the truck and trailer on a snow-covered, gravel area, by the motel, took his hold all and locked the truck. He walked through the snow, in his rigger boots and arrived at the motel reception. An hour later, he was showered and changed. Food arrived. He ate and watched a pod cast, on his laptop.

*

Next morning, Cliff set out, just before dawn. He arrived in Commerce City, a suburb of Denver and drove to the address, which was in an industrial estate. He parked the truck and a man in a hi-viz came over. He put the window down. "Here to pick up a load, for Sweetwater Farm." Cliff said. "Got your purchase order?" The man asked. Cliff opened the email, on his phone and held it up. The man scanned the QR code, on his RF gun. "OK, I'll get that, for you." He jumped into the fork lift and disappeared, into the big-box building. A little later, Cliff's trailer was loaded, with shrink-wrapped pallets of goods. He hit the road again, heading through Denver, on the I25. He was relieved to find that the weather was a little less wild, than it had been, the previous day. The Sun came out, as the interstate took him through the snowy mountains of Southern Colorado. Just over the border, into New Mexico, he turned off the interstate, at Raton and headed East on Highway 87, a rural divided highway, which he had driven at least once on previous occasions. It was a little windy, on the plains. Snow blew about, flurries of it whipping across the road, in front of him. He crossed the border, into Texas Land, at Texline, around mid day. He stopped in the town, for gas and lunch, then hit the road again. He hit the I27, at Amarillo and headed South. He passed Lubbock and arrived at the farm, part way between Lubbock and Abilene. The farmer had plowed his road. Cliff drove into the concrete farm yard and stopped. The farmer came out and unloaded the trailer, with a pallet fitting, on his tractor. He paid Cliff, in cash and Cliff hit the road.

He arrived at Abilene, at around 8:30pm. The GPS took him to Gray's single wide. It was in a residential street, lined with a mixture of single wides, double wides and houses. The road was damp and the lawns had a sprinkling of snow. Bare, winter trees were dotted about. Cliff parked the truck and trailer in the street and walked up the drive, past a silver gray, 1998, Pontiac Grand Prix Coupe. He carefully climbed the wooden steps and was about to knock on the front door, when it opened. "Hey! Wassup!" Gray greeted Cliff. "Man! Long time!" Cliff replied. "Come in." Cliff followed Gray inside. The interior was cozy and comfortable. It was open plan, the living, dining and kitchen areas were all one. It was also cluttered, with books, papers, magazines, computer and radio equipment all over the living room. "Scuse the state of the place. I've been tidying up, for you coming, but it's a mammoth task. Take a seat. Dinner's ready." Cliff sat at the table. Gray served them both a beef stew, from a large cook pot. They tucked in. After dinner, they sat in easy chairs, in the living room. "You've accumulated a lot of stuff, in a few years." Cliff observed. "Well, some of it is mine. Some of it is my old man's. He past on, about two years ago." Gray said. "Sorry to hear that." Cliff said. "We knew it was coming. He'd been fighting cancer, for several years. Didn't make it any easier, though." "Dear, man, I'm sorry." "Thanks. Anyway, he left me a load of stuff. A life time's collection of all sorts. Books, magazines, tools, you name it. A lot of it is in the shed, at the back." Pause. "Do you have any family?" "Oh sure. My Mom lives in DFW, where I grew up. She's in her seventies, though and not so mobile. I go through there about once a fortnight, to see her and help her with a few things." "That's good." Cliff replied. "How about you? How's Idaho, Mountainland?" "It's good, generally. A bit cold and snowy, at this time of year." "You told me you and your girl had a kid, how's he doing?" "He's fine. He's four months old now. Vicki is basically a full time Mom at the mo. She put her side of the business on hold, for a bit. I do odds and ends, when I'm not on the road, to keep us in the game." "Sounds full on." Gray said. "Parents always say having a family is full on. They aren't kidding." Cliff replied. "I bet. I never had kids, myself. Had a girlfriend, years ago, but no kids. Too old for all that stuff, now. And always too busy, with work, car maintenance and everything else." "That your Grand Prix?" "Yeah, 's mine. Bought it a few years ago." "Looks good." "It's a real nice car. Something like twenty seven years old. Still drives spot on. I do most stuff myself, passes it's auto check every year, no problem." Gray said. "So, what brings you down to Texas Land, from snowy Mountainland?" "I delivered a load of irrigation gear, to a farm, about fifty miles from here, from a manufacturer in Denver." "Ah, irrigation, it's the talk of the town. Farmers are putting in new systems, all over the place." Gray said. "Is that something to do with Texas's independence?" Cliff asked. "Seems to be. I don't follow all the political stuff closely, but I have some idea what is going on. When we got independent, the government started building thorium-reactors, on the gulf coast. They de-salinate sea water. They've been building pipe lines, into the

248

interior. Some of the lines are nearly done, so farmers have started upgrading their irrigation systems. Or something like that. I think." "Sounds amazing. Texas Land is on the up." "Sure is. And we are going to be expanding soon, as well, apparently." Gray said. "Expanding?" Cliff asked. "Northwards. The Westland Government is in talks with the Texas Land Government, about merging the two countries, together." "You're shitting me." Cliff said. "Nope. On the news every day. And on the web and over the radio." "So, a big chunk of the Mid-West might end up being part of Texas Land?" Cliff mooted. "Well, if it goes ahead, it would give us access to the Canadian border, with no other borders, in between."

*

Over the following few weeks, Cliff went to and fro, shipping irrigation gear from Denver, to Northern Texas. A network of farmers, around Amarillo and Lubbock, had got his number and were getting everything that they would need, for a productive year, ahead. He stayed in a motel in Denver, after the return trips and stayed with Gray, after the outward ones. He had a video call, with Vicki and Chip, in the Denver motel nights. He listened to the local radio stations, as he drove. Gray was right, there was lots of talk, about irrigation and about the union of Texas Land, with Westland, which currently comprised Oklahoma, Kansas, Nebraska, South Dakota and North Dakota. Those States, with their smaller populations, relative to Texas, would retain their State Governments, to manage local affairs, but would be part of Texas Land. The Austin Government would be the new 'Federal

Government'. "What kind of visa are you on?" Gray asked, one night, after dinner, as they say drinking beer, in Gray's living room. "Er, dunno actually. I just swipe my card, at the border." Cliff said. "The app that goes with the card will tell you." Gray suggested. Cliff logged into the app and looked at his account settings. "I'm on a T1 Visa, it says here." Cliff said. "Ah, transport of essential goods, that makes sense." Gray said. "Just curious. There's a lot of talk about visas, at the moment. Been some controversy over who should have what, that sort of thing." "Texas has different immigration rules, to those of the USA, doesn't it?" Cliff asked. "Sure. We used to have everyone and their dog, coming across the Mexico border. The wall stopped that. Now, people have to apply for a visa and work permit." "Keeps out the undesirables." Cliff replied. "Sure. Anyone who gets caught, involved in crime, gets sent right back." "I bet that has helped to clean up the streets." Cliff said. "Wadaya know, two old guys, who used to be homeless, talking about cleaning up the streets." Gray quipped. They both laughed. "Perhaps everyone deserves a second chance?" Cliff mooted. "Yeah, I agree. That's what America was always about, the land of opportunity." Gray said. "And we seem to be getting back to that, in a round about sort of way." Cliff replied. "Opportunity to turn your life around." He added. "Sure. Not the opportunity to smoke meth." Gray replied. "Another beer?"

*

Late January, Friday afternoon. Cliff arrived home, after several weeks away. There was still snow on the ground, in Mountainland. He parked the truck and trailer and went inside. Vicki greeted him with a hug. Amy was also there, holding Chip. Vicki and Amy had cooked a pork and apple pie, with roast potatoes. They ate, then sat on the sofas and caught up. "Vicki told me a bit about your business, in Texas." Amy said. "Delivering irrigation equipment?" "Yeah. From a manufacturer in Denver, to Northern Texas." Cliff said. "And you had someone to stay with?" "Yeah. Grayson. A guy that I knew, from the camp in Pomona. He lives in Abilene." "You drove every day, for nearly three weeks. You must be exhausted." "Yeah. Pretty much. What's been happening here?" "Mom has been looking after Chip, through the day. I've been doing some work. Got some containers on route. Got some loose ends tied up, from a while back." "Amazing." Cliff said. "Seen Jesse or Sophia?" "Yeah, a few times. All good." Vicki replied.

*

Various people had warned about a bad winter, that winter. December had been cold, with some snow, which was usual, for Idaho. Early January had been colder, with more snow, again, nothing out of the ordinary. Cliff had been through several winters and had only lost a handful of days, to the weather. The Twin Falls council had various contractors out, to clear the snow. Even when they were not able to keep all of the residential streets clear, the Sierra would usually make it, out to the interstate. The interstates were usually kept clear, by contractors, now hired by the Mountainland government. On a few occasions, in previous years, when the snow drifted to several feet, he had to call customers and reschedule. They had always been OK about that. Everyone understood the Idaho weather.

Now, in early February, it started to snow, in anger. It snowed. And snowed. And snowed. Every morning, when he got up, at 6:30am, the snow was deeper. The snowplows were struggling to keep it clear. Cliff had struggled to get back home, in Vicki's Caddy, after taking Amy back to the airport, in Boise. He rescheduled his customers, into March and took over some of Vicki's work. She had trained him in freight forwarding, so that he could take on some of her work, when Chip was born. Now, he kept their income coming, without having to leave the house. One day, in the first week in February, he was in the middle of completing a customs form, online. He was on Vicki's PC, with the form on one screen and Atlas Connect on the other. Another tab was open, in the background, with an internet radio station playing. They talked about the tough winter, the Mountainland was getting. Idaho, Montana and Utah were especially bad, with wind blown snow blocking many roads. The contractors were struggling, to keep roads open. Cliff remembered the idea that he had, on the interstate, in Wyoming.

"It's not had much use. I'm gettin' too old to do this, now." Lucas said. "My old one broke, last winter. I'd had it for years. I bought this one, but I have health issues now, so I'm giving it up." "It looks like new." Cliff said, walking around the FirstTrax snowplow. He had found it on the local online ads page, with 'offers' as the price. "How much do you want, for it?" "Well, I paid about four grand for it, about this time last year, because the Mountainland Dollar was weak, at the time. But I'll not pass that

252

on, to you. How about two grand?" "Exactly my budget." Cliff said, handing Lucas a brown envelope, full of Mountainland twenties. "All yours." Lucas said, stuffing the envelope into the pocket of his fleece. The two men wrestled the plow into the flat bed of Cliff's truck. Cliff clocked Lucas's truck, parked on his driveway. "That's a Denali?" He asked. "Sure. I've had GMC, all my life. Never had anything else." Lucas said. "It looks great." Cliff said. "I've got the base model, but it's still good." He added. "They both do the same job, but mine has leather seats and all sorts of toys." Lucas replied. "You added aftermarket alloys, to yours?" He asked, looking at Cliff's truck. "No. The previous owner put them on, among other things." Cliff replied. "Some people say to stay away from aftermarket stuff, but I've had no trouble."

Cliff and Jesse fitted the plow, that afternoon. Vicki and Chip watched, from the window. Once it was on, Cliff got into the truck and cleared their street, piling snow on neighbors cars, as he went by. Jesse stood on the sidewalk and watched, glad that his Impala was off the road, on his driveway. Cliff stopped outside his drive and waved Jesse to get in. Jesse got into the front passenger seat. Cliff drove off. "Let's do another street." He said. Six streets later, they arrived home. Cliff parked on the driveway and they talked. "Any luck with my license?" Cliff asked. "Sorry. I guess I should have told you, before you went and bought this thing. The licensing process takes months. The snow will be gone, by the time you have it." Jesse replied. "No surprise there. Government will be government, even when it is not Federal. It doesn't matter, because I'm not after their money." Cliff said, then went on: "Can you do a crowd fund site, for me? It doesn't have to be an absolute work of art, just something that local people can drop a few bucks on, when they see the plow go by." "Sure. I can do that." Jesse agreed. "In return, I'll plow our street, so you can get your sedan out. How's that?" Cliff asked. "Deal." Jesse replied.

Cliff plowed the streets, of Twin Falls, for weeks, after that. He cleared residential streets, the ones that the contractors had not had time to do. Jesse advertised the crowd fund site on local ads pages and donations poured in. Residents were glad to be able to get back to their offices and get out for supplies. Cliff and Vicki discussed the business, over dinner, in the evenings. "What's an average donation?" Cliff asked. "Most are a few bucks, some are more generous. I guess, about five bucks." Vicki said. "And we're getting dozens, per day, right?" "We're making about the same as when you do your normal business." Vicki replied.

*

The following April, Saturday afternoon. The snow had thawed a few weeks earlier. Cliff had stashed the snowplow in the garage and went back to his usual business. Vicki and Sophia took the kids out somewhere, that afternoon. Jesse knocked on the door of the Miles-Wisconsin residence. It opened and Cliff appeared, in denims and a fleece. "Come in." Jesse followed Cliff inside. "Grab a seat. Beer?" "Thanks, Dude." Jesse sat on the sofa. Cliff took two bottles of beer, from the fridge and went back into the living room. He handed one to to Jesse, then sat on the opposite sofa. "Sapnin?" Cliff asked. "Ah, usual. Hey, before I forget, can I take your crowd funding site down now? It'll save me a few bucks on the server hosting." Jesse said. "Sure thing. Doubt there'll be much more snow, for another eight months." Cliff replied. "I'll keep the site for you and just upload the same one, next winter, how's that?" Jesse asked. "Sounds like a plan." Cliff agreed. "How's business?" Jesse asked. "Crazy busy. Catching up on all the stuff that has been put back, 'cause of the snow. How about you?" Cliff replied. "Also busy. Nothing to do with the snow, in my case." Jesse replied.

"Hey, have you been following the news, recently?" Cliff asked. "Sure, always." Jesse replied. "I've not really had time to follow it, properly, but Westland has now joined Texas Land." Cliff said. "Sure has. One country, all the way from Corpus Christi to Portal." Jesse replied. "Like a middle pillar, right up the middle of the of the country." Cliff replied. "Gray was talking about it, when I was staying with him, a few months back. They must have been talking about it a while." He added. "It's been in the works for longer than that." Jesse replied. "Actually, when the Westland referendum was being organized, three and a half years ago, some of the officials in the em-wip mooted the idea that their States could join Texas. So, the idea is not new." "No referendum, this time." Cliff pointed out. "No. There was, actually. It was when your kid was born, so you missed it." Jesse said. "Ah, OK. Did you go and do security, for that one?" Cliff asked. "No, there was no security. The organizers decided that it was not necessary." Jesse replied. "I guess DC does not exist, any longer. So, there is no deep state to put a wrench in the works." Cliff said. Pause. "Well, the deep state kinda does still exist, but not so much in DC and they don't have the same power that they used to have." Jesse replied. "How do you mean, still exist? How? Where?" Cliff asked. "It's complicated. But, for a start, the deep state has always been trans-national. DC was part of it, but not the whole of it." Jesse replied. "You mean, like, the City of London, the Vatican, Brussels?" Cliff interjected. "Sure and more." Jesse replied. "Also, what does deep state mean, really?" He asked. There was a long pause, as Cliff thought about that.

"Well, I guess, it depends who you ask. Different people have different ideas about what it means. Some people see it as the 'military-industrial complex'. But, I was part of that, for most of my career and I know that it's not what many people think. America never needed foreign oil, for example. We have more than enough of our own." "What is the military industrial complex for, then?" Jesse interjected. Pause. "I guess it's all about control. It's sold to the public as defense. It is that, to some extent. But, it's also about re-engineering the politics of nations, to bring them under a multi-national umbrella." Cliff suggested. "So, that's the motivation, but what do you think it actually *is?*" Jesse asked. "Well, I guess it's a network, of people, in positions of power. Politicians, CEOs, financiers, military." Cliff suggested. Pause. "You think they're the top of the pyramid?" Jesse asked. Long pause. "No. I'm sure there are people, in the shadows, controlling them." Cliff replied. "So, 'We the People' don't stand a chance?" Jesse mooted. "I guess, in essence, we don't know exactly what the deep state is, because we are outsiders. We just know that people, who are further up the pyramid, steer us in one direction, or another and we don't know where they are taking us, until we get there." Cliff replied. Pause. "So, what's the point of the independence movement, if we don't know where we're going?" Jesse asked. Cliff stroked his beard. "Another beer?" He asked. "Fuck, yeah. I need one, for this conversation." Jesse replied.

Cliff brought another two beers, from the fridge. He sat down again, on the sofa. "Honest answer. I dunno. You're the independence guru." He replied. Jesse: "OK. See, why most people don't understand the world? It's because they see it in black and white. It's all them, or all us. In reality, It's never all them, or all us. Neither side has all the power. The elite have power, in some ways. They control media, governments, corporations. But, We the People have power in other ways." "What power do we have?" Cliff interjected. Pause. "Think of an ocean. What can one drop do, on it's own?" Jesse asked. "Not a lot." Cliff replied. "What can an ocean do?" Jesse asked. "A lot." Cliff replied. "So, who has the power? The people, or the elite?" Pause. "Well, I guess there are billions of us and thousands of them." Cliff replied. "Exactly." Jesse replied. "So, how does the independence movement fit into that picture?" Cliff asked. "I think you know the answer, already, you just need to think about it." Jesse replied. Cliff went silent, for a minute, or so. "The ocean has washed the power away, from DC, I guess." He said. "And does the ocean know it has done so?" Another long pause. "Some of the drops do." Cliff offered. "But, in aggregate, it does not?" Jesse asked. "I guess not." Cliff replied. "But, the change of direction has still happened, right?" Jesse asked. "Yeah, I guess." Cliff replied. "So, who has the power, *really?*" Jesse asked. "The ocean?" Cliff offered. "But the ocean doesn't know shit." Jesse said. "OK, you got me. I'm lost." Cliff admitted. "What drives an ocean? What makes the ocean currents flow?" Jesse asked. Cliff thought about it, then replied: "The Sun."

Chapter 17

Deep Tech

One month later, Monday, mid-May, Calgary, Alberta. Cliff sat in his truck, with the air con and the radio on, waiting. He was parked, just in front of the door of a big-box building, his trailer behind him, inside the building. Around him, was the cleanest industrial yard he had ever seen. Acres of perfect concrete, bounded by a few feet of manicured grass, with a tree every few feet and a high, chain link fence, beyond that. Behind him, a large industrial unit, full of tools and equipment that were way above his pay grade. Guys in overalls and a few in lab coats used a gantry crane to load the load onto his trailer. They were taking their time. They had asked his permission to drill holes in his trailer, to which they would bolt a special rig, to take the load. Normally, if anyone asked to drill holes in his trailer, he would put the phone down. But, at the price these guys had offered, he agreed. He had suggested that they use the holes, that were already in the trailer, for his motorcycle rig, but they needed exactly what they needed, for their special load.

At about mid-day, the load was on, secured and the fibre-glass cover secured, over it. The site foreman instructed him that he could go. Cliff drove forward, carefully, to the gate, looked both ways and pulled out, into the street. Behind him, was the most valuable load that had ever been on his trailer. So valuable, that the sender had insisted that they use their own insurance, rather than his. He drove Westbound, through Foothills, which he reckoned must be one of the largest industrial estates on Earth. He turned onto 52nd street and headed South, on the divided highway. He arrived at a set of lights and stopped, in the left hand lane, with his left flasher on. The lights changed and he drove off carefully, turning left, heading Eastbound on Highway 506, Glenmore Trail. He accelerated gently, checking his rear view mirror now and again, to make sure the load was fine. He took the ramp off, onto Highway 201 and headed South again. He relaxed a little, having navigated the city. He was now on the main ring road, around Calgary and would shortly be heading across the Canadian plains, towards the Mountainland border. The radio played, music, jabber, music, jabber. He was cruising at about 50mph. Up ahead, a car's flashers went on. He started to slow. Other cars and trucks were slowing down. All the traffic seemed to be slowing. Damn. There must be an accident, somewhere ahead. He slowed down, behind the car in front, in the right hand lane. All of the traffic on the carriageway started to creep along, at about 10mph. It kept moving, at 10mph. Kept moving, kept moving, kept moving. 5 minutes went by. 10 minutes went by. Still, the traffic crept down the divided highway. Motorcycles lane-split, through the traffic, at about 20mph, making slightly better time than the rest of the traffic. Was this normal? Did Calgary usually have severe traffic congestion? Cliff wondered.

He re-tuned the radio, around various stations, trying to find some Calgary news. He found a station that had a news bulletin and listened. They reported various local news, then an article about the congestion. There was a 'go slow', organized by a truckers union, in protest at the proposals by the Ottawa Government, to electronically tag all trucks and trailers. Several trucks were driving around the ring-road, counter-clockwise, at 10mph, holding up thousands of other trucks and cars. This was not good, for Cliff. He had a drive of three days, ahead of him and did not want to be held up. The client had contacted him months earlier, to organize transport, for their highly important load. This was the highest paid, highest pressure job in his trucking career and he wanted it to go smoothly. He zoomed out, on his GPS screen, to get a bigger picture, of the area. The road had rounded a corner, to the right and was now heading West. In about a mile and a half, he would be taking the ramp off, onto Highway 2, to head South. He did a rough calculation, in his head. 60 minutes, divided by 10mph, equals 6 minutes per mile, times 1.5 miles, equals 9 minutes. Cool. 9 minutes was not a problem.

He turned off, onto Highway 2. The traffic in front continued to do 10mph. The large volume of traffic would take some time to pick up speed, Cliff thought. He drove along at 10mph, for a while longer. He was in the right lane and the road went into a long, slight curve as it left the suburban areas of Calgary. There was slow moving traffic, as far as the eye could see. Time went by. 10 minutes, 20 minutes, 30 minutes. The traffic was not picking up speed. The go-slow-trucks had not continued around the ring-road, as the news seemed to suggest. They were clearly, now, heading South, on Highway 2. And he was stuck in a queue, behind them. This would not do, he had to turn off. He took a ramp off the divided highway at Okotoks and headed East, on a rural highway. At last, he was able to get moving and cruised at about 50mph. The vast, agricultural plains of Western Canada slid by the windows of his truck. The sky was the biggest that he had seen, endless blue, from horizon to horizon. The area was sparsely populated, just a farm or a house, here and there, beside the road, or off in the distance.

The GPS continually re-calculated, trying to put him back on the main route, but he ignored it and carried on, down one rural highway, after another. After about an hour and a half, he passed the town of Nobleford. He arrived at another major route, Highway 3. As he approached it, he saw a large volume of traffic on it, moving slowly. Damn. He had hit another protest. He was on the ramp and had no choice but to join the road. He did so and crept along, at 10mph, with the other traffic. He zoomed out again, on the GPS. The town of Lethbridge was about 10 miles away. It was already late afternoon. He had planned to cross the Mountainland border and stay the night in Shelby, or Great Falls, Montana, but would not reach them until late evening, at that rate, even if the protest stopped at Lethbridge. He decided to stay the night in Lethbridge and turned off the main highway.

Cliff found a motel with large, diagonal spaces and parked the truck and trailer across two of them. He set up the camera, that the client had supplied, in the rear of the truck, pointed it at the trailer and powered it on. It booted and the blue LED indicated that it had connected to the 4G network. The clients 24 hour security team would now be able to see the load, from their office. He went inside, paid for a room , showered, changed and ordered food. He opened the Freight Watch app on his phone, to make sure that the load was visible on the camera. He called his contact, at the company and advised that he had been held up and was staying the night in a different location, to that which had been planned. She thanked him for his call and let him go. After dinner, he booted his laptop and read some news. Then he went to cog dot com, to see if there was any information on the Canadian trucker protests. He found an article on the site and started to read it.

The Canadian Legislature had brought forward a bill, to make the electronic tagging of all commercial trucks and trailers in the county, compulsory. Politicians in Ottawa, the Capitol of Canada and the media in Toronto, argued that tagging was necessary, to enable the Federal Government to manage emissions of green house gasses, from trucks. They argued that they needed to monitor and reduce the mileage of trucks, forcing truckers to work part time, perhaps three days per week, in order for Canada to meet their carbon emission targets. The truckers argued that such limitations would prevent them from being able to balance their books, putting many of them out of business. Self employed truck drivers would have to sell up and take low paid jobs, or no jobs at all. Cutting back the haulage industry would also reduce the supply of goods, to stores, creating shortages and pushing up prices. The politicians countered that argument, suggesting that the Government could manage the supply of goods, through rationing. At the bottom of the article, was a link to the truckers' website. Cliff had been a little annoyed at the protest, earlier in the day. He tended to support grass-roots political movements, but also needed to make a living. Now he saw that their ability to make a living was threatened, so he decided to support them. He clicked on the link and their page opened in another tab. He donated about $100 MLD, equivalent, in Tron coin, from his crypto account.

*

Next day, Tuesday, 9:00am. Cliff drove Southbound, down Highway 62. He guessed that the main route, Highway 4, might be at 10mph again, so he took the back road, out of Lethbridge. The road twisted and turned, through the bleak and windswept hills of Southern Alberta. The rolling hills and endless, tree-less grassland looked a little like an alien planet. He drove past a cattle ranch, now and again. He drove through the hamlet of Del Bonita and arrived at the rear end of a queue, at the border crossing. Usually, the more remote border crossings were quiet, but clearly, some people had the same idea as he had and avoided the main route. The queue moved forward, one vehicle length, at a time. About 30 minutes and some paperwork later, he was in Mountainland. He cut through Cut Bank and an hour or so later, he was on the I15, heading South.

After stopping for lunch and diesel in Helena, Montana, Cliff called Vicki. "Hi Cliff." Her voice came over the truck's speakers. "Hey Babe. How you doin'? How's Chip?" "We're fine. And you?" "I'm good. I'm just South of Helena. I'll be home at about seven thirty, PM, tonight." "OK. I'll have dinner ready, for you." "Thanks, Babe." "Take care." "Sure, see you later." Cliff continued South, through the mountains of Montana, Mountainland. He arrived home at 7:30pm and reversed the trailer, past the house, into the rear yard, so that it was out of sight of the street, as an extra layer of security. He set the camera and went inside. Vicki greeted him and they sat down for dinner. She had cooked steak, fries and broccoli. Chip sat in his high-chair and ate ground steak, ground fries and ground broccoli. "How's your day been?" Cliff asked. "Busy. Been juggling Chip and ISO containers all day. You?" "Today was OK. Got a clear run, down the interstate. Yesterday went awry. There was a trucker protest, in Canada. Lost some time on that." "That'll make your delivery late?" Vicki asked. "Maybe half a day. I called the client, yesterday and told them that I'd been delayed. They're OK with that. They are more concerned with security, than speed." Cliff replied. "Our back yard is probably more secure than a motel parking lot." Vicki mooted. "Sure thing." Cliff agreed. "Plus, we can tell our grand kids that we had a classified aero engine parked outside our house." He added.

*

Next day, mid-day. Cliff drove down Highway 93, through Nevada. Overhead, a hot Sun and blue sky. The arid mountains of Northern Nevada slid by the windows of his truck. He passed through the small, remote town of Eli and continued, South. He was in the only State that had not officially declared itself a new country, or part of a new country. Nominally, it was still part of the USA, which no longer existed, or something. Some Las Vegas residents wanted it to be part of Pacifica, others of Rangeland. Some people, mostly members of the Church of Utah, mostly in Northern Nevada, wanted to join Utah. It was a State of limbo. The Nevada Government, in Carson City, managed the everyday affairs of the State, or Country, or whatever it was. Mid-afternoon, Cliff turned off the 93, onto the 375 and drove through the hamlet of Crystal Springs. He continued on the Extraterrestrial Highway. Just before the hamlet of Rachel, he turned left, off the highway, onto an unmetalled road. It was a long straight road, which lead him across the arid plain, towards a range of mountains, in the distance.

*

Some weeks later, early June. Cliff's successful delivery of the aero engine had lead to further contracts, for the client and their associates. The combination of his military background, professionalism and can-do attitude had hit the spot. Miles-Wisconsin Transport was on the up. It was a Friday and Cliff was giving himself a long weekend, as things were going so well. He had taken Vicki's Monte Carlo, which had not had much use, in recent months and drove to Pocatello, to show it to a prospective buyer. He had said full price, if he were to deliver it. The buyer drove a hard bargain, trying to get it for half price, offering a mish-mash of Dollars and cryptos. Cliff politely declined and drove home.

He would have been annoyed, except that it was a nice day in late spring, for a run in a classic sports car. He arrived home in the early afternoon. He parked the car back in it's place, in the rear yard, on the gravel, next to the garage. He locked it and walked away, towards the house. He glanced over his shoulder at it. The car that did not want to be sold.

He went inside and Vicki greeted him. She had cooked ham and eggs. They sat at the dining table and ate. Chip ate ground ham and ground eggs, in his high chair. Cliff clocked that there was something different, about the living room, but could not figure out what it was. Vicki had changed something. What could she have done, in the few hours that he was away? "Have you moved some furniture?" He asked, glancing at the sofas and bookshelves. Pause. "How do you define furniture?" Vicki asked. "The moveable articles in a household that make it suitable for living or working." Cliff replied, reading from the browser, on his phone. "By that definition, yes." She replied. "What have you changed?" He asked. "I spy." She replied. Cliff scanned the room. "Is that a new TV?" He asked, looking at the flat screen, hanging on the wall, over the wood burning stove. "It's not a TV. The TV is away, to a thrift store. It's that thirty two inch monitor that I bought, a while ago. It sat in it's box, in my office, for over a year." She said. "Yeah, I never got around to setting it up. Been busy." Cliff said. "Well, I had some spare time, so I set it up." Vicki replied. "You put it up on the wall, by yourself?" Cliff asked. "Well, actually, I got Jesse to do the bracket thing, at the back. I did the rest." She replied. "What's it connected to?" He asked. "That mini-PC, that sat in it's box, in my office, for over a year." She replied. "Hmm, OK. And what's the PC connected to?" He asked. "The internet." Vicki replied, simply. "I hope you don't mind the TV going away." She added. "Do I mind? Pretty sure you watch about ninety five percent of the TV in this house. No, I don't mind. Just surprised that you would make such a change." Cliff said. Pause. Vicki looked at Cliff, glanced at Chip, then back at Cliff. "I want him to grow up with alternative media, not New York media. I want him to have a free mind, like his Dad."

*

A few months later, Sunday afternoon, mid September. Vicki and Sophia took the kids out shopping, or something. Jesse joined Cliff in the back yard, for a few beers. They sat on garden chairs, in denims and t-shirts, in the shade of one of the trees. They talked a bit about Jesse's current project, then Jesse asked Cliff about his business. "I'm getting some more specialist work now, moving high-security goods, for defense contractors." Cliff said. "Sounds interesting, what sort of things?" Jesse asked. "Classified stuff. They don't tell me much about it. The first job was to move an airplane engine, from Calgary to Groom Lake Airbase. I got stuck in a go-slow, truckers were protesting the electronic tagging, but I still delivered the load in time." "Good." Jesse replied. "I gave the Canadian truckers a donation. Got to support other working people." He added. "Same here. I gave them some of my Tron coin. I would not want to be in their situation." Cliff replied. "I haven't seen anything about it, online, I guess the Canadian Government

267

backed down, in the end?" Cliff asked. "No, they didn't. The protests went on for weeks. Now, some of the Canadian States are holding an independence referendum." Jesse replied. "Wow! Really? Canada copying the US, I mean, former US. I like that." Cliff said. "Which States are involved?" He asked. "All of the North and Western States; Alberta, Saskatchewan, Manitoba, Yukon, Northwest Territories and Nunavut." Jesse replied. "There's an article about it on cog dot com." He added. "Canada has a lower population density than us, especially in the West. Are those States going independent as a block?" Cliff asked. "They're having a three-way question, on their ballots. Remain in Canada, go independent as a block, or go independent and join Texas Land." Pause. "Seriously?" Cliff asked. "They want to join Texas Land?" "Well, I guess we find out, after the referendum." Jesse replied. "When's the referendum?" Cliff asked. "Next week." Jesse replied. "Let me guess. You're going to do security for it and you want me to come along?" Cliff replied. "No. I asked one of the guys in the Idexit Party about that. They have their own security, they don't need us." "If they do vote to join Texas Land, that'll make one country, all the way from the Gulf of Mexico, to the border with Alaska." Cliff pointed out. "Not only that, but some people are suggesting that Alaska might join Texas Land, at some point." Jesse said. Pause. "One country, all the way from Galveston, to Prudhoe Bay. That would be something." Cliff replied. "I was gonna say, 'but it'll never happen', but I keep saying that, then it happens." He added. Jesse laughed. "You're sounding like an old timer, now." He said. "Sure. Chuck does not understand independence.

Larry does. Some old timers get it, others don't" Cliff replied. "Talking of family, how's Chip?" Jesse asked. "He's fine." Cliff replied. "He'll be one year old, next week."

Chapter 18

Victory Lap

Two years later, September, Monday. Cliff drove up the I5, Northbound. He had stayed the night with Kirk and Dot, in Portland, after picking up his load, in the California Bay area. It was an overcast day, in Pacifica, with showers on and off. On his trailer, a Cadillac CT5 Blackwing, in black. It belonged to Frank Olson, a friend of Kirk's Dad. He was a motor-sport enthusiast, retired from his job at a tech firm in San Francisco. He had flown out to Anchorage, a few days earlier, to be ready to take delivery of his car and make other preparations. He would be taking part in the Cannonball Cruise. The endurance race had been organized by some of the senior members of several of the independence parties, along with retired racing drivers, auto manufacturers and various sponsors. It was to celebrate the joining of Alaska, Yukon, NWT, Alberta, Saskatchewan and Manitoba, with Texas Land. They were racing from Anchorage, to Galveston, Texas.

Cliff reached Tacoma, Washington, mid morning. He drove through the suburban areas, took an exit off the interstate and turned into the industrial area of the docks. He turned off the 509 and the GPS took him to the truck staging area, next to the Blair

Waterway. He turned into the yard and found a diagonal space. He parked in it, along side semi trucks and trailers. He turned off the engine and waited. A man in a hi-viz vest came over to his truck. He put the window down. "You're here for the Anchorage ship?" The man asked. "Sure, to deliver the car." Cliff replied, pointing a thumb to the trailer." "Are you taking the truck and trailer on board?" The man asked. "No. Just dropping the car. Someone is coming, on the ship, to drive it on board." Cliff replied.

*

Two days later, Anchorage. Frank stood on the quayside, watching, as tugs maneuvered the ConRo ship into the dock. The process was slow, the gray and white behemoth turning slowly, 180 degrees, in the Knik Arm. Trucks and ISO containers were visible on the top deck. After a while, it was moored. The doors opened and trucks started to disembark, followed by cars. Frank noticed that many of the cars were competitors. Sports coupes, sedans and hot hatches, with numbers on the doors and sponsors logs on the body panels. He spotted his Caddy. It drove down the ramp, off the ship and into the parking lot. Frank walked towards it. Jerry, the driver that he had hired, got out. "Hi, hows it going?" Frank asked. "Fine thanks and you?" Jerry replied. Fist pump. "There's your car." Jerry handed the key to Frank. "It's fine, but feel free to have a look around it." He held a clipboard and pen, as Frank looked around the car. "Perfect. Thanks" He replied and signed the sheet. A few minutes later, he drove the car through the streets of Anchorage, to his motel.

Friday, early morning, in the town of Palmer, about 35 miles North of Anchorage. It was a sunny day, with a blue sky and a cumulus cloud, here and there. About two-dozen cars parked in a large parking lot, next to the Alaska Fairground. Drivers worked on their cars, making last minute checks, topping up fluids, packing spares and tools into the trunks and rear seats. Some stood and talked. Frank looked around the lot. The competition was varied. A Lamborghini Aventador, an Aston Martin DB11, a Ferrari Daytona SP3, a Rolls Royce Wraith, a Polestar 1, a Subaru BRZ and many other similar models. The scrutineers worked their way around the lot, making sure that none of the cars had illegal modifications, such as nitrous oxide injection, or slick tires. He ate sandwiches and peanuts and swigged water, from a bottle, as he would not eat again, until later in the day.

Late morning, the staging started. The Lambo was first in the queue. It stopped at the start line, then the organizers let it go. One car after another, each one minute apart, set off. Frank joined the queue and worked his way forwards. The Ferrari was in front of him and stopped at the line. One minute went by, then the flag went down. The Ferrari drove off, with a crackle from the exhaust. Frank drove up to the line and stopped. One minute went by, then the flag went down. He accelerated away from the line, out onto the road. He turned right, onto AK-1, heading North-East. He accelerated hard, up the road, the car's 668bhp V8 whisking the car up to nearly 100mph. The forest of Alaska went by, in a blur. He slowed down, to about 60mph, for a series

271

of bends, carefully keeping the car off the barrier, on the right hand side. He cut across the yellow lines, using the full width of the road. The Police had closed the road, for about half a day, to allow the rally to get going, so there would be nothing coming the other way. The Glenn Highway twisted and turned, up the North bank of the Matanuska River. Frank piloted the car up the road, as quickly as he safely could. Much of the road had no barrier, with nothing but soil and trees between him and the river. He straddled the yellow lines and mostly kept between 70 and 90mph.

He passed through the remote town of Glennallen, turning left and heading North. The highway took him deeper still, into the wilds of Alaska. He would have liked to catch up with the Ferrari, but did not. He checked his rear view mirror, every-so-often and had not seen any other car, behind him. Then, he spotted daytime running lights, on the rear horizon. Someone was gaining on him. He kept going, building his pace, just a little. He checked the rear view mirror, again, as he neared the end of another straight. The car was gaining on him. It was black. He tried to remember which car was black. Ah yes, the Rolls Royce. That car was about the same power as his, but heavier. It should not be gaining on him. Still, there was about 4,000 miles still to go. He had decided, before the race, that he would pace himself. Snake and hare. Or something like that. He carried on. The Wraith gained on him, gradually, until it was right behind him. But, they had reached the first stop. Just as it caught up with him, he arrived in the small town of Tok. He drove into the gas station and brimmed the Caddy with gas. Other cars, in the race, were there. The Wraith pulled in, behind him. The driver, an Arabic-looking guy, got out and started to fill the car.

A few minutes later, the car was full and gas paid for. Other drivers had parked on the gravel area, by the gas station and were eating and talking. He was tempted to stop, for a break, after about 200 miles and 3 hours drive. But, he also liked the idea of getting a head start, on the other competitors. He hit the road. He headed east, on AK-2. The road was straight and he got some speed up. He hit 120mph and checked his rear view mirror. Headlights were visible, in the distance. The driver of the Wraith had the same idea as him. The road became twisty and he had to slow a little. He carried on. Endurance could win, just as well as outright speed. He was going to use a bit of both and hopefully, win the race. The driver of the Wraith kept trying to catch him, projector-bean lights visible in his rear view mirror, down all of the straights. It was the battle of the Brit and the American, on the North American continent, more than two and a half centuries after the last battle. So far, the American was struggling. But, they had 4,000 miles to go.

Frank had studied the route and had a good idea where he would stop. He crossed the border, from Alaska, into Yukon. There was no border control, since Yukon had seceded, from Canada and joined Texas Land. He carried on. The road became a little gravelly, stones clattering on the Caddy's chassis. He slowed a little. The Wraith caught him up. It's rectangular headlights and chrome grill appeared in his rear view mirror. Damn. Hours of driving had made him slow, at little too much. He picked up pace a little, managing to stay in front.

There was no other traffic, on the closed road, so there was nothing to stop an over take. He cornered hard and accelerated hard, out of the bends. The Caddy could pull away, out of the turns, being lighter, but the Wraith would use a little more top speed, down the straights, to close the gap. Frank concentrated hard, working the controls, using all his skill and the cars abilities, to stay in front. The Brit stayed right on his tail. They arrived at Haines Junction. There was a t-junction in front of him. Damn. He slowed to a stop. He had studied maps of the route, but did not remember a t-junction. He glanced at the GPS. It told him to go left. His slight hesitation, at the junction, allowed the Wraith to pass him, turning left and flooring it, up the hill. He turned left and followed it. He tried to catch up, but the Wraith driver was going all out. He managed to keep up, just. There were a few hundred yards, between him and the other car. They drove on, mile after mile, a similar gap between them. The Wraith driver would not let Frank catch up. Frank would not let the Brit get away. Stalemate.

8:00pm. Frank had been driving for about 10 hours, almost non-stop and was exhausted. But, he did not want to let the other guy get away. Fortunately, they came to a set of lights. He came up behind the Wraith and stopped. It had it's flasher on, indicating left. The driver was stopping at White Horse. Whew. Frank went into town and found a motel, for the night.

*

Two days later, Great Falls, Montana, Mountainland. Cliff turned off 6th Street, onto American Avenue. To the right, was a rail yard, with a large area of gravel. On the gravel were two-dozen race cars, some of them on stands, others being jacked up by the driver and teams. Cliff drove slowly, through the lot, looking for the black Caddy. He spotted it, in the far corner, drove over and reversed in beside it. Unusually, the trailer was not attached to his truck. He got out and Frank got out of the Caddy. "Cliff." "Frank." Fist pump. "How's it goin'?" Cliff asked. "Not bad, thanks, you?" "Yeah, early start, but good." Cliff dropped the tail gate. They took out the alloys, with tires fitted. Frank put his trolley jack under the car and lifted each corner, in turn, unscrewed the studs with a cordless impact driver, swapped the wheel, then went onto the next corner. Cliff took each of the wheels, with the worn tires and put them in the flat bed of the Sierra. Then he gave Frank the can of 0w40 fully synthetic engine oil. Frank jacked the car again, put a stand under and dropped the oil, into a drain can. He replaced the plug and filter and filled the engine with fresh oil. Cliff took the can of old oil. "How much am I due you, for today?" Frank asked. "Don't worry about it, just now. I'll add it to the bill for hauling the car to Tacoma. How's that?" "Cool. Thanks." Frank replied. Pit stop complete, Cliff hit the road and headed for home.

*

As soon as Cliff was away, Frank hit the road again. The Caddy was now on the aftermarket alloys and sticky Yokohama semi-slick tires, that he had bought, for the second half of the cruise. The I15 went in the wrong direction, so the route went along Highway 87. Anyway, most of the remaining route would be on rural highways, as local authorities did not want to close large sections of interstates, for a race. That would be too disruptive. He had two very long days ahead of him, one from Great Falls to Denver, then, the final day, Denver to Galveston. Cliff had delivered the goods, promptly and he had gotten out of the pit stop before any of the other cars. He would try to do the same in Denver. The organizers had booked motels rooms, for all of the competitors, which were included in the up-front fee that he had paid. He had the idea that he would go past Denver and stop somewhere further South, to give him a head start, in the morning. He would have to pay for his own motel room, but it would be worth it, if he won.

He hammered down the 87 at 100-120mph. Theoretically, as the road was closed, he could go faster, but it was cattle country and there was an outside chance that one of the locals might not know, or have forgotten that the road was closed, that day. The Caddy whisked past entrances to ranches. Hills, grassland and power lines went by in a blur. About 11:30am, he arrived in Billings. He stopped for gas, brimming the Caddy. He did not stop for lunch, having had a large breakfast, so that he could drive all day. He hit the road again, heading down the Old US 87, towards Hardin. At Hardin, he joined the I90, as prescribed, as there was no suitable rural highway, from there. The Southbound carriageway of the interstate was closed. Being on the interstate enabled him to make good time, passing small towns, such as Crow Agency and Sheridan at interstate speeds. Between the two, he crossed the State line, from Montana into Wyoming. At Buffalo, the route took him onto the I25. He arrived at

Casper at about 3:30pm, stopped for gas, then headed South again, on Highway 487, across the arid plains of central Wyoming. None of the other competitors had caught him up, so far. The route took him through Laramie, then continued, down the 287. The road came down, out of the hills, to Fort Collins. The Denver-Fort Collins area was too busy, to have any highway or interstate closed, so competitors were expected to join the usual traffic. Any speeding tickets would be their own problem. Frank decided to use the I25. He joined it and headed South, immediately finding himself in traffic. He drove along, at about 75mph, in the outside lane, through the mixed urban and agricultural region. The motel booked by the organizers was on the North side of the city, in Thornton. He passed it, in the early evening and continued down the I25, around the Denver down town. The road became more and more congested, as it went through the city. Four lanes crept along, at 10-20mph. Modern apartment complexes and office blocks loomed, at the side of the interstate, in the evening Sun. A while later, he arrived at Castle Rock and exited the interstate. He checked into a motel and went for dinner at a Mexican restaurant.

*

Next morning, Frank got up at 6:00am and was in the car, before 6:30. The closed route was some distance away, at the town of Limon, so he had to drive on open roads, a while longer. He took the 86, across country. The other competitors would also make an early start, he reckoned, as it was the last day of the cruise. They would be setting out from the North side of Denver, assuming that they had not done the same as him and paid for other motels. If so, they would likely take the I70, East, out of town, which would be congested. Hopefully. He drove the highway at about 80mph, a bit higher than the speed limit, but not a ridiculous speed. It was cattle and sheep country. The sides of the road had barbed-wire fences, but there was always an outside chance that livestock could escape. An altercation between a big beast and a 700bhp Caddy would be messy.

He reached the 287 after 7:00am. After that, it was the same highway, all the way, until Amarillo, where it became the I27. Then, back to the 87, at Lubbock. He stopped for gas, every 200 or so miles, to brim the thirsty Caddy. The day wore on, as he blasted across the plains of Texas. The scenery became gradually greener, through the day, as he went deeper into irrigated, agricultural land. The 83 hit the I10, at Junction and he was back on open roads, for a while. There was little traffic on the interstate and he made good time. He arrived at San Antonio, in the late afternoon. The traffic was denser on the 1604 loop and he had to slow down. After San Antonio, he was back on the I10, which was less congested, but still not a closed road. He had driven about 1,000 miles that day, had been on the road about 12 hours, minus a few minutes, here and there, to stop for gas. He was exhausted and things were about to get worse.

He took the exit, off the interstate, onto the 183, as per the instructions, heading towards Gonzales. Headlights caught his eye and he checked his rear view mirror. The Wraith was behind him. Damn. They arrived at Gonzales. The towns speed limits were still in effect, as the route went right through the town. Frank slowed down, to 35mph, as he came into the suburban streets. In a flash, the Wraith pulled out and went past him. Shit. It kept to about 40mph, then, leaving town, it accelerated hard. Frank kept up with it, but could not get past it, even on the closed road. The two cars raced down the 183, through the woods and farmland. Frank considered crossing the yellow lines and drag-racing the Roller, down a long straight stretch, but knew that they had about 180 miles, still to go. Snake and hare. He stayed on the Wraith's tail, far enough back to be safe, near enough not to let it get away, as they hammered down the 111, at around 100mph. They drove through Bay City, which had closed roads, so they did not need to stop at lights, but were supposed to keep to the speed limit. The driver of the Wraith did about 45-50mph, through the town, obviously, hoping that Frank would do the speed limit. Frank kept to the same speed, keeping between the yellow and white lines, watching carefully, for pedestrians, or drivers who took a chance and dodged around the 'road closed' signs. They continued down the 35, through towns and villages. It was well into the evening and starting to get dark. Frank was exhausted beyond words and running on adrenaline. Still, the end was near. He would need to make his move, soon. Luckily, they were on closed roads, right up to the finish line. As they drove past a wildlife refuge, on the 2004, another set of lights appeared, in his rear view mirror. Damn, another competitor. He had to get past, now. There was a straight stretch, about 8 miles long. They were doing about 120mph, as they entered the straight, straddling the yellow lines.

Frank pulled to the left and accelerated hard. The Wraith also accelerated. 130, 140, 150, 160 mph. Frank was past it. The Rolls's top speed was 155mph, the Caddy could do 200mph. He did about 160-170mph, passing an oil refinery. The Wraith could not keep up. He had to slow, for some bends, but had enough distance between him and the other guy. He arrived in Hitchcock, turned right at the lights and accelerated down Highway 6. The Wraith was in his rear-view mirror, as he drove up the ramp, onto the I45. The Southbound carriageway was closed, as the organizers knew that the racing would be full-on, near the end. The other carriageway was full of traffic. Frank drove down one of the middle lanes, across the Galveston Causeway, hitting about 140mph. A strong cross-wind tugged at the car and made him back off, to about 120mph. The Wraith was heavier that the Caddy and the cross wind affected it less, so it closed the gap, coming close, behind Frank. But, they had crossed the causeway and were now on Galveston Island. They rounded a left hand turn, Frank keeping close to the barrier, the Wraith trying to get past, on the outside. The finish line came into view. Frank cut across the lanes, in front of the Wraith, hit the exit ramp and braked, as he went through the trap. He had won, by inches.

He drove down Broadway Street and turned into the large, gravel area, that was being used for the competitors. He parked the Caddy and got out. He was tired and weary, from head to foot, but he had done it. Crowds of people, on the roads, around about, cheered, waved and blew air horns. A barbeque and beer was available, for the tired and hungry drivers. The Wraith parked next to the Caddy and the driver got out. "Frank." "Ayaz."

Handshake. "That was some driving, ras-
dik."

Chapter 19

A Little Palace on the Prairie

"It was the guy in the Cadillac, that won it." Cliff
said. "One like Vicki's?" Jesse asked. "No. A CT5
Blackwing. More than twice the power of the CTS.
Still, cool that a Caddy won." Cliff replied. "Sure.
Did you watch the race, on TV?" Jesse asked. "No.
Online. Vicki says no to TV, says it would be a bad
influence, on Chip." Cliff was in the passenger seat
of Jesse's Impala. Jesse was driving them, up
Highway 18, in Eastern Wyoming. They were going
to meet some friends of Jesse's and stay a few
days. It was a thank you, from one of the leaders of
the independence movement, to Cliff and Jesse, for
their work, leafleting suburbs, securing referenda
and pursuing ballot traffickers.

The race was a celebration of the union of Alaska,
North and Western Canada, the Mid-West and
Texas, into one giant country – Texas Land. North
America's borders had been settled, for about a
year, after nearly a decade of change. After Texas
Land had been formed, British Columbia had joined
Pacifica, to make another giant country, from San
Diego, to Fort Nelson. Idaho, Wyoming and
Montana had decided to stay as Mountainland. They
could join Texas Land, but they liked their country
the way it was. And the name 'Mountainland' had
become popular. Trade deals, with Texas Land and

Pacifica, did the trick. Rangeland made the same decision. Utah stayed stubbornly independent. The Church of Utah insisted it had nothing to do with that. Nevada was still arguing. Lakeland and New England were settled enough as they were and also made trade deals with Texas Land. Eastern Canada, namely; Ontario, Quebec, Labrador, Newfoundland, New Brunswick, Nova Scotia and Prince Edward Island had joined New England, the whole country being run from Albany, New York. The only source of change was that Tallahassee was in the middle of joining negotiations, with Austin, for Southland to join Texas Land. Next year's Cannonball Cruise would go from Anchorage, to Miami. Maybe.

They turned right and headed towards the small town of Edgemont. They crossed the border, into Texas Land, using Jesse's NAMCV. A few miles down the road, Jesse turned off, onto a gravel road. "Pretty remote, huh?" Cliff said. They were in the middle of the prairie of South Dakota. "Makes Twin Falls seem like a metropolis." Jesse quipped. They topped the brow of the hill and saw their destination, ahead of them. "Wow, big house." Cliff said. "Anton has money." Jesse said, as they approached high, black, steel gates, between concrete pillars. A camera spotted them and the gates swung open. They passed through and continued down the road. Hedges grew on either side of the road, beyond the manicured grass verges. They arrived at the house and drove into a large turning circle. Jesse parked near the front door. "No one here?" Cliff asked. "Huh?" Jesse replied. "There's no car." "Their cars'll be in the garage."

They got out of the Impala. Cliff was in brogues, beige chinos and and sharp, pressed, white shirt. Jesse wore denims and a t-shirt. Cliff stood and looked at the house. It was enormous. "Not quite what I expected." He said. "What did you expect?" Jesse asked, opening the trunk. "I dunno. Something prettier. Maybe, like something on the Vegas strip." He said. Jesse laughed. "A bit utilitarian for your taste?" He asked. Cliff surveyed the white box, with acres of tinted glass. "It's like a gigantic sandwich, on white bread." The door opened. A tall, slim, 60-something, man in Cuban heel boots, expensive black denims and a Hawaiian shirt appeared. "Welcome. I'm Anton. Come in." They followed him inside. "This is Cliff." Jesse introduced his friend and neighbor. Cliff and Anon shook hands. "I'll show you your rooms." Anton lead them through the mansion, upstairs, to the second floor. Their rooms were large, with hard wood floors, en-suite bathrooms, queen size beds and floor to ceilings windows, leading to balconies, with views of blue sky and prairie, as far as the eye could see. They unpacked their bags and went back down stairs. They found Anton in the kitchen. "Like a drink, before dinner?" He asked. "That would be nice, thanks." Jesse said. "What do you guys normally drink?" Short pause. "Mostly beer, but whatever you're having is fine." Jesse replied. "I just took a bottle of Chateau-le-Rennes, from the cellar, fancy a glass?" "Sure thing. Thanks." Jesse answered, for both of them. Cliff was busy, checking out the granite worktops, marble floors and stainless steel range. Anton poured three glasses of wine and handed one to each of them.

"Fancy a tour of the house?" Anton asked. Jesse glanced at Cliff. "Sure thing, thanks." He answered. "Yeah, that would be awesome." Cliff added, realizing that he hadn't said much. Anton lead them back out, into the main living room. "This is the lounge." He said. Cliff looked up to the ceiling, which was as high as the roof of an aircraft hanger. Neo-chandeliers hung from it. A mezzanine floor, with steel and wire balustrade, ran along the top of the kitchen and dining room. A wide, marble staircase lead up to the second floor. The room had marble floors, floor to ceiling windows, all white walls, leather sofas and a 70" TV. "Come." Anton signaled them to follow him. They followed him through a rabbit warren of corridors, all with marble floors, lined with book cases and ornaments. Anton took a left turn, through a doorway. Jesse and Cliff followed him, into a movie theater. Rows of seats, enough for two-dozen people, faced a 20' long wall. A projector was built into the rear wall. "We can catch a movie later, if you like." Anton quipped, then lead them back out, into the corridor. He lead them into a games room, with pool and billiard tables. Then into the dining room, then into another, smaller, more low-key lounge. "Come see the basement." Anton said. He hit a button, on the wall, in one of the corridors. A moment later, they were in an elevator, going down to the basement. He lead them through more corridors, into an office. It had several desks, with large monitors and PCs. He lead them into a server room. Inside was a stack, running several servers, switches, routers and a CCTV unit. He took them back out of the office and into the corridor. He took a key-fob, from his pocket and pressed a button. A book case slid to one side, exposing a

284

steel door. "Welcome to the panic room." He said. He opened the door and they went inside. Inside, was another whole house, about the same size as Cliff and Vicki's whole house. Anton took them through, to the rear of the house-within-a-house. He opened another door and they found themselves in a gun room. AR rifles, bolt-action sporting rifles, lever-action gallery rifles and hand guns of every kind, hung on the walls. "Nice collection." Cliff complimented him. "Forty years worth." Anton replied and lead them back out. They went back upstairs. Anton lead them to a large, indoor swimming pool, then on, into the garage. The garage was tucked away, at the rear of the house and was the size of a good-size industrial unit. It had gray-painted, concrete floor. Inside, were about a dozen cars, ranging from a Range Rover, to a Maybach S580. Cliff spotted a red Ferrari Daytona SP3. "Were you in the Cannonball Cruise?" He asked. "Sure. But I lost, to some dickhead, in a Cadillac." Anton replied. They went back to the kitchen.

*

Mrs. Delilah Lake-Shmee had arrived home, in her Bentley Bentayga, from a 36 hour shopping trip, to Denver. She was a tall, elegant, blond lady, in mid-heel boots, denims and a top. Anton introduced everyone to everyone else. Anton and Delilah served bison rib-eye steaks, roast potatoes, asparagus and hamburger gravy. They sat around the oak dining table and ate dinner. After dinner, Anton loaded the dish washer. They all sat in the big lounge and talked.

"What do you do for a living?" Anton asked Cliff. "I have a haulage business." Cliff replied. "I drive a truck and goose-neck trailer." He added. "Ah, OK. I wondered if you were in the tech business, like Jesse." "What do you do?" Cliff asked Anton. "I'm retired now, but I was in the defense industry." Anton replied. "I was in the military, myself." Cliff replied. "Which service?" Anton asked. "The Army, for about ten years, then the Special Forces for a few." Cliff replied. "What made you leave?" Anton asked. "I was medically discharged." Cliff said, pulling his trouser leg up a little. "I like to show off my bionic leg." He quipped. "Ha! Nice!" Delilah laughed. "Let me guess, IED?" Anton asked. "Sure. I had to have it amputated, just above the knee. Now I have a transtibial prosthesis." "How do you manage?" Delilah asked. "I manage fine. My truck is auto, I can't drive stick, 'cause I don't have a clutch foot. I learned to walk again, years ago, now. I have managed most of what I have tried, since." "It must make your life difficult, using a prosthetic limb." Delilah said. "Kinda. But I am used to it now. I have my morning and evening routine, like everyone else, but different." "Are you married?" Delilah asked. "Sure. My wife is called Vicki. We have a son, aged three and a daughter aged two." "Having a young family is the busiest time of your life." Delilah said. "Sure. But, Vicki is amazing. She looks after Chip and Aurora, runs her side of the business and keeps house." Cliff replied. "And I do as much as I can to help her, on days when I'm not on the road. And we have amazing neighbors." Cliff glanced at Jesse. "And you helped us with referendum security." Anton said. "And we appreciate that, so, thank you." He added. "Hey, anytime." Cliff replied. "How do you like your re-configured country?" Anton asked. "I like it, just fine. I like Mountainland. There's still paperwork, to plow snow, but that doesn't matter, 'cause I just crowd-fund my snow clearance operation. I have to drive across borders, everyday and my customers have to pay import taxes on their goods, but, we all pay less tax, overall." Cliff said, then asked: "How do you like Texas Land?" A knowing smile crossed Anton's face, for a second. "I like it. I like it a lot. I'd rather deal with the Austin Feds than the DC Feds, any day." He replied. "I'm getting used to crossing an international border, to go shopping, in Denver." Delilah said. "You go all the way to Denver, for groceries?" Cliff asked. "No. There are supermarkets in Rapid City, about an hour North of here. I go to Denver sometimes, to see the girls. It's about five hours from here, so I stay in a hotel for a night, or two."

*

The three guys spent the following few days doing outdoor pursuits. They buzzed about the local trails, on quad bikes, rode mountain bikes and tried some of Anton's rifle collection, on his private, 200 yard range. One afternoon, Delilah joined them on their private tennis court, for a few games of tennis. In the evenings, after dinner, the four people sat in the lounge and talked.

Cliff, to Anton: "What did you do, in the defense industry?" Anton: "Many different things. I grew up in a double-wide, in DFW, Texas. My dad worked as a welder, for a rail company. When I was in my teens, half a century ago, now, I knew I would do something similar to him; mechanics, engineering, of some sort. When I left high school, I applied for an apprenticeship, as an engineer, at an aircraft company. They hired me. I completed that and worked for them, for a number of years, working on all sorts of military aircraft. In my late twenties, I went back to studying and won a scholarship to Massachusetts Institute of Technology. I did an undergraduate degree in mechanical and electrical engineering. I went back to work for the company, for some years, working on more advanced projects. Then I went to work for a different aerospace company. They're based in Denver, but the work took me all over the world. When I was about forty five, I started my own business, back home in DFW, making specialist materials, for aircraft and satellites. That was over twenty years ago. A few years ago, I hired someone to manage the business and I managed the build, of this place." Cliff: "That's quite a career." Anton: "Well, I've achieved a fair bit, I guess. I know people who have achieved a lot more. A guy that I went to school with, became a billionaire, in the fashion industry." Jesse: "But, you have also done a lot in the political sphere." Anton: "True." Cliff: "How did you get into the independence movement?" Pause. Anton: "I know people, who were involved, in the movement, decades ago. They persuaded me to get involved, on the strategy side." Cliff: "I didn't know that the movement went back decades." Pause. Anton: "As far as Joe Average knows, it didn't. But, among the business elite and some in the military, there was talk about State secession, going back decades. Actually, probably longer." Cliff: "What you're saying would certainly sound strange, to Joe Average. Most people think of the independence movement as being primarily a grass roots movement, rather than something organized, by elites." Pause. Anton: "Well, there are always elements of both, in any political movement. The ideas come from the elite, but nothing actually happens, until the people of the country make it happen." Jesse: "What Sophia calls 'people power'." Cliff: "Ultimately, the people do have the power, because there are many more of us, than there are billionaires, or DC bureaucrats." Anton: "But, how do you define 'people' and how do you define 'elite'? Where do you draw the line, between the two?" Pause. Cliff: "I guess, I see it like this. Many people, especially on the left, talk about the wealth gap. But, a wealthy person might know very little, about, say, the political direction that a country is going to take. So, they are not much different than Joe Average. Perhaps they *are* Joe Average, but with a higher standard of living." Anton: "Exactly. Being wealthy does not automatically make you an insider." Cliff: "I that case, I wonder what *does* make a person an insider?" Anton: "Again, it depends how you define 'insider'. It's all a matter of degree. How inside is inside?" Pause. Anton again: "And inside what? Someone might be a member of one club, but not a member of another." Cliff: "Or a member of the deep state." Anton: "The biggest mistake, that many people make, about the deep state, is that there isn't one. There are many." Jesse: "I agree. I have realized, over the past decade, or so, that the affairs of the elite are highly complex and there is as much fighting and in-fighting, among them, as there is among ARS members and independence guys."

Delilah: "My friends in Denver like to talk politics. They know that I'm married to a guy who's involved in the independence movement and I get the feeling, that they are careful what they say, in front of me. But, I'm still able to glean some interesting things, from them. For example, Jody is a PA, to the manager of a chemical company and she is very sociable, she talks to anyone and everyone. She says that many of the people in Denver don't really understand the independence movement. Some are supportive of it, some not so much. People have gotten used to the current situation and are happy enough, being in Rangeland, but still don't really get what was behind it." Cliff: "Well, I guess what was behind it, was one deep state, in a battle, with another." "Sure, but, they don't understand that, because, as Anton said, many people see the deep state as one. They see it, that the deep state, or the shadow government, or whatever, has changed direction." Jesse: "I think that increasing numbers of people are starting to figure out that our movement is essentially about resistance, to increasing authoritarianism, in DC, or, I should say, what was DC." Anton: "Exactly. Which is why it is important to have more than one deep state. Joe Average does not see the approach of a more authoritarian world. He just goes about his day-to-day business. The authoritarians, in the 'authoritarian deep state', if we can call it that, can easily sell him ever more security, in return for taking his freedoms. Unless, the 'freedom deep state', if we can call it that, steps in and steers things, in a different direction."

Cliff: "I find that, when I tell people, that I was in the Special Forces, in many cases, they are curious what that means. I can talk about it, in general terms, but there's a lot that I can't talk about. For example, I can tell people that there are not just

Deep Underground Military Bases in North America, but all over the world. I can't say where, exactly, but I have been into underground bases in Europe, Latin America, the Middle East and Australia." Delilah: "And the next question is, to do what?" Cliff: "Various things, mostly classified. But including, for example, hostage rescue." Anton: "You rescued hostages, from underground military bases?" Cliff: "Sure, on a number of occasions." Anton: "How do you do that?" Pause. Cliff: "Methods are also classified." Delilah: "What sort of hostages?" Cliff: "That's also classified." Anton: "Which governments were holding the hostages?" Pause. Cliff: "Ditto. But ...Let's put it like this. It's not all about government. There are other players, in the game." Delilah: "You mean, such as, the private sector?" Pause. Cliff: "Let's put it like this. Joe Average, in general, thinks that we are alone, in the universe." Delilah: "But, we are not. Its just that, that is also classified. See, what I wonder is, now that DC does not exist, who is keeping all the classified information classified?" Jesse: "DC still exists, but as a museum, not a seat of government." Anton: "Now that there is a lot less government, it is likely that some of the technologies, that I and others like myself, have worked on, will find their way into the commercial sector. In the private sector, secrets only stay secret, until someone finds it more profitable to sell them, than to monopolize them."

Chapter 20

A few weeks later, Saturday morning. Cliff's alarm went off. He grabbed his phone, from the bedside cabinet and turned the alarm off. It was 7:00am. He got out of bed, went to shower, then put his leg on and dressed, in his usual desert boots, khaki cargo pants, shoulder holster, with his 1911 and black polo. He took his overnight bag and opened the door. He walked down the long corridor, with it's vinyl floor, plain white walls and low ceiling. He exited the building, out into the Nevada, early morning Sun. He walked across the large, concrete parking lot, to his truck, pressing the key fob as he neared. He put his bag in the back and got in. He drove out of the lot and down the road, to the building where his trailer was parked.

"Morning." He said, to a man in a hi-viz vest. "Is my trailer ready?" "Is yours the twenty foot box trailer?" "Sure." "No, Sir. It'll be another hour and a half." "Cool. I'll go get breakfast." Cliff drove back up the road and parked, in another parking lot, near the staff canteen. He was a civilian contractor, but he was still allowed to use the canteen. He went inside, took a clean tray, from the stack and went to the counter. "What're you having?" The young guy, in a white apron, asked. "I'll have the ham and eggs, thanks. The young man took a plate, from the stack and dished out bacon, ham, fried egg, toast and tomatoes. Cliff paid, with a $10 US note, found a table, sat and ate. He always took the opportunity to spend some of his stash of US dollars, on trips to Nevada, as it was the only country, in North America, that still accepted them.

After breakfast, he still had some time to spare, so he decided to take a wonder, around the site. He had wondered, how much his card would give him access to, on previous occasions, but had not wanted to push his luck. Getting caught somewhere that he should not be, might be a difficult one to explain, to the site security. He was supposed to be there to collect, or deliver, a load, not to go nosing about in who knows what. But, he was in a curious mood that day. Also, there were few people around the site, it was unusually quiet.

Cliff walked out of the canteen and went to an office building, nearby. It was built from cinder block, more substantial than some of the other buildings, on the site. He went to the door and swiped his card, on the reader, expecting it to flash red. It flashed green. He pushed and it opened. He was in another corridor, like the one in the dorm. He walked down it, deeper into the building. What would his pretext be, if someone asked him, what he was doing there? Looking for the gents, that would do. He found an elevator. Next to it, was a swipe card pad. Here goes, he thought and swiped his card on it. Green. The elevator doors opened. He stepped in. The doors closed and he hit the button, to go down. The elevator went down. The doors opened and he stepped out, into another corridor. He walked down it. On either side were doors, some all wood, painted white, others white, with a window. He stopped at one with a window and looked through it. An office. Desks, chairs, PCs, monitors, filing cabinets. On, to the next one. More of the same. Then, he came to a lab. He peered through the door. Work benches, white coats hanging on pegs, all sorts of equipment, that he did not recognize. He swiped his card, on the card reader. Red. Damn. It was not an access all areas pass, after all. He continued, down the corridor, trying this door and that. All of them flashed red. He went back to the elevator and got into it. Cliff still had some time. Perhaps, he thought, he should check out another level? He hit the button again and went down another level. The doors opened and he stepped out.

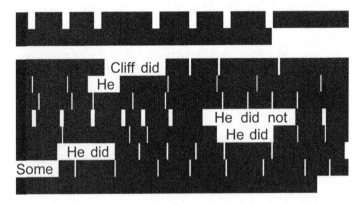

Later that morning, Cliff arrived at Highway 375. He turned right, heading South-East. It was the usual, sunny, Nevada day. He passed through Crystal Springs and headed down Highway 93, Eastbound. He passed through the small town of Caliente and carried on. A few miles later, he took a short-cut, along Highway 319, a minor road, through the hills. He swiped into Utah, with his NAMCV card, arrived in Cedar City, at around 1:00pm and went into a gas station. He brimmed the tank with diesel, bought sandwiches and had lunch, parked at the side of the gas station. He looked out, over the Sun-drenched mountains and plains, of Southern Utah. Too bad, that ████ ████ ████ █████████ ███ ████   Never mind, better luck next time.

He hit the road, heading North, on I15, up Utah's Central Valley. At Sulphurdale, he took the exit, onto the I70 and headed East. The I70, through Eastern Utah, was one of the loneliest roads, in North America. It crossed some of the most arid land, on the whole continent. Rocky, sandy ground stretched in all directions, as far as they eye could see. Scrubby vegetation was dotted about over the land scape. Mesas and rock formations loomed, in the distance. Around 7:00pm, he crossed the border, into Rangeland, using his NAMCV and continued. The interstate followed the Colorado River, into the mountains, passing through tunnels and canyons. Wooded slopes and craggy tops, towered over the road. It got dark. He carried on. The radio played; music, jabber, music jabber. The truck's projector beam lights lit, mile after mile, of yellow and white lines. He passed small towns; Silverthorne, Georgetown, Idaho Springs. Later that evening, he reached Denver. He followed the I70, around the city. Industrial buildings, flood lit rail yards and skyscrapers glided past the windows of the truck.

Cruising down the Dwight D. Eisenhower Highway, he saw the sign, for Denver International Airport. He took the ramp off the interstate, onto Pena Boulevard. He followed the road, under a flyover, then over the interstate, heading North. He followed the road around to the right, then took the exit, onto the ███████████████████████   Finally, the GPS told him that he had arrived, at his destination. He was at a red and white barrier. The barrier raised and he drove into a compound. A few buildings were dotted about, with various vehicles, parked outside of them. A man in a hi-viz vest stopped him. He put the window down. "I have a delivery for ██ ██ ██ ██ ██ ██ ██." He said. "Can you reverse your trailer into that building, please?" The man said. Cliff turned the truck and trailer around, then reversed the box trailer, into the vehicle doorway, in the building, under the watchful eye of Blucifer.

Chapter 21

Battle Rappin'

Friday afternoon, September, some years later. Cliff drove up the I84, towards home. He had gotten his commercial license, for Mountainland, which covered him to drive semi trucks and trailers, in every country, in North America. He was driving his 2018 Freightliner Cascadia Sleeper. His new truck was in silver gray, with a raised roof and a Detroit 400 engine. The Texas Land Government, in Austin was building a superhighway, from Miami, to Anchorage, called the Pan-American Highway. When complete, it would be the greatest highway ever built, anywhere on Earth. It would move people, goods and resources, across the North American continent, from one end, to the other. It included rail roads, alongside, to move the heavier materials and run high speed passenger trains. Cliff had long term contracts, to haul loads of construction materials, to the Montana and Wyoming sections of the road and rail road. That gave him some greater financial security, which was good, because it helped him and Vicki to raise Chip and Aurora.

He arrived at his unit, which he had bought, in a corner of an industrial estate, in Twin Falls. The door opened, as he approached. He drove the truck inside. A few minutes later, he was in the Monte Carlo, driving the 7 or 8 blocks, to his house. He arrived home and parked on the drive, next to Vicki's Caddy. He got out and went inside. Chip and Aurora ran to the door and greeted him, with their usual weekend excitement. Vicki greeted him with a hug. She'd had a busy week, as well, with the freight forwarding business, which had moved to the garage, refurbished by Cliff, so that Aurora had a bedroom. The family sat around the dining table and ate steaks, fries and salad. Chip drank beer, Vicki wine, the kids orange juice. They talked, catching up with each others' news, from the week. After dinner, the kids played on their X-Boxes. Vicki tidied the kitchen and Cliff loaded the dish washer. They went through to the living room and sat down, on the sofa. "Ah, I forgot." Vicki said. "Something came for you, in the mail." She handed him an envelope. It was a high-quality, sage green envelope, with his name and address, in blue hand writing. He opened it. Inside, were several sheets of high quality paper. On it, written in fountain pen, was a poem.

To Cliff

A homeless man hobbles

Military career wasn't a doddle

He was struck hard and low

But inside, he's still an Noble

Unbelievable adversity

On these streets, city

It rains in California

' though he was born here

Serving one's country provides little recognition

When you come to buy a gun and ammunition

Friends don't let friends go without

Especially when they've been World about

He knows not why he plys his craft

Money and pleasure and pain and graft

People and Gods afar look on

Mostly right and sometimes wrong

Cheaters never win and

Winners never cheat

Arcana v. Frank

Was never a dead heat

A standoff at sea

A fence around a fence

Moves and Counter Moves

Rivalry, play and dance

Army International at the State Capitol

According to the media, perfectly rational

They think we have just stones and sticks

No   idea   of   the   little   guy's
tricks

Separation of Church and State

Something that few are likely to hate

Drastic changes give some people fears

Reality, in the middle, no need for tears

Anti Reactionary Society, to End

Hate, Oligarchy and Laissez-fair Economics

Hate their parents and hate all hicks

They're the ones with the stones and sticks

Brandon, lets go vote

Seb Frank's rallies were a mote

Xerox'd ballots in vans and tunnels

Fake signatures, full to the gunnels

Questions of management and finance

Come and go and play and dance

Uninitiate's fog and cloud and doubt

Slowly clears, along the route

Traveling this way and that

Little by little, they re-draw the map

Events here and there seem unconnected

Slowly but surely, a new World is perfected

Maybe Military and Magick Mix?

Secret Societies' grades and picks

See secret language of Kelly and Dee

Or war time writings of Al' Crowley

Pagans believed in Gods of weather

Rain dances and head dresses of feathers

Magick is science beyond the observer

Things they do on Earth, our mother

Secret elites continental re-imaginings

States of the Nation now National Fledglings

Soldiers and men with rifles on slings

These are some of our favorite things

A new World is born

Old World we mourn

As Above, So Below

As Below, So Above

Next door, lives my handler

Strange and curious, as the Mandela

Turns out, stakes could not be higher

Under one roof, Elohim and Ghia

Secret technology, on the road

Governments, think they are owed

A change of the Guard, yet unknown

Where we go one, we all go

Who would guess

People in casual dress

A story about cars

And Humanity, going to the stars

A Little Palace on the Prairie

Earth, Water, Fire and Airy

Magick is always performed in secret

You'd know that, people of the Sarkel

Their methods: many and various

Ours: Awakening and Democracy

Not their age of Technocracy

But our age of Aquarius

Take care,

Anon.